A DUKE ALWAYS
Gets What He Wants

Rebecca Leigh

ISBN: 978-1-66783-036-0 (printed)

ISBN: 978-1-66783-037-7 (eBook)

Chapter One

London, England 1812

The air felt rather heavy and thick tonight as the carriage moved through the streets of London's fashionable Grosvenor's Square in Mayfair. It was the beginning of the season and most of the ton's aristocratic families had descended upon town to showcase their wealth and their daughters if they were unlucky enough to have any. He himself had generally looked forward to the season. It was a time of mischief and carnal pleasures for him and his two good friends. Being the heir to a duke-dom had always opened doors to him but since coming into his title, he had discovered that regardless of his wicked reputation he was still most sought after.

He was the exceedingly wealthy and very powerful Ethan Gray, Duke of Hawksford, known to his friends as Hawk. At eight and twenty years of age, he was in the prime of life. Nothing was beyond his grasp. His influence was remarkable, but his reputation was one of a devilish rake. He had taken great care to cultivate his reputation to such a pinnacle and took pride in making certain he was known for his debauched and decadent love of carnality.

And while normally he would be eager for the London season to begin, this year would be different. This year his aunt would be bringing his sister Catherine out for her first season. With Catherine attending many of the same balls and society functions as himself, he would have to reign in his baser instincts and conduct himself more appropriately. Hopefully,

Catherine would find a husband soon and his stint for playing proper guardian would be over and he could resume his typical interests.

His carriage came to a stop in front of the home of his oldest friend and fellow lover of lasciviousness, an equally rich and powerful duke in his own right. The carriage door opened and his friend, Michael Shelbourne, Duke of Leicester climbed inside. "I assume that tonight's entertainment will be worth me breaking an engagement with the fair and very eager to please Lucy Davies," Leicester said as he shut the carriage door.

The two of them had grown up as friends and became even closer since their days at Eton when they were just young boys. Along with another young lord, Charles Newberg, Marquis of Rockhurst and heir to the Duke of Avanley, the trio became notorious troublemakers at school. All three being heirs to powerful and wealthy dukedoms, they were given lots of leeway with their shenanigans. Now that they were older, they were the biggest rakes in London. Mommas scurried to find and protect their daughters from the dangerous or devil dukes as they were sometimes called. The devil dukes themselves thought it was rather amusing, since those same mommas and pappas would jump at the chance to see their daughters become duchesses if any of them were inclined towards marriage. But they were more interested in bedding women rather than wedding them and that made them very dangerous indeed.

Hawk gave his friend a half smile before turning to look out the window of the carriage as it rolled through the streets of Mayfair. "I'm sure you can spare one night away from your mistress to attend Almacks."

Leicester's face lost a little color. "I must not have heard you correctly, did you say Almacks?"

"Unfortunately, I did."

Leicester quickly rapped on top of the carriage signaling them to stop before reaching for the door. Hawk put his hand out to stop him. He leaned out the window and told his driver to continue, then faced his friend who by judging the look on his face was not pleased with their destination.

"Have you lost your bloody mind?! Why in the name of heaven would you want to go to Almacks? It is hot, stuffy, boring, nothing to drink but tepid lemonade and no doubt will signal the old dowagers that we have decided to seek brides for ourselves, not to mention the fact that we are not on the best terms with the patronesses or have you forgotten that little fact."

"I understand your hesitation, but I do not have a choice. Catherine is in town with my Aunt Louisa. She is making her debut at Almacks tonight and my aunt seems to think it will be better for Catherine if I am there supporting her."

His friend narrowed his eyes slightly. "Catherine can't be old enough for a season, can she?"

Hawk nodded. "She should have made her presentation last year, but she was still in mourning after the death of our parents. She is eighteen and firmly convinced that if she doesn't find a husband soon, she will be a spinster for the remainder of her life."

Leicester laughed heartily. "The sister of the Duke of Hawksford will have no trouble finding someone to marry her. While that explains your need to be in attendance, I am not sure why I have to suffer as well."

Hawk lazily picked a piece of lint from his black coat before looking back at his friend. "You owe me."

At his words Leicester leaned back against the carriage and accepted his fate. "Yes, I do. If you hadn't distracted Lady Julia's father, she would have had me trapped like a rat. Marriage to her would have been unbearable, not to mention the fact that I am not sure I could have gotten through the bedding part of the ordeal."

Hawk smiled. He had indeed saved his friend from the parson's trap when Lady Julia Smithers had colluded with her father to trap the young duke into marriage. No man wanted to be trapped, and Lady Julia wasn't exactly a beauty. She was short and about forty stones overweight with a pox complexion, not to mention her nasty personality. It would have been hell on earth for Leicester to be leg shackled to the shrew, so while

Lady Julia had Michael trapped in the drawing room of a party they had attended, he had distracted the lady's father long enough for his friend to escape the clutches of the female who damned near held him hostage.

The carriage came to a stop and the two men alighted to be met by the third member of their trio, Charles Bedford, Lord Rockhurst. Rockhurst was the worst of the three of them. His father had been strict and puritanical when he was growing up and he was determined to make it his lifelong mission to be the exact opposite. In fact, looking at him now, Hawk wondered whose bed Rockhurst had just climbed out of to join them. His hair was slightly ruffled and clothes wrinkled, and it appeared he had gotten dressed on the fly.

Rockhurst buttoned his coat and smoothed back his hair. "I thought we were banned from Almacks?"

Leicester straightened his cravat. "That was only for one year, but I am sure the patronesses will not be overly pleased with you if the lemonade becomes spiked again."

Hawksford grinned as he recalled the memory. "We will all be on our best behavior tonight. My sister is counting on it and Aunt Louisa will rake all three of us over the coals if we do anything to hurt her chances this season."

"I can't believe our little Catherine is old enough to be on the marriage mart. Remember how she used to chase after you, Leicester? Always saying that the two of you would marry," Rockhurst said as they walked up the steps to enter the assembly rooms.

"Yes, unfortunately I do remember. Hopefully, she has outgrown her fascination with me."

"As if I would ever permit you to marry my sister," Hawk replied as they came to the entrance.

The three of them entered and waited to be announced. They were an intimidating lot. All of them over six feet tall with strong athletic builds.

They knew exactly how they appeared and grinned slightly as they were announced. The three of them were no stranger to the adoring ladies. Not only were they rich and held lofty titles, but they were handsome as hell and had been told so by scores of ladies since they were youths. Their confidence bordering on arrogance made it look as if they were on the prowl for their next meal and every lady in the room felt her temperature rise if any of them looked her way. The patronesses eyed them warily as if daring them to disturb the realm in which they reigned supreme. The three smiled and nodded to them a silent agreement that tonight they would indeed behave as was expected. Hawk looked around the room admiring the new flock of ladies being presented. While they never dallied with young unmarried ladies of the beau monde, it certainly didn't hurt to see what would be on the menu a year or so down the road. They were about to make their way over to speak with Lord Carrolton with whom they had also attended Eton, when they met an insurmountable wall.

"You're late."

"My apologies, Aunt Louisa," Hawk said as he bowed deeply toward his aunt giving her a smile, he hoped would forgive this indiscretion.

The older lady gave him a half grin. Hawk reached down and kissed her cheek. "Too afraid to attend alone I see." Leicester and Rockhurst took a step toward her. "All three of you being present tonight will certainly start the gossip tongues wagging."

Leicester reached for her hand and placed a kiss above it. "I told Hawk exactly the same thing just a few minutes ago in the carriage. God forbid my mother hear of my attending."

She laughed. "I am surprised you didn't try to jump out of the carriage upon discovering your destination."

"He tried," Hawk said causing his aunt to laugh again and Leicester to grunt in disgust. "I am here as you requested. Where is Catherine?"

"She will be escorted back to me as soon as her dance with Lord Filligrew is over. She has been given the nod to waltz, as has Lady

Persephone. Hawk, you will dance the first waltz of the evening with your sister and one of you," she said pointing to Rockhurst and Leicester, "will throw yourself on the altar of sacrifice and dance the first waltz with Persephone. After that you may go to your clubs or wherever you wish to be. But I will expect escorts throughout the season, Ethan."

His aunt and his mother were the only people that ever called him by his given name. It warmed his heart a bit. "I will be at your service." He bowed at the waist and watched as his aunt sailed along the floor back to her place with the other dowagers.

"Who is Lady Persephone and why are we obligated to dance with her?" Lord Rockhurst asked once her ladyship was out of hearing.

Hawk scanned the room looking for his sister. "She is the daughter of Viscount Radcliff."

"Viscount Radcliff? I don't believe I know him," Leicester said as he winked at a young lady staring at him from across the room.

"He hasn't been in England for the past fifteen years or so. When his wife died, he left Persephone in the care of my aunt and he left to go explore Egypt or Greece. He considers himself an amateur archaeologist."

Leicester put his hand up to his chin. "Persephone?" Realization struck him. "Dear God, is that the hoyden that used to come stay with Catherine when they were little girls still in the nursery?"

Hawk's smile widened. "You remember?"

"Bloody hell! Yes, I remember her putting a frog in my boot that Christmas I came to stay with you." He rolled his eyes to heaven. "Rockhurst you will have to be tonight's sacrificial lamb and dance with her. The last time I saw her she was covered in mud and Hawk's mother was having a fit because she and Catherine had been digging in the dirt for worms, probably to put in my bed no less."

Hawk laughed again at his friend before he heard Lord Rockhurst say under his breath, "Consider me sacrificed."

They all three looked up to see his aunt Viscountess Mulford coming toward them with his sister and quite possibly the most beautiful woman he had ever seen. She had golden blonde hair curled and pinned up in an elaborate coiffure with a few ringlets falling alongside her face and the back of her neck. She had a peaches and cream complexion, but it was her eyes that drew him to her. They were a deep blue, the kind of blue you would see out on the open ocean, framed with thick dark lashes. He allowed his gaze to travel down to where he could see the swells of her breasts along the edge of her modest bodice. Her figure was curved in all the right places where a man desired curves to be. She was exquisite. He had never seen anything like her before and the hunter in him instinctively knew that he would have this woman in his bed. His mind was drifting to those thoughts when his aunt cleared her throat loudly to get his attention.

"Your graces, my lord, of course you all know Lady Catherine, but may I present Lady Persephone Carlisle." Both ladies sank into deep elegant curtsies.

Lady Catherine was the first to speak. "I was afraid you wouldn't come, Hawk."

He reached over and kissed her cheek. "I would trapse through Dante's Inferno if you asked, dear sister."

She rolled her eyes slightly and glanced over at Persephone. "I told you he truly was a devil."

He turned to see Lady Persephone smile and if he thought her beautiful before she was positively radiant when she smiled.

"I am very pleased to see you again, your grace. It has been quite a few years," Lady Carlisle said as she looked up at him.

Leicester stepped forward and took her hand. "This isn't our first meeting either, my lady. I remember you from a few years back as well." Hawk watched as he saw his friend expertly pull her closer.

She gave him a quick little wink. "Don't be afraid, your grace. I no longer put frogs in people's shoes."

He raised her hand to his lips. "My dear, for you I could endure a few frogs."

Lord Rockhurst stepped in and took her hand from Leicester, "My lady, I believe they are about to play the first waltz, would you do me the honor?"

"Certainly, my lord." She turned back to Hawk. "Your grace, thank you for your hospitality in allowing me to stay with Catherine during the season."

He bowed to her and watched as Lord Rockhurst escorted her onto the floor. He then looked to his aunt. "My hospitality?"

She waved her hand dismissively in the air. "We will discuss it later, but I would like to move into Hawksford House for the season. It is much grander than my townhouse and since Catherine is your sister, I think it is fitting that we stay there."

His sister pulled lightly on his arm. "The waltz, Hawk. You are to dance with me."

He gave his aunt a parting look that said they definitely would be discussing things further and moved to take his sister onto the dance floor.

As the waltz began, he couldn't help but notice the way Lady Persephone moved gracefully with the music. He also couldn't help but observe the way Rockhurst held her much closer than was necessary or even proper. The irritation he felt at watching her being held in another man's arms surprised him.

"Are you going to stare at her the entire time we dance together?" his sister asked as she looked up at her brother.

"I am sorry, love. You do look lovely tonight. Are you having a good time?"

"I am indeed. Although I am looking forward to more lively parties. Almacks seems rather dull." She wrinkled her nose and for a moment she looked just as she did as a little girl when she was made to eat something she did not like. He really couldn't believe his baby sister was old enough for a season. She was beautiful in her own right. He could see that she and Lady Persephone were destined to be the diamonds of the season. He looked up and caught the eyes of the lady in question. She quickly looked away turning her attention back to Rockhurst. He smiled, eager to begin the chase.

"You are doing it again, Hawk," his sister said bringing him back to the present. "You are just like every other man that sees her." She laughed causing him to raise one eyebrow silently asking for an explanation. "Unfortunately for those men, Persephone is not after a title and wealth. She isn't even sure she wants to marry and if she does it will only be for love."

"Then she is naïve," he replied without much feeling.

"You are such a cynic, Hawk. Some people do marry for love. Not everyone in the ton marries for a title."

He grinned scathingly. "Who am I to shatter your illusion."

She beamed at him before saying, "By the look on your face earlier I am sure you had not been aware of Aunt Louisa's plan to launch us into society from Hawksford House."

Hawk twirled her faster. "I was not aware of her plans, but she is correct. You are the daughter and sister of a duke, and you should be at Hawksford House."

"Thank you, Hawk. Aunt Louisa's house can't compare to yours. Besides it's my home too, at least until I am married."

"It is a bachelor's residence, my residence. So, some adjustments must be made. I will have Billings make arrangements," he said as they continued to twirl around the ballroom.

She waved a hand dismissively. "Yes, yes, we know all about your reputation and how the three of you are called the dangerous dukes."

He narrowed his eyes and gave her a firm look. "What the devil do you know about my reputation?"

"I can read you know. And there is seldom a week when one of you is not mentioned in the scandal sheets."

His expression darkened. "I would think Aunt Louisa would not allow you to read filth, most of which is not true I might add."

She laughed again. "I bet a good bit is true."

"We will not discuss this further," he said sharply. "If you are to stay at Hawksford House, I will go stay with Leicester."

Catherine gasped. "You can't do that. You're my brother. How would it look if you took no part in seeing me well settled? Persephone and I will be no trouble at all."

He looked back to where the lady in question was still in the arms of his friend, Lord Rockhurst. Indeed, having Lady Persephone under his roof would be interesting.

The three dangerous dukes, Persephone knew she would see them while she was in London. It had been years since she had seen Catherine's brother the Duke of Hawksford and even longer since she had seen Leicester. As a young girl she had always thought them handsome, but seeing them now, they were not merely handsome, they were magnificent. The scandal sheets and newspapers had not done justice to their descriptions. The entire assembly room took pause when they were announced, and the air took on a certain heat as they moved around the rooms. As a close friend of Catherine Gray, Hawksford's sister, she had grown up hearing the tales of the three gentlemen. Catherine would often mention how the three got in trouble while at school and how she had overheard her father and mother in despair of what would become of his grace if he didn't stop behaving like a hellion. After the three left Eton, she and Catherine had searched the gossip sheets for any news or stories about them. Catherine was desperately in love with Michael Shelbourne, the Duke of Leicester. Ever since she was a little girl, she had followed him around and when the two girls were alone, she talked of him as if he were a knight in shining armor. Therefore, the tales of their love affairs broke Catherine's heart a little every time she read about Leicester in the papers. And their love affairs were widespread and, in some cases, rather shocking. Persephone often wondered if there was any truth to the stories. Aunt Louisa had always told them that gossip was greatly exaggerated and that mollified Catherine to an extent. But after seeing the three gentlemen tonight she was more convinced that the stories were accurate.

Persephone glanced over Lord Rockhurst's shoulder as they danced the waltz to catch the eyes of the Duke of Hawksford. For a moment she thought his dark eyes almost looked predatory as if he was stalking his prey. A shiver went through her as she contemplated that thought.

"Are you cold, Lady Carlisle?" Lord Rockhurst asked as he twirled her once again around the room.

She quickly tore her eyes away and looked up at her partner. "No, I am quite well, my lord."

He smiled. "You know he is not nearly as much fun as I am."

Persephone felt a blush creep up her neck. "I'm not sure who you are speaking off, my lord."

He leaned a little closer to her ear. "Hawksford, hasn't taken his eyes from you since you crossed the ballroom to greet us."

"I'm sure you are mistaken, my lord."

He pulled her closer still knowing he was pushing the boundaries. "As you say, my dear. Tell me, are you glad to be in London?"

"Exceedingly so. I am looking forward to the events of the season," she replied with a bright smile.

He glanced up to see Hawk narrow his eyes at him, obviously not pleased with him for holding her so close. "Do you ride? I would be honored if you and Catherine would join me tomorrow for a ride through Hyde Park."

Her face brightened. "I would love that, of course I will have to ask Aunt Louisa if she has made other plans."

The music came to a stop, and he took her elbow to lead her to where Catherine was waiting with her brother.

"Thank you for the dance, my lord."

He bowed deeply. "It was indeed my pleasure and I look forward to our …ride tomorrow."

The three of them watched as the ladies were claimed for other dances by eager young lords.

Leicester nudged Hawk. "Let us be off now. I have an opera singer waiting for me."

Hawk turned to him. "Later," he then narrowed his gaze at Rockhurst. "What the hell are you about, Charles? You know you were pushing propriety by holding her so close. The gossip sheets will be talking about that dance tomorrow."

Rockhurst shrugged his shoulders. "It will not be the first time I have been mentioned in the scandal sheets."

Hawk leaned closer and said seriously. "But it will be hers. Keep in mind that she is an innocent, and off limits unless you wish to marry the girl."

Rockhurst was unperturbed by his friend's comments. "Is marriage what you were thinking of when you were staring at her the entire time while she was dancing with me? Because I have seen that look before, my friend and while a romp between the sheets might have crossed your mind, I would bet money that matrimony was not the path that led you there."

Hawk took a deep breath. "I am just looking after the girl's reputation. After all, she will be a guest under my roof and a dear friend to my sister. Not to mention that my aunt loves her like she was her daughter. Just keep that in mind in your interactions with her." He looked toward the dance floor one more time to see her smile at the young lord leading her through the quadrille. "I have done my duty here. Let's go to White's, I could use a drink."

"Finally, someone is making sense," Leicester replied as he turned for the door. "If we hurry, I just may be able to visit Lucy's bed tonight after all."

The three of them left the assembly and waited for their carriage to be brought around. Hawk thought about his friend's words and knew they were true. He did want Persephone in his bed and marriage had not entered his mind. Perhaps he should keep his distance and focus his attention elsewhere. He had not taken a mistress in a few months since he had broken off the arrangement with the French opera singer Josephine Arnaud. A visit to an eager young widow or unhappily married woman of the ton might be in order. Then he could focus his energies on getting his sister married and returning his home back to a bachelor residence.

The next morning

The Duke of Hawksford leaned back against the doorframe of his study and watched as a mountain of trunks and luggage were brought into his house. He had spoken with his butler Billings and his chief housekeeper first thing that morning to explain what was about to descend upon them. Being the professionals and the efficient servants that they were, things were immediately taken into hand, and he felt sure the transition from a bachelor residence to a home containing three women, two of which were debutantes, would be smooth. At least as smooth as it could be. His aunt finally entered the house after informing one of the footmen to make sure her trunks were unpacked first as Lady Catherine and Lady Persephone would be arriving later. She noticed him standing there, arms crossed, brooding over his dilemma and walked toward him. He stood to the side and allowed her to sail past him into his study. Closing the door behind him he walked past where she had taken a seat and moved to the front of his desk so he could face her.

"Don't look so miserable, Ethan. I'm sure the girls will be no problem at all. I venture to say you will probably not even notice a disruption in your day-to-day activities." She looked up at him and smiled.

He nodded. "If you knew my day-to-day activities, Aunt Louisa, you would certainly hope that they would be disrupted." He saw her blush slightly. "But since ladies will be present in my home I will try to be on my best behavior."

"Excellent. I am sure the ladies will have no trouble in finding husbands. They are both beautiful and while Persephone's dowry can't compare to Catherine's, it is still healthy," she said as she started to get up from her chair.

"Has her father abandoned her? Does he not wish to make certain she finds a decent match?" he asked speaking of Persephone.

His aunt sat back down and turned her head to side slightly. "Once her mother died, almost immediately, he left for Greece. I write to him once a year to inform him of her progress and wellbeing. He seldom writes back and never writes to Persephone." She shook her head in disgust. "You would think it would bother the girl and perhaps it does to a degree, but she never mentions him." She looked up at her nephew. "She has been an immense joy to me these past few years and I will see that she is successful. Her beauty is beyond compare and her heart is just as special. She is very much like her mother and her mother was an angel. I miss her friendship even after all these years."

He crossed his arms over his chest as he leaned back against the desk. "Where are Catherine and Persephone?"

"They are riding in the park with Lord Rockhurst. I'm sure they will arrive any moment now." She leaned forward and placed her hand on his arm. "Don't look so menacing. Rockhurst would never do anything to hurt the reputation of your sister, and he seemed quite smitten with Persephone."

Hawk wasn't sure why he felt angry at her words. "Rockhurst's reputation says otherwise."

His aunt laughed as she made her way out the door. "So does yours, my dear, so does yours."

Perhaps it was because as a duke he had always gotten what he wanted. He had been spoiled as a child, and as an adult he still managed to get his way most of the time. Maybe that was the reason he felt as if Rockhurst was invading his territory. He needed to spend more time with Persephone, because he was certain that like all other attractions he had formed with beautiful women in the past, it would grow cold quickly, and he would lose interest. He had already lay awake last night convincing himself that he could not have her in his bed since she was untouched. With her being off limits to his bed, he was sure his desire for her would fade.

Lord Rockhurst had arrived at Aunt Louisa's townhouse earlier than expected, so she and Catherine rushed to get into their riding habits not wanting to keep him waiting. She had been looking forward to their ride since he had offered to take them the night before. Hyde Park was the gathering place of the beau monde. Anyone that wanted to be seen would be there. They entered the park and Persephone marveled at all the carriages and horses. Since she and Catherine were new to the London scene, they were also a peculiarity. Everyone seemed to be watching them as they rode, wondering who they were and why they were in the company of the

Marquis of Rockhurst. Persephone smiled at several gentleman who tipped their hats to her as they passed.

"I told you I would be envied," Lord Rockhurst said as he sidled his horse closer to her.

Persephone glanced over at him. "Everyone is just curious."

Charles laughed. "It is obvious you have not been circulating about the ton. Everyone here is curious, that is correct. The males of our class are trying to figure out who you are and no doubt how much of a dowry you carry with you. Not to mention your familial connections." He nodded toward a group of gentlemen on horseback staring at them and talking amongst themselves as they passed. "The women on the other hand are much more devious. You are competition, simple as that, and as you are beautiful, they are right now trying to decide whether it is to their benefit to befriend you or cut you." He saw that she was indeed listening intently. "As Catherine is the sister of a duke, an unmarried one at that, I feel certain they will wish to befriend her if only to try to get Hawksford to the altar." He leaned over a little bit closer. "You on the other hand are in a different position."

Persephone cocked her head to the side curious as to where the conversation was going. "What do you mean, my lord?"

"Simple really, since you are living under the same roof as Hawksford but are not a relative, all the marriage minded ladies seeking to become a duchess will see you as a threat, an extremely beautiful menace to their plans."

She laughed at that. "You sound so sinister, my lord. Let me assure you I am no threat. The duke has no interest in me. I'm sure he is counting the moments before we are out of his way."

The marquis glanced over at her and winked. "I wouldn't be so sure, my dear."

Before she could question him further, Catherine rode along beside her again. "I certainly feel as if we are on parade. My cheeks are hurting from smiling and nodding so much as we pass by everyone."

Two gentlemen rode over to them. "Good morning, Rockhurst. We were hoping you would introduce us." They smiled and nodded toward the ladies.

The marquis pulled his horse to a stop. "Lady Catherine Gray, sister of the Duke of Hawksford and Lady Persephone Carlisle, daughter of Viscount Radcliff may I introduce Viscount Denmore and the Earl of Mooreland."

"It is a pleasure to meet both of you ladies," the viscount said as the earl managed to squeeze his horse between Persephone and Lord Rockhurst.

"You must be new to London, my lady. A lady as lovely as yourself would not have escaped my notice, I assure you," Lord Mooreland said as he leered at her.

Catherine smiled brightly at both gentlemen. "This is our first season in London, my lords. Both Lady Carlisle and I have been traveling with my aunt the past year."

"Ahh, that is why we have not seen the two of you. Hawksford must be thrilled to have you back home, Lady Gray. Where are you staying while in London, Lady Carlisle?"

Persephone looked over at the marquis. A shadow had come over his face and he was wearing a dark frown and she wondered if the two gentlemen were suitable. "I am also staying at Hawksford House as I am in the guardianship of the duke's aunt."

"Very nice. Two beauties under the same roof. Rockhurst you are indeed a lucky man to be trusted by Hawksford with what I am sure he considers priceless treasures," Lord Mooreland said as he looked over the ladies again.

At this, the marquis rode forward and took the reins of Persephone's horse to pull her away from the earl. Catherine nudged her horse forward as well. "As you say Mooreland, I am trusted. Good day gentleman."

Catherine looked over her shoulder as the three of them rode away. "My goodness the viscount is certainly handsome. And I feel sure the earl has fallen in love with you already Persephone."

"Don't be ridiculous, Catherine. He was just being flirtatious."

The marquis still had a frown on his face. "I am sure Hawk will not be happy that Mooreland has met the two of you. He is a rake after all."

Persephone laughed causing him to turn in her direction. "As are you, my lord."

At this he gave her that jaunty one-sided grin. "That I am, my dear. But no two rakes are the same. There are rules gentlemen should follow when it comes to seduction. Mooreland does not follow them. Don't let yourself be caught alone with him."

Catherine leaned over closer and whispered to Persephone. "I'm sure the same thing goes for my brother as well as Rockhurst and Leicester."

Persephone smiled brightly and turned her attention back to the parade of carriages and phaetons through the park. By the time they were heading back to Hawksford House she had smiled so much her face was beginning to ache. Lord Rockhurst had introduced them to so many of the glittering members of the beau monde, she knew there was no way she would remember everyone. Most were cordial, a few of the ladies tried and failed to hide their jealousy at them being in the company of the marquis. Overall, it had been an enjoyable morning.

As soon as the horses came to a stop in front of Hawksford House grooms came forward to take the reins and stand at the head of the horses. Lord Rockhurst first went to assist Catherine and then came to her. He lifted her to the ground as if she weighed nothing at all. "Thank you, my lord."

His hands were still on her waist as he leaned a little closer. "It was my pleasure, my lady."

He stepped away and Persephone reached up to rub the side of her horses' neck and as she did so, the horse sidestepped and stepped on her foot. "Oh my!" The groom immediately took a firmer hold on the horse and moved him over a step.

Catherine ran over to her. "Persephone! Are you alright?"

She instantly bent down to grab her toes. "My goodness that hurt, but I will be fine. Thank goodness I had on riding boots."

Lord Rockhurst came to her side and took her elbow to help her stand. "What the hell?"

Catherine frowned at him. "She will be fine, accidents happen."

Rockhurst looked toward the house where he saw Hawk watching from the window. He grinned as he looked back to Persephone knowing full well the storm he was about to provoke.

"Well, we don't want to take any chances." With that he swept her up in his arms and started toward the stairs.

Hawk was watching out the window of his study as the trio rode up to the front of the house. His fists clinched at this sides as he watched his friend lift Persephone from the saddle.

"What the hell is wrong with you, Hawk?" Leicester asked from where he sat in the study.

"Charles is back with Persephone and Catherine."

Leicester took a drink of his brandy. "Well, it is about time. Was he planning on keeping them at the park for the entire day? I can't believe you would trust him with your sister. Her reputation could be in tatters as we speak."

Hawk looked away from the window and back toward his friend. "Catherine is safe with him; she is just a child."

"She didn't look like a child last night," Leicester mumbled under his breath before getting up to stand beside his friend at the window. "From the looks of things, you may not have to worry about one of your little problems for much longer."

Hawk gave his friend a harsh look, "What do mean by that?"

"Just look for yourself. Have you ever seen Charles so attentive to a lady?"

"I have seen Charles attentive to a great many ladies," Hawk said as he glared at his friend.

Leicester gave a short laugh. "Not young marriageable ladies. Perhaps he has an eye on Persephone for himself. His father is constantly harassing him about getting married and setting up his nursery. It would solve both of your problems and she would be off your hands."

Hawk's frown deepened. "Charles is not interested in marriage."

"All of us have to marry at one time or another if not for only to proliferate our lineage," Leicester said frowning as if the thought perturbed him.

Hawk continued to watch from the window as Persephone leaned over but he couldn't see what she was doing. Then suddenly Charles swept her into his arms. He shrugged off the restraining hand Leicester placed on his arm as he walked out of the study just as the front door was opened and Charles came in with Persephone in his arms, Catherine following right behind them.

"What in the....?" He stepped right in front of them and immediately took Persephone from him into his own arms.

Rockhurst looked over at Leicester and gave him a wicked grin. "Horse stepped on her foot. I was taking her to her bedroom."

But Hawk wasn't listening and had already started up the stairs. "You will not be going anywhere near her bedroom!"

Charles smiled down at Catherine who stood there with her mouth agape. "I would give them a few minutes and then perhaps go notify your aunt." He gave her a wink before walking over to where Leicester stood in the doorway of the study.

Persephone had been more than a little surprised at the duke's actions. "It really is nothing, your grace. I can walk."

"If you can walk, why was Rockhurst carrying you?"

"I'm not certain, but I can assure you I am perfectly capable of walking." It was obvious he had no intention of putting her back on her feet. She didn't know if she should be angry or mortified. The emotions she was feeling being held tightly against his chest, breathing in his scent as his strong arms held her close were not either.

When they reached the top of the stairs, he looked first one way then the other and asked, "Which room is yours?"

If she wasn't so embarrassed, she would have thought the confused look on his face comical. "Well, I'm not certain, your grace since I have literally not stepped foot inside your home before now."

He looked down at her and his mouth turned up in a one-sided grin. Fortunately, a maid rushed to assist them. "Which room has been assigned for Lady Carlisle?"

"Right this way, your grace," the maid said demurely after dropping into a deep curtsy. She then led the way down the hall to a bedchamber on the right and opened the door for them.

"That will be all," Hawk said dismissing the maid without even looking back at her. He walked quickly over to the bed to set Persephone down before dropping to his knees and reaching for her foot.

Persephone didn't have time to marvel at the opulence of her bedchamber before she felt him removing her boot. "My goodness you are all making such a fuss over nothing." She moved her foot away and pushed the skirt of her riding habit back over her ankle. "That's not even the right foot!"

Without asking he reached for her other foot and quickly removed her boot and stocking to examine the damage. "Doesn't appear to be broken or injured severely," he said as he allowed his hand to move over her tiny foot to her smooth slim ankle.

Persephone could feel her blush rising. "I told you it was nothing." She shivered as his hand moved slowly from her ankle up to the calf of her leg. She quickly recovered her senses and pushing her skirt down again she jumped up from the bed. "I appreciate your concern, your grace but as I said it was unwarranted. I am perfectly fine." He stood up from his position at her feet and loomed over her. She instantly tried to take a step backward, but unfortunately the bed prevented her escape.

He leaned closer and looked at the way her lips formed a perfect pink bow and imagined pulling her bottom lip between his teeth as he kissed her. He dragged his gaze away from her mouth to those deep blue eyes of hers. "I am glad that you weren't hurt." He reached up on impulse and touched the side of her cheek slowly letting his fingers move down toward her chin.

Persephone inhaled sharply at the familiarity but couldn't seem to take her eyes from his face. By God he was handsome, and she could imagine women swooning at his feet on a regular basis. A loud cough from the doorway pulled her from his trance. He lowered his eyes before looking up and once again giving her a devilish grin before taking a few steps backward.

"My goodness, Hawk. Are the gentlemen of the ton always so impulsive? I have been stepped on by my horse countless times and no one has bothered to sweep me up and carry me around," Catherine said as she walked further into the room.

He turned and walked toward his sister. "Lady Carlisle is our guest. I was being a good host."

Catherine's eyes danced with laughter. "Yes, you must be a good host. If word gets out about this, you will have a horde of ladies falling in the street in front of the house or throwing themselves onto the front steps from their carriages." She saw his eyes narrow. "Perhaps I should make Billings aware in case more rescues are needed."

"Mind your tongue, Catherine. I'm not opposed to sending you to a convent." He turned and gave Persephone a deep bow before walking out of the room shutting the door behind him.

Once they were alone Persephone took a deep breath and sat back down on the bed.

Catherine came and sat beside her. "What the devil was that all about?"

Persephone shook her head. "I have no idea."

Catherine let a small giggle escape her.

"What's so funny?"

"It's nothing really. Just that you have been in London less than a week and already you have had two of the most sought-after men of the ton carrying you around in their arms. What sort of girl has that kind of luck?"

Persephone stood and walked over to the fireplace. "I'm not sure I would call it luck, but I have learned one important lesson today."

Catherine cocked her head to the side. "And what lesson is that?"

"That your brother is dangerous. While I do love your family and I am so appreciative of your brother allowing me to stay here with you for the season, I have no intention of falling for his charms. I am not going to be caught in a bad situation. I am not ready to marry and if I do decide to one day it will be for love. Besides, your brother is not in the market for a wife."

Hawk left Persephone's room and made his way back downstairs to his study where he found both Rockhurst and Leicester lounging in the two chairs in front of his desk enjoying his best brandy.

Rockhurst was the first to notice his entrance. He leaned back further propping his feet on the edge of his desk. "I hope Lady Persephone is doing well. She gave us quite a scare."

Hawk did not miss the use of her given name. "It was nothing serious. Which makes me wonder why you thought it was necessary to carry her into the house?"

Rockhurst took a sip of his drink before saying, "I was merely being cautious. What gentleman would not jump at the chance to carry such a beautiful woman in their arms? Besides, I only meant to carry her to her bedchamber to prevent further injury to her foot."

Hawk came round to sit at his desk. "You have no business being in a young lady's bedchamber."

"Did you just deposit her at the top of the stairs then?"

Hawk gave his friend a hard stare. "Get your feet off my desk."

Rockhurst chuckled as he put his feet back on the floor.

Leicester stood from his chair. "You are both ridiculous." He sat his glass down on the desk and headed for the door. "I'll see you later tonight at White's."

"Are you not attending the Beaumont's ball this evening?" Hawk asked.

"I'm not inclined to set the gossips to thinking I'm in the market for a bride. I think I will seek more pleasurable pursuits tonight." His lips lifted on one corner in a devilish smile as he withdrew from the room.

Rockhurst stood as well. "I believe I will take my leave as well. But I will see you later at Beaumont's."

Hawk opened the ledger on his desk, but his mind was not on numbers and accounts. He was thinking of a slim delicate ankle and the lovely lady attached to it.

Chapter Two

Persephone watched as Catherine twirled around for the third time in front of the mirror in her dressing room. "You look beautiful, Catherine. That color definitely suits you better than the white gowns we had to wear to Almacks."

Catherine was wearing her newest ballgown made of a deep rich lavender light muslin with a silver gauze overlay on the skirt. Tiny diamonds were sewn on the skirt, and she shimmered in the light from the candles as she spun around again admiring herself.

"Do you think Leicester will ask me to dance?" she asked as she tugged on one of her brunette curls that was draped over her shoulder.

"If he is there, he might. But if not, there will be scores of gentlemen lined up to dance with you," Persephone said as she stood up and straightened the skirt of her gown. She also was wearing one of her favorite ballgowns. With her fair complexion and light blonde hair, she always thought she appeared washed out in the white or light-colored gowns expected of debutantes. Tonight, she wore a silk gown of royal blue with the same color gauze overlay. It had flowers embroidered in silver thread across the bottom of the skirt. Her golden curls were pinned up in a fashionable coiffure with a few curls framing her face.

Catherine gave her a wink. "Just wait till Hawk sees you in that dress."

Persephone rolled her eyes as she pulled on her white elbow length gloves. "Don't make more of it than it is, Catherine. We should go downstairs; you know how Aunt Louisa hates waiting on us."

Just as they were to leave the room there was a knock at the door. Catherine opened it to find her lady's maid Lillian holding two black velvet jewel cases. "Excuse me, my lady, but I was given these by Mr. Billings to bring to you. His grace had them brought out from the family collection for the two of you to wear tonight.

Catherine reached out and took the boxes from her maid. "Thank you, Lillian." She walked over to the dressing table with Persephone following behind her. "How thoughtful of Hawk to let us wear the family jewels. I can't wait to see what he picked out for us. She opened the first case and it held a stunning sapphire and diamond necklace with matching earrings and a bracelet.

Persephone gasp when she saw the jewels. "Oh, my goodness! They are beautiful." She reached out to touch them as if she couldn't believe they were real.

"These must be for you, Persephone. They will look lovely with your dress." She put that box aside and opened the second one to see that it contained a beautiful amethyst and diamond necklace with matching earrings and a comb for her hair. "Oh my, I remember my mother wearing this set."

"Here let me put the necklace on for you, Persephone."

Persephone shook her head. "Oh no, I couldn't wear something so luxurious and part of your family's collection."

Catherine paid her no heed. "Don't be ridiculous. If Hawk didn't want you to wear them, he would not have sent them to you. It would be insulting if you refused." She turned her friend around and fastened the necklace around her neck. "Now, my turn." She took the amethyst necklace from its case and handed it to Persephone.

Persephone placed the necklace around Catherine's throat before putting on the rest of the jewelry and heading downstairs to join the duke and Aunt Louisa.

The duke was waiting for them at the bottom of the stairs. Persephone thought he was a strikingly handsome man. He was dressed all in black except for his white shirt and intricately styled cravat and his coat fit him to perfection. She could see now why the papers always talked about how women would lay their hearts at his feet.

He offered his hand to her as she reached the bottom step. "Ladies, you both look lovely."

Persephone felt the warmth of his hand through her glove. "Thank you, your grace, for allowing me to wear your family's jewels. I am honored and I promise to take good care of them." She absently reached for her neck and touched the cool stones resting against her throat.

His gaze followed her fingers as they glided over the stones coming to a stop at the larger sapphire resting right above the valley between her breasts. His mind began conjuring images of her wearing nothing but the necklace. He forced his gaze back up to her face. "It is my pleasure, but I believe it is your beauty that makes the jewels look so exquisite."

Persephone blushed at the flattery.

"Where is Aunt Louisa?" Catherine asked breaking the spell.

He dropped Persephone's hand and moved toward the front door where Billings was waiting to help him with his greatcoat. "She is already in the carriage. Shall we join her?"

Catherine took his arm and Persephone followed behind them as they made their way to the ducal conveyance. He handed Catherine into the carriage first to sit beside their Aunt Louisa, then he helped Persephone inside and climbed in to sit next to her.

Persephone wished Catherine had sat beside the duke. She clasped her hands in her lap as he moved an inch closer barely touching her skirts with his leg.

Catherine gave her a mischievous grin. "I really am surprised you decided to join us tonight, Hawk."

Aunt Louisa patted her knee. "It is his duty to see you well matched, dear child. As the sister of the Duke of Hawksford you will be most sought after and not always by the best gentlemen. It is your brother's responsibility to see that he keeps the fortune hunters and rascals at bay."

"Who is going to watch over Persephone?" she asked giving her aunt an innocent smile.

"I will be pleased to help keep the rascals away from Lady Carlisle as well," he said as he looked across the carriage at his sister.

Aunt Louisa smiled and clapped her hands together. "Excellent! What better chaperone could you have?"

Persephone kept her gaze straight ahead not wanting to look over at the man beside her.

When the carriage joined the line of others waiting for their turn to drop off their passengers, Persephone became more excited. She leaned forward to see out the window. Torches lined the drive up to the large mansion and she marveled at the many fine carriages lining up and the elegantly dressed men and women alighting from them. Their carriage came to a stop and a livered footman with a white heavily powdered wig, opened the door. The duke was the first to alight from the carriage. He assisted Catherine and Aunt Louisa before reaching up to take her hand. She placed her gloved hand in his and felt a shiver as he squeezed lightly.

As they walked up the steps to where the major domo was waiting to announce them, he leaned over and spoke. "Before the other gentlemen here request all your dances, I would ask you to save a waltz for me."

She looked over at him. He gave her a mischievous grin before straightening his shoulders and raising his chin a notch higher transforming into the formidable duke that he truly was before being announced. She thought he looked very regal standing there and as he entered the room, she didn't miss the way ladies began fanning themselves a little more vigorously as he drew near.

Catherine walked up beside her and took her hand. "Isn't it grand, Persephone? The season is going to be so entertaining."

She and Catherine made their way further towards the ballroom and were indeed besieged by gentlemen asking for their dance cards. As the first gentleman claimed a dance, she glanced over to where the duke was having an intimate conversation with a beautiful lady in a low-cut red gown who was doing her best to display her bosom to the upmost advantage. She saw him give the lady an exasperated look before his eyes caught hers. He held up his glass of champagne in salute and nodded slightly to her. She gave him a half grin trying not to laugh out loud as the lady pressed her chest into his arm almost spilling his champagne. Persephone turned her attention back to her dance partner, Lord something or other, as they moved further into the center of the ballroom.

Hawk gave the lady beside him a harsh look after her unwanted attention nearly caused him to spill his drink all over his new coat made by Weston. "Excuse me, madam."

He walked away leaving her in a huff and went over to where Rockhurst and Leicester were standing off to the side of the room. "I would have thought the two of you had more pleasurable pursuits tonight than Beaumont's ball."

Leicester shrugged his shoulders. "We felt it necessary to come to your aide in the event you needed help. Your Aunt Louisa is already in the card room and since you seem to be unable to take your eyes from Lady Carlisle, someone needs to be here to watch over your sister."

Rockhurst took a sip of his drink as his gaze followed a young married lady passing by fluttering her lashes at him over the top of her fan. "I'm here simply looking over the wares hoping to find a lovely bed sport partner for the evening." He turned back to his friends. "Perhaps that is what you need, Hawk, a quick tumble in the sheets. I hear Lady Milton is high spirited in the bedroom. I'm not speaking from firsthand experience, but I have heard rumors."

"I am not in need of a bed partner at the moment. My main concern is chaperoning my sister this season," he said as he absently scanned the ballroom looking for her.

Rockhurst smirked. "Not to mention the delicious Persephone."

Hawk gave him a slight frown which drew his brows together. "You shouldn't speak of her in that way."

Rockhurst raised one eyebrow. "I speak about a great many ladies that way."

Leicester grumbled loudly. "You are both exasperating. If I must stand here and listen to the two of you all evening, I'll go mad." He nodded toward the dance floor. "Don't you think Lord Farthington is looking much too pleased with himself after dancing with Catherine. He is a bloody bounder and should be warned away from her."

Hawk gave his friend an odd look. "Catherine has too much sense to be taken in by Farthington, but I will speak to her later tonight. Right now, I see she is with Lord Keeling and he is a more than honorable fellow and would certainly make her an excellent match."

Leicester downed the remainder of his drink. "As you say, how do you feel about Mooreland because it seems he is about to claim Lady Carlisle's next dance, which if I am correct is to be a waltz."

Hawk handed his drink to a passing footman. "Excuse me gentlemen, I believe this is to be my dance."

Persephone had just finished a quadrille with Lord Falconbridge when she heard a familiar voice behind her. "Good evening, Lady Carlisle."

She spun around. "Lord Mooreland, how good it is to see you again."

He bowed at the waist and took her hand and raised it to his lips. Persephone tried to suppress the desire to pull her hand away and wipe it on her dress. "You are indeed the loveliest lady in the room. I hope you have been enjoying the evening's festivities."

She smiled tentatively. "It has been a lovely evening; the Beaumont's have a magnificent home."

He still held her hand in his. "The next dance is a waltz, and I would be honored if you would consent to dance it with me."

She opened her mouth to reply when a strong deep voice answered for her.

"Sorry to disappoint you, Mooreland, but I believe the lady has promised this waltz to me." Hawk reached over and removed her hand from the earl's.

Lord Mooreland straightened, and Persephone could see he was angered by the duke's interference. "Your grace." He bowed slightly just enough not to be insulting. "Lady Carlisle, perhaps another time." He turned and walked out of the room.

"Oh my, he isn't happy with you at all."

Hawk took her hand and moved her further onto the dancefloor. He put his hand on her waist and drew her closer as the strains of the waltz began. "I am not concerned with Mooreland and neither should you be."

Persephone tried to ignore the warmth she felt as his hand rested on the small of her back as he guided her through a spin. "I see you were able to extract yourself from the clutches of the lady in the red dress without any damages to your coat."

He smiled disarmingly when he looked down at her and her heart lurched a little. "Escaping the clutches of ambitious females is a skill I have cultivated over the years."

"Yes, I have read of your exploits."

He noticed the teasing sparkle in her eyes and the charming dimples on her cheeks when she grinned, and he couldn't decide if he should be irritated that she knew so much about his past or enchanted by the tongue and cheek way she referred to it. "I still can't believe Aunt Louisa allowed the two of you to read such rubbish." He pulled her a little closer. "And only a small portion of the stories are true."

"I would love to hear the story of how Leicester tried to walk the tightrope when the acrobatic performers were at Vauxhall," Persephone said as he twirled her faster. The duke was an excellent dancer and made her feel as if she were floating. At times she thought that if he did not have such a tight hold on her waist, she would lose her footing as they spun around the room.

Hawk felt completely enthralled by her smile and wit. "It was an exciting evening, and I am ashamed to admit that we all had been drinking more than we should. But luckily Rockhurst had enough sense to stop him before he broke his fool neck."

"And where were you, your grace?"

He gave her that devilish look again. "I was occupied elsewhere."

"That is exactly what the scandal sheets said."

He frowned for just a moment then quickly changed the subject. "Tell me, have you found the evening stimulating? Have any gentlemen caught your attention?"

"Everyone has been very nice except a few ladies that sent me nasty looks when it was mentioned that I was staying at Hawksford House, but alas the search for a husband must continue. Not that I'm really interested in marriage."

He laughed at her comment. It was unusual enjoying being in the company of a woman who wasn't lying beneath him. Typically, the company of females grated on his nerves. The constant talk of ribbons, hats, dressmakers, and idle gossip was enough to drive him mad. But talking to Persephone was a pleasure and that was something he had not expected. "It's jealousy because you are exceptionally beautiful. Ladies will always try to shun those they think are competition. And what do you mean that you are not interested in marriage? Isn't that what every young female is after?" The dance ended and he found himself reluctant to release her.

"Most young females, yes." She smiled at his look of perplexity. "You are too kind, your grace. Thank you for the dance." She curtsied and then turned to greet the next gentlemen waiting for her.

He made his way to the card rooms where he found Leicester and Rockhurst engaged in a game of hazard. They looked up as he walked up to them. "Care to join us? The dice seem to favor me tonight and you can afford to lose a great deal," Leicester said as his friend sat down.

Hawk signaled for a footman to bring him a drink. "No, I think I will keep my blunt tonight."

Lord Rockhurst took a drink from the footman as well. "You know they have her on the betting books at Whites."

Hawk gave him a curious look. "Who?"

"Lady Carlisle."

Hawk shrugged his shoulders. "Those fools will wager on anything. What exactly are they betting on?"

Rockhurst cursed under his breath as he lost again. "There are actually two bets on the books. The first being who gets her to the altar and the second whether she will be in your bed before she gets there and after that dance tonight, I will wager the odds just went up on that score."

Hawk shot to his feet the anger he was feeling threatening to burst forth. "I will see that anything linked to her name is removed from the books and I will ruin anyone that thinks to challenge me."

Leicester threw the dice again. "For God's sake, Hawk sit down. You know as well as I that this is not the first time ladies have been on the books at Whites."

"It will be the last time this particular lady is on the books." He took a seat again holding his anger at bay.

Rockhurst leaned back in his seat. "Don't you want to know who they are currently saying has the best chance of marrying her?"

"Not particularly," Hawk said as he took a drink of his champagne.

"Well, it isn't you. Believe it or not I am currently in the lead for that honor," Rockhurst said amused by his friend's expression.

Hawk laughed. "You must be joking."

"I don't know why you are so surprised. I have to marry sometime and even though I am a mere marquess at present, I am the heir to the Duke of Avanley." He shifted forward a bit. "I am quite a good catch. Besides, I was seen with her in the park."

"This is ridiculous. I should put a stop to this nonsense." Hawk stood from his chair. "I'm going back to the ballroom to resume my role as chaperone."

Leicester stood as well gathering the money he had won from his friend. "Rockhurst you are no longer making it interesting. I grow tired of winning your money. I think I will leave and go visit Lucy. She is still upset with me for canceling the other night." He grinned rakishly. "I must make it up to her."

Both gentlemen managed to weave through the crowd to the edge of the dancefloor avoiding the gaze of expectant ladies hoping for an invitation to dance. They stood watching as both Catherine and Persephone danced with two young lordlings who looked completely enamored. Catherine swirled past them smiling brightly at her partner.

"I thought you were leaving. Don't you have an eager lady waiting for you?" Hawk asked as he glanced over to his friend.

Leicester watched the dancers. "I'll buy her a bracelet instead. Excuse me."

The dance ended and Leicester walked over to where Catherine stood talking to her partner. When he walked up the young lord took a step back and lost a little of the color in his face. He bowed quickly. "Your grace." Then turned and scampered away.

Catherine tried to hide her excitement. "Did you really have to scare him away?"

"It is not my fault he ran like a rabbit," Leicester said as he took her elbow and led her to the refreshment table. "I just wanted to remind you to be careful. Some of the gentlemen I have noticed you dancing with are not suitable."

Catherine looked over at him wrinkling her forehead in annoyance. "You have appointed yourself my guardian then?"

"Since your brother is otherwise preoccupied, I feel it is my duty to assist you as I would my own sister."

At his words Catherine felt her heart break just a little. "I am not your sister nor your responsibility, your grace. Excuse me." She turned to walk away but he grabbed her arm and turned her back around to face him.

"Don't be senseless, Catherine, I am only trying to help you."

She felt tears gathering in her eyes. "I don't need your help." She quickly walked away hoping to find Persephone before anyone noticed her distress.

Persephone was standing at the edge of the ballroom near one of the sets of open doors that led out onto the terrace talking to Lord Williamson and Lord Bentley when she saw her friend heading in her direction.

It took all of Catherine's resolve to keep it together as she made her way over to the trio. "Excuse me, gentlemen but I would ask Lady Persephone to join me on the terrace for some air."

"Certainly, my lady. Would you like us to join you?" Lord Bentley asked sweetly.

Persephone recognized her friend's distress. "We will be only a few moments. Perhaps you could both get us a drink from the refreshment table, and we will rejoin you shortly." That seemed to appease them and when they walked away toward the refreshments, Persephone quickly ushered Catherine out the doors onto the terrace which was luckily empty at the moment.

"Oh, my dear, what is the matter?" Persephone asked as she hugged her friend.

"It's Leicester. He pulled me aside and lectured me on making sure I was dancing with suitable gentlemen. He sees me as a sister." She sniffled and wiped her eyes. "I have loved him since I was twelve years old, but he is never going to see me as anything but Hawk's sister."

Persephone understood her friend's disappointment. "I think he will come around in time. Who could not love you?"

Catherine smiled through her tears. "I don't know what I would do without you, Persephone. You are right. I shall not give up hope."

They stayed on the terrace a few minutes longer making certain no one would notice Catherine's discomposure before joining Lords Bentley and Williamson back inside.

After dancing a few more times. Aunt Louisa emerged from one of the card rooms and announced she was ready to return to Hawksford House. The duke summoned the carriage and they said goodbye to their hosts before he handed the ladies up into the carriage. Once they were all inside, he shut the door.

"Aren't you coming with us, Hawk?" Catherine asked.

"I'm going to join Rockhurst at our club. I will be home much later." With that he knocked on the side of the carriage to signal the driver to drive on.

Persephone looked down at her hands and wondered if he was really going to the clubs or if he was meeting a lady. There were plenty at the ball sending him provocative looks and she was sure they would welcome him into their beds. She sighed heavily wondering what it would be like to have the same freedom as a man. She shook her head slightly. It was none of her business what the Duke of Hawksford did in his spare time. She was here to enjoy the pleasures of the season with her friend, not to be seduced by London's most notorious rake.

Chapter Three

After such a long, stimulating night Persephone thought she could have fallen right to sleep, but as she tossed and turned in her bed, she realized sleep was not going to come easy for her. She blew out a frustrated breath and decided she would go get a book to read from the library. She got up from her bed, put on her wrapper, and grabbed the candle on the table beside the bed. The hallways were dark, and all the servants would be asleep, so she quietly made her way down to the first floor to the library. She was surprised to see the room partially lit and thought perhaps the servants had forgotten to extinguish a candle burning. She moved over to the bookcases but startled at the sound of a familiar deep voice.

"You couldn't sleep either?"

Persephone turned quickly. "Your grace, I wasn't expecting to see anyone at this time of night."

As he stealthily moved out of the shadows into the light, she could see he had discarded most of his evening attire and was wearing just his white shirt which he had opened at the neck allowing her a glimpse of dark hair on his chest and his black trousers.

He stopped a few feet from her. "So, what has you out of bed at this time of night?" He took a sip of what she thought must be brandy before setting the glass down on a nearby table.

Nervously she began to fidget with the tie on her robe. "I couldn't sleep, all of the excitement of the evening I suppose. What about you? I thought you would still be at your club."

He had the devil of a time concentrating on her words as he watched her fingers tug on the silk ribbon tied just below her breasts. "Whites held no amusement for me tonight. I preferred to be home." He looked up and caught the smirk on her lips.

"If you aren't careful, your grace, your reputation will take a hit. If word gets out you preferred the quiet of home to a night of debauchery at your club your standing as a rake could be ruined."

He took three steps forward till he was inches away from her. "It's your reputation that you should be worried about. You are standing in a poorly lit room alone with me at an ungodly hour of the night." He reached out and took the ribbon that tied her robe in his fingers. "Me choosing to be alone with the most beautiful woman in London would only bolster my reputation."

For a moment she wanted to lean into him, feel his strong arms come around her, have him kiss her, but she came to her senses before she did anything so incredibly stupid. She pulled her ribbon from his fingers. Falling for the duke's charms was the last thing she needed to do. She moved away from him closer to the bookshelves. "I will just grab a book and leave you to your solitude." She turned to read the spines of the books, but she could sense him moving behind her.

She quickly grabbed a book off the shelf and turned to leave. But as she moved to pass him, he reached out and took the book from her. He read the title and looked back at her with one arched eyebrow. "I had not realized you were so interested in animal husbandry."

She glanced at the book and her cheeks instantly flamed.

He chuckled at her look of embarrassment. "I think you are trying to escape me, Persephone. Do you not enjoy my company?"

She wished the floor would just open and swallow her. "It isn't that I don't enjoy your company and our dance this evening but…."

He moved so quickly that she didn't have time to think. "I'm going to kiss you, Persephone."

He put his hands on either side of her cheeks and tilted her face up to his. As he was lowering his lips to hers, he stopped. Her eyes were closed tight, and her lips slightly parted. She had a look of complete innocence. "Have you ever been kissed before, Persephone?"

She opened her eyes and blinked. "No, well when I was twelve the baker's son in the village stole a kiss." She lowered her lashes, and her cheeks turned a lovely shade of pink.

He smiled and his voice softened. "Do you want to be kissed?"

She raised her eyes to his. "I'm not sure."

He cocked his head to the side quizzically. "You're not?"

Her brow furrowed and she bit her bottom lip before trying to explain. "You see, being kissed by you I think would be nice."

"Nice?"

"Yes, nice. But it might also be a mistake. I'm sure you kiss very well at least that is what the…."

He looked irritated as he finished her statement for her. "Scandal sheets say?"

She did have the good grace to look embarrassed. "Yes, but we would never suit."

He took his hands from her face and stood a little straighter. "I'm not sure if I should be insulted or relieved? Never have I been rebuffed before I even kissed a lady. Now that I think of it, I have never been rejected… ever."

She couldn't help but grin and reached out and absently touched his hand. "Oh no, I didn't mean it that way. But if we were discovered you might have to propose marriage and we both know marriage is not at the forefront of your mind nor is it in mine."

He reached around and wrapped an arm around her waist to pull her closer into him. "You are overthinking things, Persephone. One kiss doesn't always lead to marriage." He took his fingers and lifted her chin. "One kiss, just a taste," he whispered as his lips lowered to hers.

As soon as his lips touched hers, he knew one kiss would not be enough. She tasted sweet and her innocence was like an aphrodisiac to him. Her lips parted and he took full advantage to let his tongue mingle with hers. She was hesitant at first, but a fast learner. He was surprised when she nibbled lightly on his lower lip, and it spurred him to pull her tighter. He let his hand move from her waist to cup her perfectly rounded backside. She sighed against his mouth. He broke the kiss to look down into her upturned face. Her eyes were still closed, and her lips were pink and slightly swollen from his kiss. He thought she could not have looked more beautiful. He moved to kiss her again when her eyes opened, and she stepped back.

Persephone wasn't sure her legs would hold her, but she did manage to move a step away from him. "My goodness, that was very…"

"Don't you dare say, nice," he said wrinkling his brow.

She reached up and touched her lips. "No, that was much better than nice, your grace."

"I think you should call me, Hawk."

She shook her head. "That would never be proper."

He smiled that smile that made her toes curl. "You are much too concerned with being proper, Persephone. It will certainly be alright for you to address me as Hawk, most of my close acquaintances do so."

"Alright, if you insist, Hawk. But I'm not sure we should make a habit of being alone, again."

He stalked her as she took a few steps backward towards the door. "We are definitely going to make it a habit of being alone, my dear."

Persephone started to argue with him, but with the predatory gleam in his eyes she decided it would be best to retreat and gain her wits before facing him again. She turned and left the room hurrying back up the stairs to her bedroom.

Hawk watched her go and wondered what had come over him. She was beautiful, no question about that, but he had beautiful women before and none of them kept him from getting sleep at night or made him want to strangle every man that looked in their direction. There was something about Persephone that got under his skin. He had hoped that a kiss would cure him of his craving, but unfortunately it had only heightened his lust for her. He reached for the remainder of his brandy and swallowed it in one long swig. What was it going to take to get Persephone Carlisle out of his thoughts?

Persephone leaned back against her bedroom door after she had closed it. The things she read in the scandal sheets about the Duke of Hawksford did not do him justice. She placed a hand over her rapidly beating heart. Her lips still tingled from his kiss. She had known it would be a mistake to let him kiss her. How would she ever be able to be in the same room with the man and not want to drag him into the nearest coat closet? How would she ever be able to kiss another man without thinking of his scorching kiss?

"Damn it," she said to herself as she walked over to the bed. If she thought sleep was hard to come by before, it would be nearly impossible now.

Persephone closed her eyes and sighed as her lady's maid tried to apply some creams and lotions that would help make her look less fatigued. "It will be alright, Sarah. I am only tired and I'm sure once I have a good breakfast and get some fresh air I will look and feel much better."

"Yes, my lady," Sarah said as she pinched her cheeks trying to put some color on her face.

Thankfully, she was saved from any more of her maid's ministrations when Catherine burst through the door. "Persephone! You must hurry and come downstairs. Loads of flowers are being delivered with notes of affection from gentlemen we met last night at the ball. Aunt Louisa says we must be ready to greet callers this afternoon." Her friend walked closer. "One of the arrangements for me even had a love sonnet accompanying it." She laughed and plopped down in a chair beside her. "This season is going to be so much fun."

Persephone stifled a yawn. "I'm sure it will be. Although, I'm not sure I can stand too many more late nights."

Catherine grabbed her hand and pulled her from the chair. "Don't be such a ninny. Come see everything."

Persephone stumbled along behind her friend down the stairs where there were indeed at least a dozen beautiful flower arrangements waiting for them. "Oh my, there are so many!"

"And more to come I'm sure of it," Catherine said excitedly.

Aunt Louisa came out of the parlor. "Girls let's join his grace for breakfast. We can't stand around all day gawking. You must be prepared for callers."

They followed her into the breakfast room and Persephone stopped short when she saw Hawk standing at the head of the table. She didn't know how he did it. He looked immaculate and in no way as if he had any trouble sleeping at all.

"Good morning, aunt." He walked toward his Aunt Louisa and kissed her cheek before pulling a chair out for her.

A footman rushed over to hold chairs out for Catherine and herself .

"Good morning, Catherine, Persephone," he said nodding in their direction.

Catherine smiled brightly at her brother. "Good morning, Hawk."

"Good morning, your grace," Persephone said as she tried and failed to avoid eye contact. He winked at her, and she looked quickly away towards the food on the buffet.

"Did you see all the flowers Persephone and I have received this morning, Hawk? We were quite the success last night," Catherine said as a footman set a plate of food before her.

Persephone kept her eyes downcast even though she could feel his gaze on her.

"There was never any doubt in my mind that the two of you would be a success. You look tired this morning, Persephone," he said in a teasing voice.

She glanced up quickly to see him smirk. "I'm sure I will be fine after some breakfast and perhaps some fresh air." She stabbed her fork into her a sausage. Was he deliberately baiting her?

Aunt Louisa took a sip of her tea. "You know we will be besieged with callers this morning, Ethan. I was hoping you would be home today. After all, I'm sure you will know some, if not all, of the gentlemen. It would be helpful to have some inside information, so we know who is acceptable and who is not." She reached over and patted Catherine's hand and then Persephone's. "I do want to make certain my girls find the best possible matches."

"You know that I don't intend on marrying my first season, Aunt Louisa and Persephone isn't looking for a husband either. Can't we just have fun this season and not feel as if we were on an auction block?"

Aunt Louisa gasp. "Don't be crude, Catherine."

Catherine looked over at her brother. "Do you think any of your friends will be calling on us today, Hawk?"

Persephone knew her friend was thinking of the Duke of Leicester. She glanced over at the duke and wondered what his thoughts would be if he knew Catherine was in love with his best friend.

"I will be in my office meeting with my secretary on estate matters today so I will be at home if you have need of me." He then stood from his chair. "I hope you ladies enjoy the attention you receive today. I would caution you to remember that not all men are honorable and there are quite a few fortune hunters this season." He stopped behind Persephone's chair. "When you are ready to take some air, I will be happy to escort you."

Persephone tried to avoid the strange look Catherine and Aunt Louisa gave her. "I'm sure you are much too busy, your grace. My maid will be glad to join me."

He placed his hand on the back of her chair and although no one else could see, she felt his fingers lightly touch the back of her neck. "I insist. As soon as you are finished with your breakfast I will be waiting." He bowed slightly to his aunt before turning and leaving the room.

"My word, whatever has gotten into Hawksford?" Aunt Louisa asked as she eyed her over the rim of her teacup.

Catherine was not nearly as obtuse. "I think he fancies you, Persephone."

Persephone nearly dropped her cup and cringed as it clanked against the saucer. "He is just being a good host."

Catherine giggled. "Yes, I'm certain that's all it is."

Persephone stood up ignoring her friend's sarcastic comment and not wanting to endure Aunt Louisa's questioning stares, she left the room and found the duke talking with his secretary just outside the door to his study. "Excuse me, your grace."

"Ah, there you are, Lady Carlisle. I was just telling Mr. Phillips that I will be back in about an hour. Shall we?" He offered her his arm.

She placed her hand on his sleeve. "We can just take a stroll in the garden. I know you are busy."

"I thought we would take a short stroll through Mayfair." He grabbed her hand when she went to pull away.

"Mayfair? That really isn't necessary. The garden will be fine."

"As you wish." He led her back through his study and out the double doors to a path that led to the small gardens behind the house. Once out of sight of the house he stopped beside a bench and motioned for her to take a seat. "I don't come out here often, but this seems like a quiet place where we can enjoy the morning."

Persephone sighed heavily. "I don't mean to be rude or insulting, but we really shouldn't be doing this."

"Doing what?"

She waved an exasperated arm around. "This! Walking in the garden together alone and certainly not after what happened last night in the library."

He sat beside her. "Did you not enjoy what we did in the library? I found it rather pleasurable."

She rolled her eyes. "Of course, I enjoyed it. Any woman would enjoy being kissed by you. I would venture to say you are an expert in that arena. But we cannot continue. Your sister is already suspicious after you offered to walk with me this morning. And can you imagine how disappointed in me your aunt would be if she found out about last night or caught us kissing again."

He took her hand and brought it to his lips. "We should enjoy the pleasure we bring to each other. I will make certain no one discovers us. After tasting you last night I find myself craving more."

She licked her lips and shivered as his words. He was definitely good at this. Pleasure would be assured if she allowed this to continue. "Regardless, I am here, in London, to enjoy the season not to husband hunt as others might think. If we were to be discovered it could be disastrous for both of us. While I agree that it would be enjoyable, it would not be wise."

This was new to him. He was a duke and used to getting exactly what he wanted. Women had always thrown themselves into his path at every opportunity, so for this woman to deny him didn't sit well. He found himself getting a little angry. But he was good at seduction and perhaps he would have to put a little more effort into getting what he wanted. He stood and offered her his hand to help her up. "If that is what you think is best."

She felt a mixture of relief and disappointment. He had agreed to her request but was it what she truly wished. Last night she had thought of little else but his kiss. Now she had been successful in convincing him to never kiss her again. Her heart sank a little at the thought of never being in his arms again but instead she said, "I think it would be best."

"I will agree on one condition." He still held her hand. "I require you save me a waltz at every ball we attend."

She looked at him suspiciously, "A waltz at every ball will get people talking about us."

He shrugged his shoulders. "They already gossip about me at every turn, as you are quick to point out in the scandal sheets, but I also require you play a game of chance with me on nights we do not attend a ball."

She put her hands on her hips. "For some reason I feel as if I am a lamb being led to the slaughter. What's the wager in this game of chance?"

"A kiss"

She shook her head. "No, that's a ridiculous wager. I'm sure you are an expert at games of chance which leaves me at a disadvantage, not to mention doing the exact thing I am trying to avoid."

"You are too smart for your own good." He put his hand to his chin as if in deep thought. "Alright, I will agree if you promise a waltz at every ball and on nights we do not attend a ball, you will spend at least one hour with me."

Her eyes narrowed as if she were trying to discover the plot. "I'm not sure you understand."

He took her hand and placed it on his arm as he began walking back toward the house. "I understand perfectly. You feel it is unwise for us to engage in carnal pleasures. I find that I enjoy spending time with you, so I proposed a compromise."

She blushed at the words carnal pleasures as was his plan. He needed to throw her off balance or she would reason things out and not agree to his scheme.

He stopped before they reached the house. "Are we in agreement then? One waltz and one hour in my company."

She took a deep breath. "I need to think on this."

He put both hands around her waist and pulled her into his chest. He leaned down and kissed her softly until he felt her hands clutch the lapels of his jacket then he deepened the kiss. He loved the way she felt against him and was reluctant to let her go but too much might shock her. He just needed to kiss her enough to get her to agree. He lifted his lips from hers and whispered. "Do you acquiesce?"

Persephone wasn't sure she was capable of coherent thought, but she felt herself nodding in agreement.

"Excellent. Now we should go back inside before Catherine comes looking for you."

Persephone did not say another word as he led her back toward the house. Once she was at the foot of the stairs he bowed deeply over her hand. "I will see you later, Persephone." He then turned to go back to his study to join his secretary.

3 hours later

Aunt Louisa had been correct, they had been besieged by callers all afternoon. Persephone was beginning to struggle with keeping up with the conversations and the names of the gentlemen. Catherine was smiling sweetly at Lord Whittington or Wallington; she couldn't remember and more than once she found her eyes getting heavy as she struggled not to yawn. Aunt Louisa would be appalled at her lack of manners if she broke out in a wide unladylike yawn right now.

"Lady Carlisle, . . .are you alright?" Lord Philmont asked causing her to sit more upright.

"Yes, I'm perfectly well, my lord. Pardon me for my lack of attention. Since we are new to London it has been difficult to adjust myself to city hours."

He reached over and patted her hand, an action she felt was patronizing. "It is perfectly understandable that you would be more comfortable keeping country hours. But I'm sure it will not take long to adjust to the late nights of London."

She tried to smile without her face showing the irritation she was feeling. "Yes, I'm certain we will adjust."

"Do you like the opera, my lady?" he asked obviously wanting to continue the conversation that she desperately wanted to end.

She blinked a few times trying to stay alert. "I love the theater. I have been a few times with Viscountess Mulford."

He clasped his hands together. "Excellent. I have a box, although not nearly as large and elaborate as Hawksford's box, I do think it has an excellent view of the stage."

"It sounds lovely, my lord."

She was saved from trying to come up with more to say when the duke entered the chamber. The gentlemen all rose to their feet and bowed respectfully as he outranked everyone in the room.

He stopped beside Lord Philmont. "Good afternoon, Philmont."

Lord Philmont gave him a thin-lipped smile. "Hawksford, I don't believe I have seen you in Parliament lately."

The duke took a seat beside her on the settee. "I have been seeking more pleasurable pursuits lately." His eyes glanced over at her just enough so she would notice but the young lordling would not.

Lord Philmont puffed his chest out a bit. "I find nothing more pleasurable than doing my duty and serving my country."

Persephone tried not to cringe. Lord Philmont was young, and she hoped the duke would not be offended by his remark. She was sure he was just trying to make himself sound significant in front of such an important peer. She bit the corner of her bottom lip waiting to see if Hawk would eviscerate the young lord.

The duke did not seem bothered by the comment, he simply grinned in that devilish way of his before responding. "If Parliament is the most pleasurable thing you have engaged in, then I suggest you expand your horizons and pursue some other interests." He then stood. "Excuse me, I must make my way about the room." He leaned over and took her hand raising it to his lips before turning and walking toward his sister.

"The man may be a duke, but he is also the biggest rogue in London. He and his friends Leicester and Rockhurst are disgraceful," Lord Philmont whispered sanctimoniously to her.

She didn't know if it was because she was so tired or if Lord Philmont just seemed to grate on her nerves, but she felt she couldn't let an insult to her host go unchecked. "My lord, the duke has been nothing but kind to me and his sister since we have been in London. It is not very gracious of you to speak of him so in his house."

Lord Philmont seemed shocked that she would dare to speak to him in such a way. "Excuse me, my lady. I meant no offense, perhaps I should take my leave."

"Perhaps you should. Good day, my lord." She didn't even bother to show him out. She took the brief reprieve to close her eyes if only for a moment.

"For a lady so worried about her reputation, you certainly will have people talking if you defend my honor so staunchly every time someone mutters an insult."

Persephone opened her eyes and sighed heavily. "He was rude, and what's more, I found him bothersome."

He smiled but remained standing. "Well, I'm afraid you may have missed out on an invitation to join him in his box at the theater."

She chuckled softly. "Yes, I'm afraid so."

"Luckily, I have a box you can use."

"Yes, he did make a point of telling me that while his box wasn't as grand as yours, it did have an excellent view."

He almost reached out and touched the dimple on her cheek. One day he would kiss it but now was a time for restraint. It was obvious she was exhausted; her eyes were not as bright as they had been the night before. "Would you like me to send everyone on their way so you could rest before dinner tonight?"

It was tempting to take him up on the offer, but she knew Catherine was having a grand time having so many gentlemen at her feet. She would not dream of spoiling it for her. "I'm sure you could clear the room with a single word and while I appreciate the offer, I could not ruin your sister's fun."

He looked over to where his sister sat with three gentlemen dancing attendance on her. "None of them stand a chance. She is just playing with them."

She was surprised that he was so astute and wondered if he knew where his sister's affections truly lay. "Catherine is so effervescent; she naturally draws men to her."

He turned to look at her and his face took on a more serious note. "What of you? What draws men to you, Persephone? Is it your unmatched beauty, your bright smile, your wit, or those eyes, eyes the color that poets write about?"

She blushed brightly and looked down not wanting to meet his gaze. "You flatter me, your grace. One thing I do know for certain is that it is not my dowry."

He smiled at her humor. "I think it is all of the above and more. I am determined to discover the more." He bowed to her and she watched as he left the room as silently as he had entered.

Chapter Four

Luckily, Persephone did manage to be able to go to her room for a couple of hours before it was time to get ready for dinner. Thankfully, they would be dining at home. Catherine was excited because the Duke of Leicester was to join them as was Lord Rockhurst. Persephone was feeling much better after a short nap. She had a feeling she would be needing her wits about her tonight if the duke insisted on an hour alone with her. How he would manage to get her alone without his aunt or sister knowing was a mystery to her, but with the duke's reputation she was sure he would think of something. Her maid was just putting the finishing touches to her hair when Catherine came in all smiles.

"Wasn't this morning fun? I couldn't believe we received so many callers." She plopped down on the bed. "And tonight, I am wearing one of my favorite gowns."

Persephone smiled at her friend. "You look stunning in all of your gowns."

Catherine motioned for the maid to leave them. Once they were alone, she looked at Persephone and said, "So, what exactly is going on with you and my brother?"

Persephone thought she had swallowed her tongue and started to cough. "I have already told you that he is just being kind and considerate."

Catherine rolled her eyes and sighed. "Yes, he has a reputation for being kind and considerate. I'm his sister, Persephone don't try to make me believe that nonsense. I have never seen him behave this way towards a lady."

Persephone stood and walked over to the bed. "You have not spent that much time in your brother's company in a good many years, Catherine. Do you truly know how he behaves with ladies?"

Catherine rolled her eyes again as she headed toward the door. "I am not blind, my dear friend, even if you are."

The Duke of Leicester and Lord Rockhurst sat in the library with Hawk as they waited for the ladies to come down for dinner. Leicester swirled some of Hawk's best brandy around in the glass before sipping it slowly. "I heard your house was besieged by callers this morning."

Hawk narrowed his eyes slightly. "Just where did you hear that, I might ask, and when did you start listening to gossip?"

"So, it isn't true?"

Hawk nodded his head faintly. "It's true. But no one seemed to seriously gain their interest."

"It shouldn't take long. They are already being heralded as the toasts of the season. I also heard at Whites that Lord Penwick is looking for a bride and has mentioned that an alliance with the Duke of Hawksford would be a good match for both parties," Lord Rockhurst said as he watched the rain beating against the windows.

"Penwick is sixty years old. He is old enough to be Catherine's father. Surely, he does not think I would marry my sister off to him," Hawk replied in disgust. "Catherine would never consent to anything so perverse."

Lord Rockhurst nodded in agreement. "I never thought she would, and I knew you would never consider it. Just letting you know that Penwick may make his intentions known to you. Has anyone caught Catherine's attention or that of the lovely Persephone?"

"It's only been a few days, Rockhurst. I'm sure both ladies will be more selective than to choose a husband in the time span of a week," Leicester said irritably as he finished his drink.

Hawk leaned back in his chair, his mind drifting to what he hoped would be a pleasant night. He was to have his one hour alone with Persephone, and while he promised not to kiss her, he could think of more pleasurable things he could do with her that didn't involve kissing.

"Hawk! What the hell is wrong with you? You don't want to go out to the clubs, you can't even keep your head in our conversation, and I bet you haven't seen the buxom Marie since your aunt came to town." Rockhurst smirked, "Could there be a reason for your lack of interest in all things wicked? And could this reason be about five foot four with long blonde curls, blue eyes, and curves that make a man, . . ."

"Enough! You are speaking of a lady not a cheap jewel of the demi monde," Hawk said as he rose from his chair, grabbing his coat and putting it on. "Dinner should be ready, and the ladies will be down soon." He walked from the room leaving his two friends smiling at each other as they moved to join him.

The ladies were indeed descending the stairs as they left the study. Aunt Louisa was the first to reach the gentlemen as they waited at the bottom of the stairs. "Ethan," she greeted him as he pressed a kiss to her hand. "Leicester, Lord Rockhurst I hope you will not mind if I extended the invitation to two other gentlemen tonight. Lord Barrington and Lord Fenmore will be joining us this evening."

Hawk frowned at this news. He had been looking forward to more time with Persephone and now it occurred to him that sharing her with the likes of Fenmore or Barrington was not appealing. "You should have informed me sooner, aunt," he replied curtly.

She waved off his comment. "They are very eligible gentlemen. Both come from excellent families and while not nearly as wealthy as any of you," piercing each one with a stare, "they do have respectable fortunes. Either of them would make excellent matches for Catherine or Persephone." She smoothly moved away from him unperturbed at his annoyance.

Leicester offered her his arm and gave her his most attractive smile. "My lady, may I escort you into the drawing room while we await our other guests."

She cackled at him as she placed her boney hand on his arm. "Your grace, you are a charmer. But don't waste it all on old ladies like me."

Lord Rockhurst offered his arm to Catherine which left Persephone alone with Hawk. "Shall we, my lady?"

She placed her hand on his arm trying to ignore the feelings she had at his touch. They walked into the drawing room just before Billings announced the arrival of Lords Barrington and Fenmore.

"Were you aware that we were to have other guests?" Hawk asked her as both gentlemen entered the room.

She leaned over and spoke softly so only he could hear. "No, but I think your aunt has been doing more research into potential husbands for Catherine and I than we had first thought. It's a pity all of her efforts are wasted." His brow furrowed as he saw her lips turn up in a brilliant smile that made her eyes sparkle for their guests.

Hawk went forward to greet both gentlemen. "Fenmore, Barrington, it is a pleasure to welcome you to Hawksford House."

Lord Barrington was the first to offer his hand in greeting. "It was an honor to receive the invitation." He glanced over at Persephone and Hawk had an instant rush of possessiveness sweep over him.

Lord Fenmore came forward as well. "Yes, I was delighted to receive your invitation, your grace."

Hawk glanced over at his aunt with a questioning look. "I'm sure you were. Let me introduce my other guests. His grace, the Duke of Leicester and the Marquis of Rockhurst, heir to the Duke of Avanley." Both men nodded slightly as Barrington and Fenmore bowed in deference to their rank.

Hawk moved a step closer to Persephone. "Let me also introduce my aunt the Dowager Countess of Mulford."

"My lady," they both said in unison. "My sister Lady Gray and her dear friend Lady Carlisle."

Both Catherine and Persephone curtsied prettily as the gentlemen moved to take their hands and kiss the air just above their wrists. It was Catherine that spoke first. "Gentlemen, we are so thrilled that you were able to join us this evening for dinner. It is always more exciting to have other guests to talk with about everything going on in the beau monde." She batted her eyelashes and Persephone wondered what her friend was trying to do.

Lord Barrington moved closer to her as Catherine seemed quite taken with Lord Fenmore. "I hope this doesn't seem too forward, Lady Carlisle, but I saw you at Beaumont's ball unfortunately, I was too late to get a spot on your dance card."

Persephone smiled sweetly at the young lord. "Perhaps I will save a dance for you the next time we meet at a ball."

The young man gave her a huge smile and Hawk groaned at the exchange between them. Leicester moved over to stand beside him. "It seems like your aunt is wasting no time."

Hawk watched as Persephone and Lord Barrington laughed at something being said between them. He gave his friend an annoyed look but was saved from having to respond when it was announced that dinner was ready to be served in the dining room.

He took a step toward Persephone, but his aunt reached out and took his arm. "Hawk, you will escort me into dinner." She leaned closer to him and whispered, "Quit glaring at Lord Barrington. You will make him nervous. I'm sure he is already apprehensive being in your presence, you are staring at him as if you wish to challenge him to a duel and that will not do." She pulled him forward. "Besides, Persephone seems to be enjoying herself and Barrington would be an excellent catch for her."

Her words did not ease the feelings he was having. He had never felt like this before. The truth struck him hard. He really would like to throw Barrington out on his arse and keep Persephone all to himself. What the hell was wrong with him? He was the devil of the ton; young women would swoon if he looked their way and mommas would rush to hide their little darlings in the event he would wish to ruin them, and here he was trying to hold in his temper as a young lordling flirted with an innocent young woman who should be off limits to a man like him.

He led the group into the dining room. His aunt sat to his right. To his dismay Persephone was seated between Lord Rockhurst and Lord Barrington. The first course was served, and he remained silent as the conversations swirled around him. His sister laughed at something Lord Fenmore had said, Rockhurst was engaged in a conversation with Persephone and Lord Barrington. She laughed again at something Rockhurst said, and he clinched his fist under the table.

"Your grace, will you be attending the Henley's ball tomorrow night?" Lord Fenmore asked drawing his attention.

Hawksford took a sip of his wine before answering. "I am not sure I will be available tomorrow evening."

"Oh, we were so hoping to go. Everyone will be there. Aunt Louisa, will we be able to go?" Catherine asked.

His aunt looked over at him briefly. "I'm sure your brother would not mind us taking one of his carriages. My dear friend Lady Hathaway is planning on being in attendance. Her granddaughter is coming out this season as well and will be performing, and I would love to hear her. She is known to be very proficient at the pianoforte."

"I would be happy to escort the three of you, with his grace's permission that is," Lord Barrington said as he smiled at Persephone.

Hawk did not bother to hide his annoyance. "There will be no need for that. If my aunt wishes to attend, I will escort her and the ladies."

A Duke Always Gets What He Wants

Lord Barrington looked chastised, and Persephone quickly tried to make him feel at ease. "I'm sure it will be a wonderful evening. Will we see you there?"

Hawk frowned as Barrington returned her smile. "I will be sure to be in attendance if you will be there, my lady."

Hawk finished the remainder of his wine and motioned for a footman to refill his glass. He wanted this dinner to be over and for his uninvited guests to be gone.

When dinner was finished, Aunt Louisa stood. "Ladies, let us leave the gentlemen to their port and go to the drawing room."

Hawk saw an opportunity and took it. "There is no need for port. We will join you in the drawing room."

His aunt gave him an irritated look but nodded in agreement. The party moved from the dining room to the drawing room. Both Leicester and Rockhurst came to stand beside him. Lord Rockhurst nudged him. "Things are going well. Both your sister and Lady Carlisle seem quite taken with the young lords."

"Fenmore is a mere viscount, Catherine is the sister of a duke, do you really think they would make a good match? He is not even in the same sphere as her, but Barrington would be quite a catch for Lady Carlisle. He seems taken with her. If he is looking for a bride, she would make an excellent countess. Her small dowry should not matter to him, he is wealthy enough," Leicester said as they continued to watch the group.

Hawk gave them both a harsh look. "Good god, one dinner and you are ready to marry her off to the man. Just because she is being polite doesn't mean she wants to marry him. It is ludicrous to think she would want to marry Barrington."

"Seeking a husband is the whole reason for a young woman to have a season; it's a marriage mart," Leicester added giving his friend a suspicious look. "Could it be that a young lady has you considering matrimony this season?"

Hawk didn't even bother answering such a question.

"It's not matrimony consuming his thoughts, it's the bedding," Lord Rockhurst said as Hawk walked over to where the two couples sat conversing with his aunt.

Leicester stared after him. "Catherine is much too young for this. She doesn't possess the maturity to handle the rakes that lurk the ballrooms of London."

"Hawk will look after his sister, and I would hardly classify Fenmore as a rake," Rockhurst said as he leaned back against the wall. "We are the biggest rakes in London and I assure you Catherine is safe from us. Persephone, on the other hand, I am not so certain will remain untouched for much longer."

Leicester nodded. "Hawk had better be careful. He knows better than to toy with the affections of an innocent. And he is not so foolish to contemplate marriage. He needs to visit one of the eager widows of the ton or a jewel of the demi monde. There are several that would welcome him into their beds."

"Perhaps, that's exactly where I will be heading this evening. Lady Bedstroke's husband left for their country estate this morning and she is lonely." He grinned devilishly.

Leicester shook his head slightly. "I assume you plan on keeping her company while her husband is gone."

"Just as long as she amuses me."

Leicester laughed at his friend then moved over to join everyone else.

Persephone liked Lord Barrington. He was very polite and easy to talk with. But she didn't miss the way Hawk stared at her or the fact that he looked angry throughout most of the dinner. As she and Catherine chatted with Lords Barrington and Fenmore she couldn't help but feel as if the duke was looming over them.

"Gentlemen, it has been a lovely evening, but it is time for me, and the younger ladies to retire. We do look forward to seeing you tomorrow night at the ball," Aunt Louisa said as she rose from her seat. All the gentlemen rose as well.

"Yes, we should be going as well," Lord Barrington said as he placed a kiss to Aunt Louisa's hand before reaching for Persephone's. "I look forward to seeing you again, my lady. I will count the minutes until I can once again see your smile."

Persephone blushed but Hawk groaned at his words and said rather sharply, "Thank you for joining us, gentlemen. Billings will see you out."

Barrington and Fenmore both bowed before heading out the door where Billings was waiting to assist them with their greatcoats.

Once they were out of earshot, Catherine turned on her brother. "Why were you so rude, Hawk? Lord Fenmore was very nice and Barrington seemed quite taken with Persephone."

"Don't lecture me, Catherine. I am not in the mood. It was time for the young lords to leave. I am not in the disposition to listen to this anymore. Aunt Louisa was tired and so am I."

Aunt Louisa stepped in before Catherine's temper got the better of her. "I am quite tired, my dear. Besides, I am sure we will see both gentlemen very soon. Now walk with me upstairs."

Catherine blew out a frustrated breath. "Good evening, gentlemen." She moved to her aunt's side. "Are you coming, Persephone?"

Persephone glanced over at Hawk who still wore a deep frown. "Yes, but I am going to go to the library before I come upstairs." Catherine gave her a knowing look and followed her aunt up to their rooms.

Hawk looked over at his friends. "I believe the two of you have other appointments this evening."

"Yes, I should have left an hour ago. It was lovely to see you again, Lady Carlisle," Lord Rockhurst said as he kissed her hand.

Leicester also took his cue to leave. "I'm sure I will see you again very soon, my lady. Enjoy the remainder of your evening."

Persephone waited till they were gone before she turned to face the duke. "Are you alright? You seemed displeased most of the evening."

He moved a step closer. "I don't like surprises. My aunt should have informed me beforehand that we were to have guests."

"Perhaps, but did you really have to make the young men so uneasy. You were quite menacing."

Hawk shrugged his shoulders. "I wasn't in the mood to be courteous. Are you prepared to give me an hour of your time?"

Persephone held up her hand to halt his advance. "As long as you remember that you are not to kiss me. We are to talk only."

"I promise not to kiss you… tonight. Do you play billiards?"

"Billiards? Your aunt has a billiard table at her home, and I have played on occasion, but I am not very good at it. Is that what you have in mind this evening?" Persephone thought his suggestion to play billiards was odd. She half expected him to argue with her about not kissing her again.

"I enjoy billiards. Perhaps I can help you improve your game." He reached for her hand and they walked down the long hallway to the billiards room. Once inside he handed her a cue stick. "Tell me something I have been curious about, why are you named after the wife of Hades?"

She laughed softly. "My father as you know is obsessed with Greek and Roman antiquities. He loves Greek mythology and always liked the story of Persephone and Hades. My mother thought it horrible to name me after the goddess forced to live in the underworld with Hades, but my father was quite insistent. She would always tell me when I was a little girl that I was not to suffer the same fate as my namesake. She told me to marry only for love or I would live in the same kind of hell. My mother felt as if my father's obsession for antiquities was as bad as him being in love with a mistress." She walked around the billiard table running her hand along the edge as she did so. "Of course, she didn't talk to me of such things. I was a child when she died. But when I was older, I found her diary in one of the chests my father had sent to your aunt's house. She had written several entries about feeling alone and neglected by my father."

She sighed heavily. "That is why I am not actively seeking a husband. I certainly will not marry for a title. I would rather not marry at all than live with a man that is not totally devoted to our marriage."

He took the first shot sending the billiard balls across the table. "Many successful marriages are built on respect, not love. Love is a difficult emotion."

He moved behind her. "Shall I help you with your shot?"

Persephone leaned over the table. Hawk leaned behind her, reaching his hand over hers as he helped her align her cue. Persephone found it difficult to breathe. This man was intoxicating. He smelled of sandalwood and pure masculine male. His breath whispered against the back of her neck causing chills to run along her spine. She took her shot and hit one of the balls into the pocket.

"Excellent," he said as his hand rested upon her hip.

She straightened and moved away from his grasp.

He studied her as he prepared to take his next shot. "You certainly had Barrington eating out of your hand tonight."

She frowned at his comment. "He was very nice. Was I supposed to be discourteous to him just because I did not fall madly in love with him?"

She found her voice rising slightly. "Which leads me to ask you a question. Why were you so rude to him tonight?"

He took his shot then stood very seriously looking her straight in the eye. "Because I don't like people thinking they can have what is mine."

Persephone felt her mouth fall open stunned at what he had said. "Excuse me?"

He walked over to her until he was a mere inch or two away. He leaned close to her ear. "Barrington can't have you, darling." His breath feathered across her ear. "I promised I would not kiss you, but I never said anything about touching you." He pulled her into his chest. He let his fingers touch the skin right below her ear and slowly make a trail down along her collarbone.

Persephone could hear the air slowly hissing between her parted lips. She shivered as his other hand moved along her waist and upward lightly grazing the side of her breast. She closed her eyes as he nibbled on her ear lobe. '*Dear god, how did any woman resist him,*' she thought as her knees got weaker but he tightened his hold and pulled her tighter against him.

"I want you, Persephone," he said again as he lifted her so that she sat on the edge of the billiards table.

Persephone felt as if she was losing her ability to think. She sighed and leaned into him as she felt his hand slide up her gown caressing the skin behind her knee. She bit her bottom lip and moaned softly.

Hawk had not intended for things to go this far. He only wanted to talk with her, but tonight set his blood to boil watching her with Barrington. He had never felt jealousy before and the desire to stake his claim on her became overwhelming. Her soft skin and the sweet sounds of pleasure she made at his touch only spurred him on further. He bent his head into her neck to breathe in her sweet scent of roses and honey. He was about to slide his hand even further up over her knee when there was a loud ruckus coming down the hallway. He quickly lifted Persephone off the table and pushed her behind him as a woman burst through the door with Billings and two footmen right on her heels.

"Ah, so this is where you have been hiding, Hawksford!"

Persephone peered around from behind the duke. A very beautiful and very angry woman stood there with hands on her hips and a fierce look on her face. Persephone had never seen her before so she was not sure who this lady could be and why she would be bullying her way into Hawksford House.

Hawk melded into his air of ducal superiority. "Billings, is there some trouble here?" His voice cracked like a whip with authority.

Billings nervously came forward. "I told the lady that you were not to be disturbed, but she refused to leave and unfortunately forced her way in searching for you. I will have her removed immediately."

The woman slapped his hand away as Billings moved to take her arm. "I am not going anywhere until I get an explanation, Hawk. I have been in town for two weeks and you have not even bothered to come to me. I have sent notes every day." She moved to look around to see Persephone hiding behind the duke's back. "Is this how you have been spending your time? Is this girl," she motioned to Persephone, "the reason you have lost interest in me?"

Persephone jumped as Hawk responded in a sharp angry tone. "Enough! Billings, escort Lady Kingsley to the drawing room."

The lady looked startled for a moment but recovered quickly. "I will not be bullied, Hawksford."

He narrowed his eyes, and his tone was harsh and cold. "Go with Billings and I will join you momentarily."

The lady huffed and her skirts rustled as she turned and practically stomped from the room. Once she was gone, Persephone moved from behind the duke.

Hawk turned and reached for her hands, but she pulled them from his grasp. "I am sorry you had to experience that, Persephone. Lady Kingsley never should have come here, and I will deal with her and return shortly."

Persephone shook her head and took a step backwards. "No, I don't think it's a good idea for us to spend any more time alone together."

Hawk once again tried to reach for her, but she avoided him. "Persephone"

She shook her head. "No, this would never work, and I am a fool for letting things go this far. I appreciate everything you have done for me, but if you insist on holding me to this ridiculous agreement I will have to leave."

Hawk felt a brief sense of panic. He was going to have to be careful with how he handled this situation. The last thing he wanted was for her to leave. "Persephone, I would like to explain all of this later."

"There is nothing to explain. I knew all about your reputation and still allowed you to kiss me. I was the fool."

He started to get angry. "Don't talk to me about those damn scandal sheets. I kissed you because I wanted to, because I have never wanted any-one so bad in my life."

Persephone crossed her arms over her chest trying to hold in her temper. "My father was completely obsessed with his antiques and his archaeology. I did not realize how much until I read my mother's' diary. She would write about her heartbreak and that his obsession was no worse than having a mistress. Do you know that he left two days after my moth-er's death? He didn't even bother to take me to your aunt himself. He had my nurse deliver me so he could rush off to Egypt or Greece or wherever else he wanted."

Hawk listened to her not quite knowing where her train of thought was heading. "I did not know."

Persephone swiped one tear away as it started to run down her cheek. She was angry and she always cried when she was furious. "I am not explaining myself very well." She reached up and pushed a stray curl behind her ear and continued, "My father never truly loved anything other than his collections and I will not ever be put in the situation my mother lived through. If that means I never marry, then that is what I will do. That is why it is so dangerous for us to play this game."

Hawk wanted to take her in his arms and took a step forward when Billings cleared his throat loudly from the doorway. "Your grace, the lady downstairs is getting very angry at having to wait so long and is threatening to come back here to confront you again."

Hawk growled under his breath. "I'll be right there, Billings."

"Yes, your grace."

When they were alone again, he moved a few steps towards her but didn't reach out to touch her. "We are not finished with this, Persephone."

Persephone narrowed her eyes at him. "Yes, we are, your grace and I mean what I say. Don't you have a guest waiting for you?"

He knew she was angry, and this was not the time to push her. There was no doubt in his mind that she meant what she said about leaving. He would just have to be patient, and patience was not something he was known to have. "I know you are angry right now but know this, I also mean what I say. You are mine, Persephone." With that he turned on his heel to go deal with Lady Kingsley. Unfortunately for her, he was not feeling the least bit charitable or forgiving.

Persephone stood there with her mouth agape at his words. She clinched her fists and headed up the stairs to her room. She didn't know if she was madder at him or herself. She knew he was a rake and fell for his charms. She quickly fled upstairs and was met in the hallway by Catherine.

"What the devil is going on downstairs. I heard yelling and saw Billings practically dragging a lady into the study." Persephone kept walking with Catherine right behind her. "Persephone? What has happened?"

Catherine followed her into her bedroom and shut the door behind them. "Ok, what is wrong?"

Persephone whirled around to face her. "I am the biggest fool in London!"

Catherine stopped short. "What?"

Persephone started pacing her bedroom. "He kissed me. I let him kiss me."

"Who? Hawk?"

Persephone plopped down in the chair by the fire. "Yes, the infamous Duke of Hawksford. I knew better."

Catherine frowned. "Did he take advantage of you?"

"No, I wanted him to kiss me. Good god, I am a wanton." Persephone covered her face with her hands.

"Was that all the commotion downstairs?"

"No, the commotion was when his mistress showed up, his very angry mistress I might add."

Catherine gasped. "Oh no. What happened?"

Persephone blushed. "We were in the billiards room."

Catherine smirked, amusement dancing in her eyes. "From the way you are blushing, I will assume you were not playing billiards."

Persephone blew out a loud breath. "Not exactly. Oh, Catherine, I am such a fool. How could I fall for him so easily? He is just so damn irresistible."

Catherine placed her arms around her friend and gave her a big hug. "He has a way about him and can be quite persuasive. But what happened with the mistress and who was it?"

Persephone rolled her eyes. "She burst in the room demanding to know why Hawk has not come to see her. She was furious."

"What did Hawk do?"

"He pushed me behind him to keep her from seeing me, but she saw me. He became very incensed and had Billings escort her to the drawing room until he could speak with her."

Catherine sat down at her feet. "And?"

"I told him I could not spend time alone with him again. It was too dangerous. Can you imagine if your Aunt Louisa had discovered us? She would have demanded he marry me and we both know how miserable we would make each other."

"And how did my brother take that?"

Persephone shook her head sadly. "He didn't take me serious, I'm afraid. He told me that I was his, and we were not finished with the discussion."

Catherine stood and walked over to the fireplace. "Hawk said that? How romantic!"

Persephone looked over at her. "Romantic? Don't be ridiculous, Catherine. He is very practiced. I'm sure he says that all the time."

"I don't think so, but you were right to tell him that it wasn't wise to be alone with him. It will drive him crazy," Catherine said as she smiled at her friend.

"I'm not trying to drive him crazy. I am trying to not go crazy myself. You know we would never suit. I could never be married to a man whose mistress just shows up at his house! Not that either of us is interested in marriage in the first place." She leaned over and rested her elbows on her knees and placed her face in her hands. "I am so angry at myself and miserable at the same time."

Catherine came over and put a hand on her shoulder. "Everything will be alright. Don't worry about Hawk. You have Lord Barrington half in love with you already and the season is just beginning."

"I don't want Barrington in love with me either." She sighed heavily. "What is wrong with me? I should be husband hunting but I have no desire to do so."

"We both agreed before we came to London, that this season was to be about having fun, not looking for husbands," Catherine said cheerfully.

Persephone felt her anger dissipate. "You're right, of course. But how am I going to avoid Hawk for the remainder of the season?"

Catherine moved towards the door. "Hawk will not be ignored, my dear. He isn't used to not getting his way. This season is going to be more interesting than we first thought."

Persephone smiled softly. "Well at least it will not be boring." Once Catherine left and she was alone she wondered how on earth she would be able to continue to resist the duke's advances. Would it be so wrong to give in and enjoy the pleasure he promised?

Hawk could not remember the last time he was this angry and if Patricia Kingsley wasn't very careful, she would be tossed out of his house on her arse and he would use all of his influence to see her ruined. Regardless of him being a known rake, he was a duke and was extremely powerful. He took a deep breath before entering the drawing room where Billings and his two footmen stood keeping Lady Kingsley from entering any other portion of his house. One nod from him and all three servants rushed from the room.

Lady Kingsley obviously did not know how close she was to her demise because she immediately walked up to him and slapped him hard across the face. "I risked everything for you, Hawk. I came to London two weeks ago expecting us to be together. You never even responded to my notes and now I know why. You were too busy entertaining young girls fresh out of the school room. Do you really think she could bring you the pleasure I can and have on more than one occasion?" She eyed him warily studying the intense look on his face and must have decided to take a different tactic to illicit a reaction. She swayed toward him and reached up to touch the red mark on his cheek.

Hawk reached out and grabbed her hand before it could touch his face. "You forget yourself, madam."

She staggered backwards as if his sharp words had struck her. "Hawk, you know I didn't mean it. We are so good together and I get so envious if I think of you with another woman. I know you have a wondering eye and it drives me crazy."

The duke's expression didn't change. "On that I will agree." Her mouth dropped open, but he continued, "Our past relationship, whatever you thought it might have been, has now come to an end. I will not deny that we shared some passionate moments, but if you think you are unique, you are mistaken."

He saw her face turn red with rage, but he continued, "In the future you will never come to my house again nor will you speak to me in public. If you care to make another scene like you did tonight, I will use every ounce of my power and influence to see that you are not invited to any ton events."

She practically spat at him. "You can't do that! You aren't exactly accepted by the ton."

"You forget again, madam that I am a duke and will be welcomed regardless. Did you also forget that I am a close friend of the Regent?"

She narrowed her eyes. "Do you think to make that little harlot your duchess now?"

He moved with lightning quickness and gripped her arms. "Listen very carefully, Patricia. I will not tolerate you saying anything about the ladies in my house. Do you understand? If I hear you breathing one negative word about tonight, I will not hesitate to make good on my promise. Is that clear?"

She must have realized her mistake. She briefly nodded and he quickly let her go. "Now, Billings will show you out. I do not expect to see you here again, ever."

With that he turned and left the room and headed back up the stairs to his own chamber, but he heard her slam the front door on her way out.

Chapter Five

Hawk sat alone in the breakfast room the next morning waiting for the ladies to come downstairs to join him. The incident with Lady Kingsley the night before and his concern over Persephone had caused him to get little to no sleep. He was nursing a raging headache and was anxious to set things right with Persephone. The footman in attendance set a plate of eggs and pastries before him. None of which seemed appealing at the moment. He looked up and stood as his aunt and his sister Catherine entered the room. He remained standing waiting for Persephone.

"You can sit, Ethan. She is taking breakfast in her room this morning," his aunt said as she moved to take a seat.

He sat back down but pushed his plate away. "I hope she is not ill."

His sister gave him a strange look. "I assure you that she is not. Persephone just wanted to sleep a little longer this morning. We have a busy day ahead of us."

"What plans have the two of you this morning? If you need an escort…."

"Don't trouble yourself, Hawk. We do not need an escort," Catherine said cutting him off.

He frowned at her not liking being interrupted. "As I was asking, what plans do you have?" he replied slowly emphasizing each word.

Catherine sighed heavily and gave him an annoyed look. "We are going to Bond Street for some shopping today. Aunt Louisa will be going as well so there is no need for you to attend us."

Aunt Louisa cleared her throat. "That is enough, Catherine. Your brother is simply concerned, and I very much appreciate him taking his duty to you seriously."

Hawk stood from his seat. "Enjoy your morning ladies." He left the ladies to their breakfast not in the mood to carry on polite conversation. He paused at the bottom of the stairs debating if he should seek Persephone out. It was one thing to have a clandestine meeting after everyone and the servants were abed, it was a totally different matter during the day when anyone could discover them. He turned to go into his study to go over some account ledgers when a footman came into the foyer with a huge bouquet of flowers followed by more footmen with equally impressive arrangements.

He waited for them to place the flowers on the tables then held his hand out for the card. The footman handed the card to him then bowed before walking away and resuming his post. Hawk scowled as he read the card. It seemed that Lord Barrington was indeed serious in his courtship of Persephone. He placed the card on the table and headed for the front door. Billings jumped to attention when he saw him.

"My greatcoat, Billings."

Billings helped him with his coat. "Shall I order a carriage, your grace?"

"No, I will walk."

"As you please, your grace."

Hawk put on his hat and walked down the steps to the street. Rockhurst would not like being roused out of his bed at this hour, but he needed a plan and Rockhurst was just the man to help him with it.

The Marquis of Rockhurst's Mayfair residence

Charles Newberg, Marquis Rockhurst jumped up as the cold splash of water hit his face.

"What the bloody hell!"

Hawk handed the pitcher of water back to Rockhurst's nervous and pale valet.

"You are fired, Harrison!" the soaking wet irate marquis shouted from his bed.

"You are not fired, Harrison," Hawk said reassuring the young man. "We tried to wake you without the water, but you were not stirring soon enough for my taste. You can't blame Harrison; he was just following my orders."

Rockhurst sat up keeping the sheets around his waist. "Why the hell are you in my bedchamber at this ungodly hour of the morning?"

"I need your advice."

At this the marquis perked up. "Advice? From me? You must be in desperate straits, Hawk if you are coming to me for counsel." He then gave his friend a smirk. "Is it a woman? Are you coming to me for suggestions in the bedroom? I am quite skilled when it comes to bedding a woman."

"More water, Harrison. He is delirious if he thinks I need his advice in that arena."

Rockhurst laughed as the valet looked from the duke then back to him again. "His grace is just jesting, Harrison. Leave us."

"Yes, my lord."

Once they were alone, Rockhurst continued, "What sort of advice are you seeking, Hawk? Does it concern a woman?"

"Get dressed. I will wait for you downstairs in the library."

Rockhurst took his damn sweet time getting dressed. Hawk was starting to wonder if he had decided to go back to sleep instead when the door to the library opened and Rockhurst walked inside.

"Alright, how may I be of assistance to you, Hawk?"

"Barrington is doubling his efforts in courting Persephone."

"Ahh, so it is the sweet Lady Persephone that brings you here so early. If Barrington is stepping into your territory just put him in his place."

Hawk sat down in one of the oversized chairs beside the chess board. "I'm afraid it's not that simple." He proceeded to tell Rockhurst about Lady Kingsley and how upset Persephone had been.

Rockhurst listened amused at the story. "So, what's the problem? If you want her, I'm sure she could be yours for the taking."

"Yes, I want her in my bed. But marriage is permanent and while we both know it is inevitable, I am not sure I would want to marry now. Besides the fact that Persephone has made it known that she is not interested in finding a husband."

"That is ridiculous. You are a duke, every unmarried woman in London thinks you are marriage material. Most of which would give their right arm to be your duchess."

Hawk stood and began pacing the room. "I'm afraid all of our escapades she has read about in the damned scandal sheets is not portraying me in a positive light. And the damn incident with Lady Kingsley did not help me either."

Rockhurst stared at his friend for a few seconds. "I think you might be in trouble, my friend."

Hawk glared at him.

"It seems that you are going to have to convince the lady that you are not what you seem. This is going to be new territory for you. You are going to have to woo her. Lady Persephone is not just going to fall at your feet nor is she going to fall into your bed," Rockhurst chuckled amused at his friend's dilemma.

"That is the most nonsensical thing I have ever heard. I am a duke, for god's sake!" He sat back down in the chair.

"I am seeing an end to an era. The Duke of Hawksford is being domesticated. Leicester and I will have to step up our lasciviousness to take up your slack."

Hawk smiled. "Are you up to it?"

Rockhurst gave a mock salute. "Absolutely."

Bond Street

Persephone smiled pleasantly as they passed the ladies and gentlemen all strolling past the fashionable shops and milliners. Lady Louisa walked before them inclining her head regally as people passed by them. The carriage was waiting for them down the street, but Aunt Louisa preferred walking so she could see everyone and more importantly be seen by more.

"You are going to love my surprise, girls," Aunt Louisa said as they reached the shop of her dressmaker. "I had each of you a new fabulous evening gown made by my favorite modiste."

"How exciting! Thank you, Aunt Louisa," Catherine said enthusiastically as she went inside the shop.

"Yes, thank you," Persephone said only to be stopped by the older lady's hand on her arm.

"Your gown is extra special, Persephone. You are so beautiful, just like your dear mother and I think this gown will certainly showcase that beauty." She gave her a wink. "And perhaps bring a certain gentleman up to scratch."

"Who do you mean, Aunt Louisa?" Persephone asked as they entered the shop together arm in arm.

The older lady looked at her quizzically then rolled her eyes dramatically. "Please, my dear. I may be old, but I am no fool."

Persephone giggled, "No one would ever accuse you of being a fool. But please don't try to play matchmaker. You know my thoughts on the matter." She wanted to say more but didn't have time to respond before seamstresses descended upon them showing them new fabrics, ribbons, and laces. All three ladies were shown into a back dressing room where two large boxes were brought out. Catherine eagerly opened her box and one of the ladies helped her pull out the beautiful peach gown from inside. It was shimmering with tiny diamond like stones and had a peach ribbon woven down the front. The overskirt was a darker color peach with white flowers embroidered on it.

"Oh, Aunt Louisa! It is stunning!" She ran over and gave her aunt a hug. "Now, Persephone it is your turn."

Persephone walked over and opened the box and gasp. Inside was a deep ruby red gown of silk. There was an overlay of black lace on the tiny sleeves and along the edge of the bodice.

"Go try it on. I want to see you in it," Aunt Louisa said smiling at the girl's excitement.

Persephone put on the dress with the help of one of the seamstresses. It was shockingly low cut, but the color was exquisite. She turned around in the mirror slowly admiring the ruby like gems sewn on train of the gown. She put a hand up to her chest and turned around to look at Aunt Louisa.

"Are you certain it's not too low? I feel as if I will pop out."

Louisa laughed, "In all my years I have never seen breasts just pop out at a ball; at least not without help." She gave Persephone a wicked wink as Catherine came out wearing her gown cut equally low.

Catherine laughed as she admired herself in the mirror. "Oh, there is no way Hawk will let me out of the house in this, Aunt Louisa. But I love it!"

The older lady waved her hand dismissing the thought. "I'll take care of Hawksford. You two will be the bell of the Hensley's ball. I hear that the prince might be in attendance and if he is there you must look your best, He is good friends with your brother, and I am certain the two of you will be introduced."

Persephone perked up at that news. It was a well-known fact that the group of friends that crowded around the prince at Carlton House were a fast set. She had read stories about the parties at Carlton House and that the Duke of Hawksford had attended some of them. She wondered what Carlton House was like and always hoped she would be able to go there one day.

Aunt Louisa noticed her look. "Don't fret, my dear."

Persephone pushed the thought out of her head and gave her a smile. "I wasn't fretting, I was thinking of how magnificent Carlton House must be. If I am ever invited to go there, I will most definitely wear this gown. I love it, thank you." She leaned over and kissed the older lady's cheek.

"Your mother was my dearest friend and since I had no daughter of my own, I feel blessed that I have you." She patted her hand. "But I promised your mother I would look out for you and see that you were properly married, and I take my duty very seriously." She reached out and adjusted the material on the dress' train. "And in this dress, you will certainly make many a man yearn for domestic bliss."

The older lady walked away to speak with the modiste, and Catherine came over and said, "In this dress, Leicester can't help but notice me. And you look like a goddess, Persephone. I can't wait for the ball tonight."

The ladies had their packages packed up and gave instructions to have them delivered to Hawksford House. They were walking out the door when Lord Barrington approached them.

"Lord Barrington, how good to see you today," Catherine said cheerfully.

Barrington briefly nodded to her, but his eyes went straight to Persephone. "It is indeed my lucky day to get to see you again ladies. Might I escort you to where you are going?"

Aunt Louisa smiled. "We have finished our business for today, but you can certainly walk us to where our carriage awaits."

"I would be delighted." He fell into step beside Persephone. "You look lovely this morning, Lady Carlisle."

Persephone gave him a soft smile. "Thank you, my lord."

He offered her his arm and she placed her hand on his elbow. "Will you be attending Hensley's ball tonight? I hear it is to be a crush, everyone has heard that the prince will be there, but it is just a rumor."

"Yes, I had heard. Do you know the prince very well, my lord?" Persephone asked genuinely curious.

He shook his head. "I have met him of course, but I am not part of the Carlton House set. I prefer more serious endeavors. The prince in my opinion is much too carefree for a monarch. He is more concerned with seeking pleasure and spending money than anything else."

Persephone didn't say anything for a few minutes as they walked. "I have heard he was very kind."

"Perhaps, when it suits him. But I should not talk of such matters to you, my lady."

This made Persephone roll her eyes. She hated being patronized simply because she was a woman. Lord Barrington had just gone down a notch in her estimation. Sarcastically she replied, "Yes, we should talk of the weather and my favorite color of ribbons or my embroidery."

He put his hand over hers. "Exactly, my apologies for not speaking of proper topics."

Persephone almost let her mouth drop open not believing he thought her serious. Thank goodness they reached the carriage. A footman came forward and opened the door for them. "Thank you for your escort, my lord."

He assisted her inside the carriage lifting her hand to his lips. "Until tonight, my lady."

Persephone sighed heavily as she sank back against the carriage cushions.

"I can't believe he thought you serious, Persephone," Catherine said as the carriage started moving. "What a bore he is."

Aunt Louisa shook her head in agreement. "Lord Barrington is a typical man. He underestimates women and their abilities."

Persephone wasn't listening. It wasn't Lord Barrington she was thinking of but rather the one man in London that made her knees go weak when he looked in her direction. Hawk was the other extreme. He was wild, worldly, powerful, and wicked. Everything she had vowed to stay away from. So, why was he the one she craved?

Rockhurst and Hawk had moved from the library and were in Rockhurst's study enjoying a glass of brandy when Leicester decided to join them.

"I wasn't expecting to find you here, Hawk," he said as he made his way over to the decanter and poured his own glass.

"I needed to get out of the house," Hawk said swirling the amber colored liquor in his glass.

Leicester took a sip. "You didn't want to go dress shopping with the ladies of your household?"

Hawk looked up at him. "You saw them?"

Leicester held out a small box. "Yes, I saw them as I was leaving the jewelers. Lucy is still pouting because I do not spend as much time with her as she would wish, and I have grown tired of her. I bought her a parting gift that I will give her tonight."

Rockhurst held out his hand and Leicester gave him the box. "Ah, a diamond brooch, very nice." He handed the box back to him. "Do you have another dove in mind to occupy your spare time?"

Leicester smirked. "As if I would tell you before I had finalized any arrangements."

Rockhurst laughed. "You are a smart man, for a duke that is."

Leicester took a seat. "I was surprised to see Barrington escorting, Persephone. He is moving very quickly. Are you sure he is not after her dowry?"

Hawk stood abruptly. "Barrington was with them?"

"I saw him escorting her to the carriage and then kissing her hand as he helped her inside." Leicester did not notice Hawk's furious expression. "I must tell you I find the man to be a bore."

Rockhurst watched as Hawk began to pace the room. "You could always kill him, Hawk."

Leicester looked to both men. "Have I missed something?"

"I believe our dear friend has fallen for the lovely Lady Persephone. Unfortunately, the lady has other plans," Rockhurst said trying to bring Leicester up to speed.

"Don't tell me that she prefers Barrington to you?"

Hawk grabbed his coat. "Barrington will not have her. I am going home. I will see you both tonight at Hensley's ball. And I am not in love."

"Prinny will be attending. I just spoke with him last night. He plans on making a brief appearance and he expects the three of us to be there. He has been receiving a lot of criticism since he became regent and wants his friends with him as a show of support," Leicester said.

Hawk nodded. "I will be there." He then turned and headed for the front door.

"I never thought I would see Hawk in such a state over a woman," Leicester mumbled under his breath.

Rockhurst shook his head. "Sadly, it's a state we all must go through eventually."

Leicester sipped his brandy. "Not for many years, my friend."

The two clinked their glasses together in a toast. "To many years and many women."

Persephone looked back at her reflection in the mirror. She had never seen a gown so stunning, nor had she worn one so low cut before. She tugged once again at the bodice. Aunt Louisa had sworn in all her years she had never seen a woman's breasts pop out at a ball, and she did not wish to be the first. Sarah had styled her hair up with a long curl hanging loose over her left shoulder. She tugged at the curl and swayed a little in the dress watching the overskirt shimmer in the light.

"Exquisite," a deep voice said from the open doorway.

Persephone turned to see the duke standing there leaning one shoulder against the door frame watching her. She instantly blushed at the compliment then remembered herself. "You shouldn't be here, your grace."

"I know, but no one seemed inclined to tell me the color of the dress you were wearing so I could have my secretary get some jewels from the collection to compliment your attire. So, I came to see myself." He let his gaze move slowly from the floor up her body pausing at her breasts before meeting her eyes. "Now I can see there is no jewel that could compare to your beauty."

Persephone inhaled slowly trying to still her rapid heartbeat. When he talked to her like that it made her want to melt into his embrace. She had to remind herself that he was an expert in making women melt and she did not want to be added to his list of conquests, nor have another incident like the night before.

"Thank you for your kindness. But jewels are not necessary."

"No, they certainly are not." He glanced one more time at her bodice. "Has my aunt seen you in this dress?"

Persephone could feel the blush rising from her chest to her face. How dare he criticize her. "She bought it for me as a surprise and yes, she has seen me in it." She was getting angry and could feel her chest rising and falling with each breath.

He took a step further into her room. "It is definitely enticing."

She whirled away from him. "Isn't that what I am supposed to do, entice a man to marry me. Isn't that the entire point of a season?"

He frowned and moved closer to her causing her to take a step backwards. "Are you trying to entice any man now? As I recall you had no wish to marry, and if you ever did, you have a very specific idea about marriage and the kind of man you wanted to marry. And I was unacceptable in that category."

She backed up more until she met the wall. His tall muscular form looming over her took the words she was about to say out of her mouth. He leaned in closer bringing his lips a fraction away from hers. She closed her eyes waiting for his touch. When it didn't come, she opened her eyes to see him still looking at her intently.

"I will see you downstairs. I will have my secretary get the rubies from my safe. They will accentuate your gown nicely."

Persephone watched him walk away and finally decided to breathe.

Hawk had never had to use more restraint in his life. It took all of his will power not to drag her into his arms and kiss her senseless. Kiss her until she forgot all about his past and her ridiculous idea of not getting married. And that dress, how would he be able to endure men looking at her and not want to knock every man on his arse that let his gaze stray to her bodice. But he had told himself that he would not be the rake tonight, but damn it was going to be a hell like he had never known before watching her dance with other men knowing they wanted her for themselves. Tonight, he would pay for his sins, and he wasn't liking the idea at all.

Persephone gave herself a few minutes before going downstairs to join Catherine and Aunt Louisa. The duke's secretary was also standing there holding a box.

"His grace told me to give this to you, my lady to wear tonight." He opened the box to reveal a necklace with a large ruby pendant encircled with diamonds.

Aunt Louisa took the necklace from the box and placed it around Persephone's neck. "Ethan must think a good deal of you, Persephone. This was his mother's favorite piece. She wore it often."

Persephone reached up and touched her fingers to the large pendant that sat just above the valley between her breasts.

"Where is Hawk?" Aunt Louisa asked as they moved to the front doors.

Billings stepped forward. "His grace is outside waiting with the carriage, my lady."

The three of them made their way down the steps to the waiting carriage. The duke looked impressive in his evening attire. When he held out his hand, she briefly looked at him before placing her hand in his. "I knew the ruby necklace would look beautiful with your gown."

"Louisa said they were your mother's favorite. Thank you for allowing me to wear them," she replied softly.

He lightly squeezed her hand and helped her inside the carriage taking the seat across from her beside his aunt.

The carriage started to move along the drive. "Is it true that the prince will be in attendance tonight, Hawk?" Catherine asked eagerly.

"He is planning on attending but don't be disappointed if he changes his mind, Prinny often does that."

Aunt Louisa snorted softly. "I wish you would distance yourself from him, Ethan."

Hawk ignored his aunt's remark and continued to sit in silence. He would like for this night to be over with quickly. He was not in the mood to chaperone his sister or watch Persephone on the arm of any other man. If things did not turn in his favor soon, he would have to go about it differently. Instead of carting her off over his shoulder and locking her up where he could have her all to himself until she consented to be his, as Rockhurst had suggested, he was taking a gentler approach. But his desire to have Persephone grew stronger every time he saw her so failure was not an option. He would have her.

The carriage came to a stop and a footman wearing a powdered wig and burgundy and gold livery opened the door. The duke stepped out first then assisted each of the ladies. Persephone's hand felt small and cold in his. He looked down at her curiously. She looked nervous. He lightly squeezed her hand causing her to gaze up at him. "Are you alright, Persephone?"

She gave him a hesitant smile and lied. "Yes, just a bit nervous tonight. I suppose it is because there are so many people here and the prince is to be in attendance." Her nerves had nothing to do with the number of guests in attendance but everything to do with him and how he made her feel. Not to mention the fact that she was still praying her breasts stayed in her bodice. "I'll be fine." She took her hand from his and went to stand beside Catherine.

"I do hope Leicester is here. He must notice me tonight," Catherine leaned over and whispered to Persephone as they made their way up the massive steps to the grand entryway.

Persephone smiled, but before she could respond they were announced by the majordomo. She and Catherine were once again besieged by eager suitors and a few older gentlemen seeking to add their name to their dance cards. Lord Barrington moved forward to greet her. The group of gentlemen parted for him as he reached her. She was surprised to see the look of what she thought was disapproval on his face.

He took her hand and placed a kiss on it before leading her away from the crowd. "I must inform you, Lady Carlisle that my mother will be most disapproving of your attire this evening."

Persephone was taken aback by his comment. "Excuse me?"

"Your gown, it is rather revealing don't you think?"

Persephone felt her annoyance rise. "You don't like my gown then, my lord."

He gave her a smile that made her stomach roll with nausea. "I like it very much." He let his gaze linger longer than was necessary on her breasts to make his point. "I just feel it is inappropriate for a lady such as yourself. My mother already has reservations about you since you are living under the same roof as that degenerate, Hawksford. I would not want her to think you were the kind of woman with which he normally chooses to associate."

Persephone took a deep breath and closed her eyes for a second to carefully choose her words. "There is no need for your mother to be concerned, my lord. I have no intention of meeting her tonight nor do I have any intention of furthering my association with you."

He grabbed her arm as she started to walk away. She bit her lip as his fingers dug into her flesh then looked down at where his hand held her. He released her but she could tell she had made him angry. "I will excuse your comments tonight, my lady. Perhaps you need some time to think about what you have said. I'm sure once you come to your senses you will wish to apologize."

She narrowed her eyes. "Do not hold your breath, my lord." She then walked away to find Catherine.

Hawk watched the exchange between Persephone and Lord Barrington with intensity. He could barely make out the words they spoke to each other, and his blood boiled when Barrington stared at her chest. He took a step forward and was only stopped by a restraining hand when she moved to walk away, and Barrington grabbed her arm.

"Easy man, she is in no danger and if my guess is correct, she is about to give Barrington the cut direct," Leicester said quietly from behind him.

"He should be glad we are in a public place," Hawk replied angrily.

They continued to watch as Persephone walked away from Barrington, head held high, regal as any queen to where Catherine stood waiting to hear what had transpired between them.

"She handled the situation quite well. There was no need for your interference."

Hawk watched her as she made her way over to the group of men and ladies talking with Catherine. She laughed at something one of them said and seemed completely unperturbed by the exchange with Barrington.

Leicester put a hand on his shoulder. "Let's go find a card game before the dowagers notice our presence. I have no desire to be set upon by a bunch of ambitious mommas and simpering unmarried misses fresh out of the schoolroom."

Hawk growled as he saw another man leering over Persephone's exposed neckline. "Perhaps we should."

He was not in the mood to converse with others at the moment, and he did not feel like dancing. He led the way leaving the ballroom with Leicester following behind him. He ignored the ladies fluttering their lashes at him from behind their fans as they passed. Another time he would have set about finding an unhappy wife or young widow looking for a night of sensual gratification, but tonight he had no interest in such things. There was only one woman with which he was concerned.

Chapter Six

Time passed slowly as Hawk watched the clock wanting this night to be over. He and Leicester had spent the majority of the ball in one of the card rooms playing a few hands and enjoying some of Hensley's best brandy.

"Excuse me, your grace. Might I have a word with you?"

Hawk looked over his shoulder surprised to see Lord Barrington standing there. He turned back toward Leicester giving the man his back. It was a direct cut and caused others in the room to take notice. Leicester raised one eyebrow as he and Hawk exchanged looks.

Barrington cleared his throat and moved around so he was facing the duke. "I would like to speak with you about Lady Persephone."

That got his attention and he replied in a stern voice. "Lady Carlisle."

Barrington looked nervous. "Yes, I should have referred to her as such, my apologies."

Hawk did not say anything, so the young lord continued. "I had words with Lady Carlisle this evening and while I feel I was justified in my opinion I could have gone about things differently. I was hoping you would speak to her on my behalf."

Leicester took a sip of his brandy curiously waiting to see how his friend responded to the request.

Hawk did not even bother to look up as he shuffled a deck of cards. "Barrington, you are not to contact Lady Carlisle again."

"Surely you aren't serious, your grace," Barrington said shocked at the duke's words. "I know when she has a moment to calm down and realize her foolishness…"

Leicester interrupted him. "I would stop now, Barrington."

Barrington did not recognize the danger. "I am hoping you can make her see how advantageous a match between us could be."

Hawk stood slowly and Leicester mumbled under his breath. "I tried to warn you."

Standing at full height, Hawksford was at a few inches over six feet and he towered over Barrington. He was an intimidating sight to most men. "Let me make myself clearer. Not only are you not to speak to Lady Carlisle again but if I ever see you put your hands on her, I will call you out. I am quite a good shot and have no plans on shooting into the air." He glowered at the younger man. "Do you understand?"

Barrington had the good sense to nod in acknowledgement and wisely walked away without further argument. Hawk's temper was holding on by a thread and if Barrington had said one more word, he probably would have punched him in the mouth.

"I feel I missed something interesting, "Lord Rockhurst said as he walked into the room.

"It was nothing," Hawk said and retook his seat as the rest of the room mumbled and went back to their activities.

Leicester leaned forward and spoke softly. "That incident will be all over London by tomorrow."

Hawk shrugged. "I don't give a damn."

"I suppose one of you will tell me what all this is about later. Right now, I have been sent to find the two of you. I have arrived with Prinny and he has sent me to retrieve you so you can join him in the ballroom. You know how he likes having his friends around him," Rockhurst said as he straightened his cravat.

Both Hawk and Leicester rose from their seats. They knew how sensitive the Prince Regent was if he thought others were criticizing him. The three of them made their way from the card room back to the ballroom. Hawk's eyes instantly found Persephone dancing a quadrille with the ancient Lord Wiltshire. While he had been reported to be quite the lady's man in his youth at seventy years of age, he was quite harmless.

They made their way to where the prince was standing with his entourage. When he saw them, he greeted them warmly. "Leicester, Hawksford, it is good to see the two of you here. Rockhurst assured me you would be in attendance."

"Hensley's ball is always the crush, your highness and as you were planning on attending, we would not dream of missing it," Leicester said as he moved to stand on one side of the monarch.

The prince's smile widened. "I hear your sister is making her debut this season, Hawk as is the daughter of Lord Carlisle. Are they attending tonight? I would like to meet them. It is said they are both beautiful beyond compare."

"I will bring them both over as soon as the dance has ended, your highness," Hawk replied as he noticed a stranger with the prince.

The prince saw him staring at the new arrival. "Let me introduce you to my guest. Comte Francisco Domingo, may I introduce the Duke of Hawksford and the Duke of Leicester, two of my most loyal friends."

The Comte bowed towards Leicester and Hawk. Both nodded before shaking hands with him.

"The Comte is visiting from Spain. I told him he will see some of our beautiful English ladies tonight," the prince said as he waved a hand toward the dancefloor.

"Is this your first visit to England?" Leicester asked.

"I visited once as a child with my father, but this is my first visit since I received my title."

The music stopped. "If you will excuse me, your highness I will go find my sister and Lady Carlisle now, excuse me." Hawk bowed toward the prince before making his way through the crowd to find Persephone and Catherine.

Catherine and Persephone were both at the refreshment table with their dance partners. When Catherine saw him, she smiled brightly. "Hawk, did you come to ask one of us to dance?"

He saw Persephone briefly glance in his direction before quickly looking away. "No, I have come to escort the both of you to meet the prince. He has asked to meet you."

Catherine grabbed Persephone's hand. "How exciting? The prince actually asked to meet us."

Persephone gave her friend a small smile then turned to face the duke. His eyes met hers and she found it hard to pull away from his gaze. He offered his arm to his sister and Persephone fell into step behind them. He escorted them back to where the prince was standing with Leicester, Rockhurst and the Comte.

"Your highness, my sister Lady Catherine Gray and Lady Persephone Carlisle."

The prince took Catherine's hand. Lady Gray, you are as lovely as I have heard. I'm sure Hawksford here has his house invaded with suitors on a daily basis."

Catherine curtsied low and blushed prettily at the comment. "Thank you, your highness."

He then moved to take Persephone's hand. "Lady Carlisle, you are also a beauty. I hope your father is well."

Persephone also curtsied low and smiled at the prince. "Thank you, your highness. I haven't heard from my father in some time, but I am sure he is perfectly well."

The prince then introduced the ladies to the Comte. Catherine curtsied and smiled prettily, but it was obvious that Persephone had caught his eye. He held her hand for longer than was proper.

"My lady, I am enchanted. Your name, Persephone, is that not the mythical wife of Hades?" the Comte asked as he continued to hold her hand.

Persephone pulled her fingers from his and blushed at the comment. She knew her name was unusual, but she hated being reminded that her mythical namesake was dragged into the underworld and forced to marry Hades. The story always embarrassed her to an extent.

She nervously looked down before responding, "Yes, my lord."

"You must tell me more about how you came to get the name. Perhaps during the next dance, I believe it is to be a waltz."

Persephone felt herself breathing a little faster. She did not wish to dance with the Comte. There was something about him, something she couldn't quite put her finger on, but it made her uneasy and a little scared. She started to panic. "I'm afraid this dance has already been promised to his grace." She looked over at Hawk who cocked his head to the side slightly and raised one eyebrow. She gave him a pleading look hoping he would not call her out for the liar she was.

Hawk stepped forward taking her hand and placing it on his arm. "Yes, indeed it is. I apologize for having to steal her away." He bowed to the prince. "Your highness."

The Comte gave Persephone a smile that made her uneasy. "Until next time, Lady Carlisle." He bowed and Persephone tightened her grip on the duke's arm as he led her away.

Hawk was not sure what had led Persephone to lie about the dance but since he had wanted to hold her in his arms all night, he was not about to throw away the opportunity. "May I ask what caused the winds of good fortune to blow in my direction?"

Persephone looked up at him. "I did not feel like dancing with the Comte. I know I must sound ridiculous, but he made me very nervous. So, I must thank you for rescuing me and not calling me out for my falsehood in front of everyone."

He pulled her into his arms placing his hand on the small of her back as the strains of the waltz began to play. "I thought I made you nervous."

She shook her head slightly and grinned. "Not in the same way."

He pulled her a fraction closer. "Did he frighten you?"

"No, not really. He just gave me an odd feeling." She looked up at the duke hoping he was understanding her. "An unpleasant feeling."

He didn't say anything, but she knew he understood. He whirled her faster and she found it hard to think of anything else when she was dancing in his arms. She felt a warmth where his hand rested on the small of her back. He was so tall that the top of her head barely reached his chin. She had danced with several gentleman at balls before, but no one danced with as much skill as the duke.

"You are very quiet, your grace."

He smiled. "I am relishing the moment, for I fear that as soon as the dance ends and you are no longer in need of my assistance, you will go back to refusing me again."

"Oh, that makes me sound like a horrible person. Please don't think of me that way. I panicked and did not know what else to do."

He pressed his hand a little firmer on her back to steer her around another couple. "I'm not complaining, my dear. I have been wanting to dance with you all night."

She relaxed a little. "I am sorry."

"There is no need to be, my love. I am happy to help you escape your many suitors any time you wish."

She blushed and whispered softly. "You shouldn't call me that. If someone hears they will make assumptions."

He looked down into her eyes holding her gaze. "Assumptions? Will they assume that I desire you, that you occupy my thoughts, that every time another man looks at you, I feel a murderous rage come over me? Let them assume what they want."

Persephone was surprised at his words. She didn't know how to respond. They finished the remainder of the dance in silence. When the music ended, he held her in his arms for a fraction longer before taking her hand and raising it to his lips.

"Shall I escort you to the refreshment table?"

"I think I would like to get some air. I'll find Catherine and she can walk with me onto the terrace."

Hawk bowed at the waist. "As you wish. I will escort you to my sister."

Catherine was not hard to find. She was standing next to Leicester on the side of the ballroom. Persephone smiled when she saw the look on his face. Catherine was staring up at him adoringly and Leicester looked as if he wanted to be anywhere but there.

"Thank you for my rescue, your grace," Persephone said as he turned to walk away.

He gave her a grin. "My pleasure, although the next time I will require some sort of payment for my assistance." He gave her a wink as he and Leicester walked away to go stand with the prince once again.

Catherine grabbed her arm as they walked toward the open balcony doors that led to the terrace overlooking the garden. The ball was a crush, and it was very hot inside. The fresh outside air felt good on her face. She breathed in a deep breath and closed her eyes for just a moment as the smell of the flowers from the garden below drifted up to the terrace.

"He is in love with you."

Persephone was startled at Catherine's bold statement. "I beg your pardon."

"Hawk, he is in love with you," Catherine said as she moved to lean against the railing.

Persephone rolled her eyes. Catherine was very fanciful. She loved her like a sister, but she was always romanticizing things. She had been in love with Leicester since she was a little girl and even though the man does not show any inclination of returning her affection, Catherine insists they are destined to be together. Persephone feared she was imagining her and her brother in the same way.

"Desire is not the same as love."

"Oh fiddle, do you not notice the way he looks at you. The fire between the two of you was practically scorching others on the dance floor. I wasn't the only one that noticed. Others were murmuring that perhaps the elusive Duke of Hawksford had been caught at last."

"Being gossiped about is the last thing I want, Catherine. I don't wish to be linked with one of the biggest rakes in the ton."

Her friend smiled brightly. "I know you have your thoughts on marriage and both of us agreed that this season would be for us, not in pursuit of a husband but what if your future happiness is closer than you think."

Persephone knew there was no need in arguing with her. Once Catherine got something in her head it took something monumental to change her mind. They stood on the terrace enjoying the night air when a voice from behind startled them.

"When I came to England, I never expected to find such attractive ladies. The women in Spain are beautiful, but none can compare with either of you."

"Comte Domingo, how very nice of you to say," Catherine replied enjoying the flattery.

He moved closer to them keeping his eyes on Persephone. "Would it be too forward of me to ask both of you to accompany me on a carriage ride through the park tomorrow? It will be nice to have such pretty guides to help me maneuver my way through your capital."

Persephone was just about to open her mouth to refuse when Catherine clasped her hands together in excitement. "We would be honored, of course we will have to seek permission from my brother and be properly chaperoned."

"Of course," the Comte replied.

"Perhaps we should go back inside, Catherine," Persephone said not liking the way the Comte kept staring at her.

Catherine looked at her friend confused at her tone of voice. "Of course, you are right, Persephone. Comte, maybe another time. I am sure we will all be tired after tonight's ball."

He nodded. "I will speak to the duke and seek his permission for another day this week." He reached for Catherine's hand and placed a quick kiss on her wrist. Persephone cringed as he took her hand in his. "Until later, my lady." He raised her hand to his lips letting his lips linger on her skin.

Persephone pulled her hand away and resisted the urge to wipe it clean on her skirt. "Good evening, Comte." She took Catherine's arm and dragged her back inside to the ball.

"I take it that you do not like the Comte," Catherine stated as Persephone continued to pull her along.

Persephone shook her head. "No, there is something about him. I don't know what it is. The way he looks at me is revolting."

"Well, we will make an excuse and not go riding with him." Catherine squeezed her hand. "I'm sure it will not take too much convincing to get Hawk to deny his permission anyway."

"Don't start, Catherine," Persephone said glancing upward in exasperation.

They didn't have any more time to discuss the matter as the next gentlemen on their dance cards claimed them and led them back to the dance floor.

The remainder of the ball continued without incident. Aunt Louisa grew tired after another two hours and Hawk called for the carriage. They were all quiet on the way home, even Catherine who normally would have been chatting away. When they arrived at Hawksford House, the duke assisted them from the carriage then disappeared inside. Persephone helped Aunt Louisa up the stairs to her bedchamber where her lady's maid was waiting for her.

"You looked lovely, tonight, Persephone. Your mother would have been proud of you." She gave Persephone a sleepy smile.

Persephone gave her a quick hug then went to her own bedchamber where Sarah was waiting for her. "Did you have a good time tonight, my lady?"

"Yes, I enjoyed myself very much."

The lady's maid moved to begin helping her with her dress.

"Wait"

The maid stopped.

"I need to go back downstairs for a moment. Please do not wait for me. I can undress myself."

The maid gave her an odd look. "I don't mind waiting, my lady. If there is something you forgot downstairs, I would be happy to go get it for you."

Persephone shook her head. "No, but I do thank you. Now go get some rest. I will see you in the morning." She didn't wait for the maid's response but headed downstairs.

There were still servants about finishing up their duties for the day. When she reached the bottom of the steps, she stopped and began second guessing her wisdom.

"Lady Carlisle, may I be of assistance?" Billings asked as he approached her.

"Where is the duke?"

"His grace is in his study, my lady. I'm not certain he wishes to be disturbed. Shall I go see if he is available?"

Persephone stepped toward him and placed her hand on his. "Oh no, please don't do that. I can wait to speak with him in the morning."

The older butler bowed to her. "As you wish, my lady."

Persephone turned back toward the stairs and waited until Billings had walked away before she quietly made her way to the duke's study. She knocked softly before opening the door a fraction of an inch. The room was dark except for the lamps burning around the desk.

She stepped further into the room. "Your grace?" She didn't see him at first. "May I speak with you?"

It was then that she saw him materialize and move to lean against the front of his desk. He was still dressed in his evening attire from the ball, and he looked incredibly handsome, but when did he not. She felt her pulse begin to speed up and she almost turned around to leave.

"If you know what is good for you, Persephone, you will not come any further into this room. I have had more to drink tonight than I care to admit and my self-control I fear may be faltering. If you come within arm's reach, I cannot guarantee I'll be able to keep my hands off you." She could see him smirk in the dim light. "Especially when you are wearing that dress."

Persephone stopped. "I came to thank you for tonight and also to ask another favor."

He stood from where he had been leaning against the desk. "The thanks are unnecessary. As for the favor, you have my attention."

She nervously clasped her hands in front of her. "It's about the Comte. When Catherine and I were on the terrace he said he would seek your permission to take us riding this week through Hyde Park." She thought she noticed him tense.

"So, the handsome Comte has changed your mind about him, and you came to me to make sure I give my approval for him to court you." His voice was harsh.

Persephone shook her head and moved forward toward him. She reached out and put her hand on his sleeve. "Oh no, you misunderstand. I don't want you to give your permission."

He looked down at where her hand rested on his arm before she pulled it away. Then he studied her face. "What happened on the terrace, Persephone?"

She shrugged her shoulders and held up her hands. "Nothing really, He just makes me feel uneasy. I don't know why. It's the reason I refused to dance with him. Please say you will not give your permission."

He stepped forward and put his hands on her shoulders. "You will be safe, Persephone. I will see that the Comte is refused admittance. Although with him being a foreign dignitary it might not sit well with the prince."

She had not thought of that. "I don't want you to do anything that will cause his highness to become angry with you. I am probably just being nonsensical. I'm sure everything will be alright."

His hands gently squeezed her shoulders. "Let me worry about Prinny." He looked down at her upturned face. "But remember what I said about saving you, there would be a price to pay." Before she could protest, he leaned down and gently pressed his lips to hers. He had told her that his self-control was vanishing where she was concerned and if she had resisted, he would have pulled away, but when her lips softened against his and he felt her lean closer into his embrace, he pulled her tighter. She parted her lips slightly and he took advantage letting his tongue mingle with hers.

Persephone wrapped her arms around his neck and leaned further into him. "We should stop now," she whispered against his lips but when he started to pull away, she intertwined her hands in his hair and pulled his head back down to hers.

He wrapped his hands around her waist and lifted her off her feet to carry her to the top of his desk where he sat her down. He pulled his lips away from hers and she instantly felt the loss, but then he pushed aside the curls that had fallen from her coiffure and began lightly kissing the side of her neck and the sensitive skin behind her ear.

Persephone sighed and angled her neck over to give him better access. Her skin prickled as he moved lower nibbling lightly at the exposed skin on her collarbone. She gripped his arms tighter. He moved back to kiss her lips again as he let one of his hands move slowly from her waist to cup her breast through the silk material of her gown. Persephone leaned into his touch marveling at how it made her feel. She wanted to touch him, so she tentatively moved her hands from his arms to place on his chest under his jacket. She could feel his muscles tense through the fabric of his shirt as she let her hands explore. He kissed her again while his hands quickly maneuvered the bodice of her gown down below her breasts. She gasped when she felt the cool air on her naked skin but when his hands covered her and he kneaded softly, she heard herself moan with desire.

Hawk couldn't believe how soft her skin was and she tasted sweet like honey. He felt himself growing hard as her nipples puckered from his ministrations. He leaned down and suckled her causing her to nearly jump from the desk. He held her still and reveled in the sounds of her whimpers and sighs of pleasure as her head fell backward. He paused long enough to look at her. She was glorious, perfectly formed and his for the taking.

"You are beautiful," he murmured against her breast.

Persephone felt her legs parting of their own volition and felt him press into her. She marveled at how hard he had become and wondered if she should touch him there. She was being very brave tonight, but she wasn't that bold, yet. She felt cool air on her stockinged legs as his hand began to slide up her skirt to touch the skin above her garters. She pulled his head back to her lips wanting more but not knowing what that more was. His fingers lightly circled the skin of her thighs and she felt warm at her center. When his fingers moved higher to lightly touch the sensitive skin between her legs, she felt as if she would expire there on the spot. His fingers glided over her crease and found her nub and began caressing her there. Persephone knew this was wrong and she should not be there, but she couldn't pull herself away. She spread her legs farther apart wanting more, needing more. Suddenly they both jumped when they heard a loud crash in the front hallway.

Hawk quickly pulled her bodice up to cover her breasts and pushed down her skirt before lifting her from the desk.

Persephone not thinking she would be able to stand on her own clung to his arm. They were both breathing heavily. Persephone's lips felt swollen, she reached up to touch them with the tips of her fingers.

"I think a servant must have dropped something in the hallway." He raked a hand through his hair. She didn't know it, but he had been damn near close to taking her on his bloody desk with the damned door open for anyone to see. He glanced at her noting the way her breasts would rise and fall with each breath.

"My apologies, Persephone."

"I'm glad we came to our senses before we were discovered." She put a hand over her heart to try to still its rapid beating.

Hawk didn't want her to leave. He wanted to lift her into his arms and take her to his bedchamber. He gave her a wicked look. "I could lock the door."

Persephone shook her head. "I had better leave, your grace. It seems like you are not the only one with self-control issues."

He watched as she quickly left the study to return to her bedchamber. Once she was out of sight he moved back over to where he had sat his glass of brandy. He lifted the glass to his lips savoring the way it burned down his throat. Sleep would be impossible after the interaction between them. But one thing was clear, she would be his. After tonight there was no way he could contemplate another man having her, tasting her, touching her, taking her to their bed. No, tonight Persephone Carlisle had sealed her fate.

Chapter Seven

When Persephone finally went down to breakfast, she was surprised to find the duke absent. Catherine and Aunt Louisa were already there and were almost finished eating. She sat down as a footman brought her a plate.

"Good morning, Persephone," Aunt Louisa said as Persephone picked up a pastry to take a bite.

"Good morning."

"Shall we go for a ride this morning, Persephone? I would love to take a gallop down Rotten Row," Catherine asked.

"It looks like it might rain this morning, perhaps we should ride another time." Just as Persephone spoke the words thunder rattled the windows.

"Well, that settles the matter. What shall we do today?" Catherine asked as she looked out the window at the darkening skies.

"Since we are going to the opera tonight, it might be a good idea to stay home and get some rest," Aunt Louisa replied before she stood from her chair.

"Opera?" Persephone exclaimed excitedly. She had been looking forward to going since they arrived in London.

"Yes, Hawk has it all arranged."

Catherine gave Persephone a small smile. "Just where is Hawk this morning?"

Persephone looked surprised at the question. "How would I know where he is? I just came down to breakfast."

Aunt Louisa gave her a curious look. "Ethan had some business to see to this morning. He will be back sometime this afternoon. Are you alright, dear?"

"Yes, I am just a little tired this morning," Persephone said as she took another bite of her pastry.

The older lady seemed to accept that excuse. "The perfect reason to take a day to rest. If either of you need me, I will be in my rooms."

She made her way out the door leaving Catherine and Persephone alone.

"Now that Aunt Louisa has left us alone, tell me what you and my brother were doing last night?"

Persephone started coughing as the bite of food she had been swallowing seemed to get lodged in her throat. She took a few seconds to recover herself. "What are you talking about?"

Catherine rolled her eyes and dabbed at her lips with a napkin. "I know you were not in your room last night and when I went looking for you, I saw you enter the study." She raised her eyebrows and gave her friend a mischievous grin.

Persephone shut her eyes briefly knowing her cheeks were turning pink. "I went to find him to inform him of the Comte's desire to take us riding and since the Comte makes me feel incredibly uncomfortable, I asked him to refuse any attempts the Comte has at seeing me."

"Hmm, and I'm sure Hawk had no problem acquiescing your request."

Persephone shook her head. "Thankfully he agreed."

Catherine tried to stifle her giggles. "Of course, he did. You probably wouldn't have had to say anything, and he would have thwarted any attempt the Comte had at courting you."

"Whatever do you mean by that?" Persephone asked crossly.

"Simple, my dear. Hawk wants you for himself and to my knowledge he always gets what he wants. He isn't going to let the Comte or anyone else for that matter stand in his way."

"So, you think that if the almighty and powerful Duke of Hawksford says I belong to him, that I have no say in the matter?"

"Of course, I don't mean that. Are you saying that you have no feelings for my brother at all?"

Persephone didn't answer and just stared at Catherine wondering just how much she knew.

"Exactly, your silence answers that question."

"You know as well as I do that your brother would never be satisfied with one woman."

This time Catherine frowned at her comment. "Don't be so quick to make assumptions, Persephone. My father was a reputed rake when he was younger, but once he met my mother, he was totally devoted to her." She reached over and touched her hand and softened her voice. "I know your father leaving you has caused you such grief, Persephone. But there are good men out there that are devoted to their families. Hawk would never abandon his family."

Persephone's smile didn't quite reach her eyes. "I just don't know what to do Catherine. I may not even marry, perhaps I will be a companion to your Aunt Louisa and travel the world. I certainly don't think I would make a good duchess. That is a daunting prospect."

Catherine laughed. "A companion? My goodness that would be a daunting task. Perhaps I won't marry either and we can travel the world together." She laughed louder as she stood from her seat. "Wouldn't we be a pair?" She placed a hand on Persephone's shoulder. "Just don't let your past cloud your judgement so you can't enjoy your future, sweet friend."

Persephone watched her friend walk from the breakfast room. She sat there a few minutes longer but couldn't bring herself to eat another bite. She had too much going on in her head, too many questions that she didn't know the answers. Was she letting her father's behavior affect how she saw her future? She couldn't deny that she had wanted what happened between the duke and her last night to happen. She knew the danger when she sought him out. Would it be possible to enjoy a few moments of pleasure with the duke with no consequences? What if she never found that kind of passion again, even with her future husband? Would it be so wrong to want a few more moments with the duke like last night? She had a lot to think about.

The Duke of Leicester's residence in Mayfair

"Do you still have friends in the foreign office?"

Leicester was surprised by the question. "Thomas Harrison is there. You remember him, he attended Eton with us, I believe he is a second or third son."

Hawk fiddled with a small figurine on Leicester's desk. "I need some information on the Comte Domingo."

"The Comte Domingo? The man with Prinny last night at Hensley's ball?"

"Yes, he has shown interest in Persephone, and she has a definite fear of him. He has made it known to her that he intends to seek my approval to court her."

"Well, that's simple enough, just don't give your permission."

Hawk leveled a serious glare on his friend. "I already intended on denying him permission. But I am interested to know more about him, when faced with an opponent I prefer to know all there is to know about him."

"I will make my inquiries and let you know what I can find out."

Hawk stood. "Thank you. I will owe you a favor."

Leicester's grin was lop-sided. "Don't think I'll forget either."

Persephone sat in the window seat of the blue morning room watching the rain, trying to concentrate on the book she was trying to read. She leaned her head against the glass and sighed heavily.

"You must be in deep thought."

She jumped at the deep voice of the duke coming from the doorway. "What makes you think that?"

He walked further into the room coming closer to her. "That sigh for one and the fact that the book you are reading is upside down."

She closed the book quickly and set it aside. "The weather is miserable today not much else to do. Your aunt is taking a nap and Catherine is upstairs drawing or painting."

"I could think of something we could do." He gave her a mischievous grin.

She actually grinned back at him. "I'm not sure that would be wise with all the servants moving around."

He shrugged his shoulders. "I can make them scatter if you wish."

Her smile grew brighter. "I'm sure you could."

"I made inquiries about Comte Domingo today."

This caused her smile to fade, and she stood quickly. "Has he contacted you?"

He took her hand and held it wanting to reassure her that she would be safe. "No, but I wanted to find out if there is reason for you to be nervous. Leicester will have his contact at the foreign office look into him and his family."

"I'm sure I am just being silly. There is probably nothing for me to fear. But I do thank you for looking into the matter for me."

He wrapped an arm around her waist and pulled her to him. "About last night, Persephone…"

She pulled away from him. Coherent thought was impossible when he held her in his arms. "Yes, I have been thinking about that."

He cocked his head to the side curious as to what she was about to say. He could tell she was nervous. She pulled her lower lip between her teeth and twisted her hands before her.

"I enjoyed last night very much."

"I'm glad to hear it." He smirked mischievously.

She took a breath. "There is an obvious attraction between us, and I think it is inevitable that we will have another interaction as we did last night."

His eyes squinted wondering where she was going with this. "I'm glad that I have something to look forward to."

She placed a hand on her chest. "Yes, well. This is very difficult for me to say, and I hope I am being clear."

"What exactly are you trying to be clear about, Persephone?"

"I'm saying that if we feel the need to do what we did last night, we should." He reached for her, but she stepped backward. "And there should be no consequences for it."

This had him confused. "No consequences?"

"Yes, I don't want you to feel that you have to marry me just because we, . . . well, because we…."

"Made love?" he finished for her.

She blushed bright red. "Yes."

He frowned slightly and narrowed his eyes. "So let me get this clear in my mind so there is no question as to what you are saying to me. You are telling me that we may continue in the manner we did last night in my study with me making love to you and I am free of all responsibilities and accountability. I can take your innocence and have you in my bed and there are no expectations of marriage?"

It didn't sound very good when he spoke it out loud in that manner. "Well, yes."

His eyes narrowed and his nostrils flared with anger. "What kind of bounder do you think I am? My god, Persephone. Do you think I am the kind of man that would do that?"

Her eyes widened in surprise. "I thought you would be pleased. You are practiced at this. You can't tell me you have not had arrangements like this with other women."

"Pleased!" His voice continued to rise. "Do you think I could do that to you? And don't you ever mention those damn scandal sheets again. I could strangle Louisa for allowing you to read that trash." He ran a hand through his hair in frustration.

"I would never make a good duchess. Don't you see? I'm not sure I will ever marry."

He was so angry he didn't want to touch her. "I don't know why you would think you wouldn't make a good duchess. Your father is a viscount and your mother the daughter of an earl. This is the most ridiculous conversation but let me end the discussion right now. I am not the sort of cad you imagine me to be and while I have every intention of making love to you, I also have every intention of making you, my wife." He held up his hand when she started to argue. "I will hear no more of this, Persephone. I will see you tonight when we leave for the opera." He left the room quickly before he said something else, or she said something even more outrageous that made his temper flare more than what it had already.

Persephone plopped back down on the window seat wondering what on earth had made her suggest something so ludicrous. Both the duke's aunt and Catherine would be mortified if they knew she had even suggested something so scandalous. She had thought it was the perfect solution.

Later that evening

Catherine didn't bother to knock on the bedchamber door, she just bounced in expecting to find Persephone as excited about their night at the opera as she was herself. But Persephone sat on the chaise lounge beside the fire. She was dressed in her evening gown but did not stir when Catherine walked over to her.

"Persephone, are you alright? Aunt Louisa is ready for us to leave. She sent me up here to see what was keeping you so long."

Persephone stood and grabbed her gloves. "I'm sorry, I didn't realize it had gotten so late."

Her friend eyed her curiously. "I thought you had been looking forward to the opera."

"Oh, I am. I just have a lot on my mind."

"Well, Hawk isn't going with us, if that is what has been worrying you."

Persephone turned back to her. "He isn't?"

"No, he told Aunt Louisa that something came up and he would try to be there but he might be late if he is even able to make it at all."

Persephone followed Catherine out of the room and downstairs to where Aunt Louisa was waiting for them. She had been dreading seeing Hawk again after their conversation that afternoon, but she couldn't help but wonder if he was still upset with her. Looking back, she was so embarrassed that she suggested something so shameful. Hopefully he would forget all about it but she was doubtful.

"There you are, Persephone. We must hurry. I don't like shoving my way through the throng of people to get to our seats in Hawkford's box." Aunt Louisa said as Billings opened the front doors.

A footman handed them into the ducal carriage and once seated Aunt Louisa patted her hand reassuringly. "I know you have been looking forward to the opera, Persephone."

She smiled back at the sweet older lady who had been like a mother to her. "I am very excited. I'm sure it will be a grand evening."

Louisa leaned over to her and said softly. "I'm sure Hawk will join us if he is able to do so."

Persephone didn't respond but turned to look out the windows of the carriage as they passed by the grand houses of Mayfair.

Once they reached the opera house both Persephone and Catherine were surprised to see the number of people attending. They followed Aunt Louisa up the stairs, nodding politely in greeting to some of the people they passed. Several gentlemen moved forward to greet them and it seemed to take them forever to reach the duke's box. It was very large and gave them an excellent view of the stage. Aunt Louisa insisted that she and Catherine sit up front so they could see the performance better and most importantly, be seen by the ton.

Persephone felt her spirits lightening as she marveled at all the grandeur around her. All eyes seemed to be watching them. She recognized several faces, some of the gentlemen she had danced with and some she had been introduced to. She did notice some of the ladies gave them resentful looks, obviously curious as to the whereabouts of the duke.

Catherine snapped her fan open then leaned over toward her. "Don't look now, but the Comte Domingo is in the box directly across from ours and he has not taken his eyes off of you since you sat down."

Persephone glanced up and locked eyes with the Comte. He gave her a smile and nodded toward her. She looked away quickly.

"Oh dear, he saw me."

"Yes, he certainly did. You couldn't have been more obvious. Why did you look at him? I told you not to look," Catherine said with a touch of irritation.

Persephone opened her fan and began fanning her cheeks. "I don't know."

The orchestra began to play music and Persephone turned her attention to the stage. She forced herself not to look back at the Comte but could feel his eyes upon her. She continued to watch the stage throughout the performance and she was able to immerse herself in it for most of the night. The singer on stage was very exotic looking with a beautiful soprano voice.

At the end of the first act, Catherine stood and said, "I would like to go to the ladies retiring room and then mingle in the hallway before the second act starts. If Persephone and I both go together, may we go?"

"You may go to the retiring room, but I don't think you should linger in the hallways unescorted," Aunt Louisa said as she began fanning herself vigorously.

Persephone stood from her chair and followed Catherine to the retiring room. The hallways were crammed with people. Some were shoving and pushing to get through the masses. At one point a group of gentlemen pushed between her and Catherine and with all the crowds, she lost sight of her. She tried to peek over the heads of the mob but she had completely lost her. She moved a little with the throng hoping to find Catherine so they could hurry back to their box. The crowd had started to disburse a bit when she caught sight of the Comte walking toward her. She quickly turned and headed back in the direction of the duke's box hoping he couldn't catch up with her. She was walking as quickly as she could while navigating through the crowd when suddenly she was shocked as a firm hand gripped her elbow and pulled into one of the curtained alcoves. She shrieked only to be silenced when firm lips descended upon hers.

She pushed at the hard chest holding her when suddenly he broke the kiss and whispered, "Hush, Persephone." She stilled and relaxed at the familiarity of the duke's voice.

"You scared me half to death!" she said as he released her.

"What the devil do you think you are doing walking about unescorted?" he said clearly annoyed.

"Catherine and I were going to the ladies retiring room. We got separated in the crowd." She put a hand over her mouth. "Oh no, Catherine. We need to find her." She moved to leave and he grabbed her arm to stop her.

"Catherine will be alright. Leicester and I both saw the two of you. He will find Catherine and escort her back to the box."

Persephone breathed a sigh of relief. "Thank goodness, shouldn't we return as well."

He pulled her back into his arms. "We will shortly. We need to let the crowds disperse and make certain no one notices us stepping out from behind the curtain together." He leaned over and pressed a light sweet kiss to her lips. "You look beautiful this evening."

She lowered her eyes. "I'm glad you came tonight. Comte Domingo is here."

"I thought he might be," He put a finger under her chin and lifted her face up to his. "Did you really think I would let you attend alone?"

"I didn't know. After this afternoon, I wasn't sure you would ever want to see me again."

He chuckled deeply. "Well, I must admit it was the most absurd suggestion I have ever heard."

Persephone didn't like that he was laughing at her. "I am sorry I suggested it. I don't know what came over me." She pushed against his chest trying to move away.

He tightened his hold. "I always want to see you, Persephone." He kissed her again, this time with more passion. She placed both hands against his chest and pushed lightly.

"We need to return to your box; your aunt will be worried."

He sighed and rested his forehead against hers. "Yes, we should. But we do need to make plans soon."

"Plans?" Persephone asked.

"Now is not the time, but soon." He peeked around the curtain to make sure the hallway was clear. "You go first and I will follow behind shortly. Wait for me down the hall and I will escort you back the rest of the way."

Persephone nodded then made her way into the corridor. She walked back toward the box then stood off to the side waiting for the duke.

"Good evening, Lady Carlisle," Comte Domingo said as he stepped around a corner.

Persephone jumped and spun around. "Comte Domingo, you startled me." She looked back over her shoulder hoping to see the duke.

"I have been waiting for you, unfortunately I lost sight of you earlier. I have been wanting to speak with you." He moved closer to her and she felt herself shiver.

"May I escort you back to your box?"

Persephone felt her heart start to race.

"She already has an escort," Hawk said in his deep authoritative voice from behind her.

Persephone felt his hand rest on the small of her back and she instantly felt more at ease.

The Comte narrowed his eyes at the duke. "I didn't realize you were here, your grace." He bowed slightly then looked back to Persephone. "We will meet another time, Lady Carlisle."

Persephone couldn't help but feel that there was menace behind his words. Hawk moved beside her and placed her hand on his arm. "You are shivering."

She looked up at him. "I can't help it. I don't know why but he is rather frightening to me."

He began leading her back toward the opera box. "There is nothing for you to be afraid of, my dear. The Comte wouldn't dare hurt anyone under my protection."

They entered the box together no doubt an act that would cause some gossip. Aunt Louisa frowned at them as they took their seats. Persephone saw that Catherine was already there seated beside Leicester.

"What took you so long?" Catherine whispered as she leaned closer to her.

"We were stopped by Comte Domingo," Persephone said not wanting to elaborate further.

"And you have been speaking with him all this time?"

Persephone gave her a cross look but didn't answer. She turned her attention back toward the stage. Catherine smiled but her attention soon drifted back to the Duke of Leicester.

At the close of the performance, Hawk stood offering his hand to his aunt to assist her in rising before offering his arm to Persephone. Catherine was wearing a wide smile as she was on the arm of the Duke of Leicester. The group left the box and began making their way to the front of the theater to the waiting carriages.

As they began to descend the grand stairway, a feminine voice called out to them. "Hawk! Hawk!" She heard him grumble under his breath before stopping.

Persephone looked around to see a very attractive lady coming towards them. She outstretched both of her hands towards the duke. "Hawk, I was hoping I would see you here tonight."

The duke nodded in acknowledgement. "Lady Sanderson, I had not realized you were back in town."

The lady didn't make a move to acknowledge anyone else. "Lord Sanderson will not leave his country seat, especially with all that mess on the continent. He is determined to hold up in the country. You wouldn't believe what I had to do to convince him to allow me to come to London."

"Lady Sanderson, may I introduce my aunt, Lady Townsend, the Dowager Countess of Mulford, and my sister, Lady Gray, and Lady Carlisle." Hawk put a hand over Persephone's as it rested on his arm.

The motion was not missed by Lady Sanderson as she narrowed her eyes slightly at Persephone before turning her smile full force back toward the duke. "I was hoping I might have a moment to speak with you about something important."

Leicester moved forward with Catherine still on his arm. "I can escort the ladies to your carriage, if you need a moment."

Hawk frowned. "That will not be necessary."

Lady Sanderson leaned forward and she put her hand on the duke's arm. "Perhaps another time, Hawk." She practically purred his name and Persephone's stomach sank.

"Good evening, my lady," Hawk said as he led them down the stairs to his waiting carriage.

Persephone didn't say anything as he handed her inside the carriage before climbing in to sit across from his aunt. Catherine was chattering about the Duke of Leicester and how handsome he was and how surprised she had been that he had rescued her from the crowd and escorted her back to the box. Persephone didn't hear most of the conversation, she kept her head turned toward the window. She wasn't angry, she just felt vacant inside.

"Persephone? Persephone?"

She jumped as Catherine reached over and shook her a little. "I'm sorry. My mind was wandering."

Catherine frowned. "This could have been the most important moment of my life, Persephone. Leicester could finally see me as a woman and not just the sister of his best friend."

"Don't be foolish, Catherine. Leicester escorted you because I asked him to see you safely back to Aunt Louisa," Hawk said causing Catherine to roll her eyes.

"Yes, yes, I know. But it could become something else."

Hawk shook his head. "Leicester is no more suitable than . . . "

Catherine smirked. "Then you are?"

He frowned at his sister then glanced over to Persephone who had her head turned to the side waiting for his reply.

Aunt Louisa saved him from answering. "Both your brother and Leicester are very suitable."

"Whatever happened to the saying, *once a rake always a rake*?" Persephone asked not to anyone in particular.

Aunt Louisa laughed loudly. "Preposterous, my dear. Many people say that a reformed rake makes the best husband."

Catherine smiled. "See, Hawk. Leicester would make an excellent husband."

His eyes were on Persephone before turning back to his sister. "Leicester is not in the market for a bride and doesn't have any plans to be for a long time. Set your sights elsewhere, Catherine."

But his sister wouldn't let the conversation go. "What about you, Hawk? Is the great Duke of Hawksford ready to settle down?"

He narrowed his eyes at her. "My plans are my concern, Catherine."

Aunt Louisa reached over and patted Catherine's knee. "Enough, my dear. Your brother's business is his own. When he is ready to marry and set up his nursery, I'm sure he will find a most suitable lady to be his duchess."

Thankfully the rest of the journey home was quiet. When the carriage came to a stop in front of Hawksford House, footmen raced down the steps to assist them. The door opened but it was Lord Rockhurst standing there. The duke descended first followed by his aunt and Catherine. Lord Rockhurst held out his hand to help Persephone.

"I hope you enjoyed the opera, Lady Carlisle," he said as he raised her hand to his lips for a brief kiss.

"What brings you here? I thought you had an engagement with your parents tonight," Hawk asked.

Persephone watched as Lord Rockhurst's expression turned dark. "It was a short engagement as they all are when my father is involved."

"If you will excuse me, gentlemen." Both Hawk and Rockhurst bowed to her and watched as she made her way up the stairs to join the other ladies.

Once the ladies were out of earshot, Lord Rockhurst said, "I have some information about the Comte Domingo I think you might find interesting."

Hawk nodded. "He was at the opera tonight and approached Persephone. Thankfully I was there. Let's go in my study where we can have some privacy."

Rockhurst followed him up the stairs and into the study. Hawk walked over to a decanter of brandy and poured two glasses. "Brandy?"

"Yes, please. A night with my father usually calls for several glasses of brandy."

Hawk took a sip. "Same thing?"

"Yes, as always. I must be responsible and marry and set up my nursery to ensure the dukedom lives on for future generations." Lord Rockhurst downed his brandy in one swallow. He paused letting the liquor burn down his throat. "Of course, he has specific potential brides in mind. But enough of my troubles."

Hawk took a seat and motioned for his friend to take the one opposite his. "So, what information do you have about the Comte?"

"I know Leicester has reached out to his contacts in the foreign office but I asked around at some of the more disreputable establishments around London. It seems the Comte has a penchant for some of the more notorious pleasure houses, the kind that cater to the tastes of depraved gentlemen." Rockhurst got up and refilled his glass. "Persephone is right to be afraid of him. The Comte gets his pleasure from inflicting pain on the women he is with. I will spare you the disgusting details but I saw the last girl he visited and I would hate to think that could happen to Persephone."

Hawk slammed his glass down on the table. "Bastard!"

"I'm sure Leicester will uncover more about him and perhaps the reason he is in London, but if I were you, I would keep Persephone and Catherine as far away from him as possible."

"I intend to do just that."

Rockhurst sat back down. "You could just marry her, then the Comte would no longer be a problem."

"I plan on it."

The next morning in Hyde Park

"It is a lovely day for a ride in the park. I'm so glad you agreed to join me, Persephone." Catherine said as she looked back over her shoulder at the three grooms following close behind them. "Although I do believe Hawk is over doing it by sending three grooms riding with us. He could have joined us himself."

"I'm sure your brother has more important things to do than play chaperone to us during the season. We have already disturbed his normal routine."

Catherine shrugged her shoulders. "It certainly won't hurt him to have his *normal* routine disrupted, besides I'm his sister."

"It does feel good to be out in the sunshine this morning after the cloudy rainy days we have had lately," Persephone said as she urged her horse into a canter.

Catherine moved alongside her. "Aunt Louisa always said that one should never waste a sunny day in England."

The two continued toward Rotten Row with the grooms following behind. Persephone smiled as she breathed in the fresh air of the park. She enjoyed being outside and when in the country, she tended to stay outside more than most ladies her age.

They heard hoofbeats coming up behind them. Catherine turned thinking to see one of their grooms but instead saw Comte Domingo and Lord Fitzwilliam. "Don't look now, but we are about to endure another encounter with the Comte."

"Goodness, what do I have to do to get that man to leave me alone?" Persephone said in irritation.

"You should be more direct. Tell him in no uncertain terms that you are not interested. Would you like me to tell him?"

Persephone shook her head. "Goodness, Catherine, you can be so malicious when you choose to be."

She shrugged her shoulders again. "Sometimes matters call for malicious."

Persephone pulled her horse up to a walk. "Might as well get this over with as quickly as possible."

The Comte and Lord Fitzwilliam came up alongside them. "Lady Carlisle, Lady Gray, what a stroke of luck to find the two of you riding this morning," the Comte said as he sidled his horse closer to Persephone.

"We were just enjoying the sunshine," Persephone said as she continued to look forward.

"Yes, we *were* enjoying our morning," Catherine said emphasizing the past tense.

The Comte glared at her before turning his attention back to Persephone. "It has been difficult for me to get a moment of your time. I have been unable to get an audience with the duke."

Persephone kept riding. "The duke is very busy as am I."

At this he reached over and grabbed the reins of her horse pulling him to a sharp stop. "I think you must be playing games with me, my lady, and I must tell you that I am growing tired of them." His voice was low and threatening.

"Take your hands from my reins," Persephone said in slow clipped tones.

Lord Fitzwilliam looked stunned. "I say, perhaps you should let the ladies continue with their ride"

"Lady Gray may continue on if she would like, Lady Carlisle and I need a moment," the Comte said still keeping his eyes trained on Persephone.

Catherine moved her horse around in front of the Comte's. "If you think for one minute that I would leave her alone with the likes of you then you are the biggest fool I have ever met."

Persephone saw the rage in the Comte's eyes and she was sure if they had not been in a public place, he would have struck Catherine for her words. She was just about to tell the Comte again to let them leave when Lord Rockhurst appeared out of nowhere on his gray stallion.

"Unless you would like for me to drag you from your horse and beat you to a bloody pulp in front of half of the best of English society, I suggest you remove your hand from the lady's reins," Rockhurst said causing the Comte to stiffen in his saddle.

"I meant Lady Carlisle no harm, I am simply wanting a moment of her time."

Once he removed his hands setting Persephone's horse free, Lord Rockhurst maneuvered his horse between the Comte and Persephone. "It looks like the lady has no desire to be in your presence and for that matter, neither do I. Fitzwilliam, you should seek a different class of friends if you know what is good for you."

The Comte practically snarled at Rockhurst. "I'm not so easily deterred, my lord. Keep that in mind and I usually get what I want."

"I meant what I said, Comte. I will not hesitate to beat you senseless, remember you are in England and I am a marquis." Who do you think the courts will favor?"

The Comte spurred his horse into a gallop and retreated leaving Lord Fitzwilliam behind. "My apologies, ladies. I had no idea he meant either of you any harm. Rockhurst, I will take your advice. Good day to you all." He turned his horse in the opposite direction leaving the three alone.

Rockhurst gave the grooms a scornful look. "I don't know why Hawk bothered to send grooms riding with you if they weren't going to protect you."

"I'm sure they would have if you had not stepped in when you did," Persephone said grateful that Lord Rockhurst happened to be in the park this morning.

He gave her a wicked grin.

Catherine came forward on her horse. "Wait a minute, did Hawk send you to spy on us?"

"I wouldn't call it spying, I am merely an extra layer of protection." He raised his eyebrows at her. "Although, you seemed to be ready to fight the Comte yourself. You are rather cheeky, Catherine."

She smiled brightly. "I will take that as a compliment."

"Shall I ride back to Hawksford House with you, ladies?"

Persephone retuned his smile. "Of course."

"Tell me, Lord Rockhurst, has my brother employed his other friends to look after us as well?" Catherine asked curiously.

"If you are speaking of Leicester, I wouldn't know."

"It's just that he joined us at the opera last night and I was wondering if it was by choice or if he was under orders."

Persephone knew her friend would be heartbroken if she thought the only reason the Duke of Leicester had sat with her and escorted her at the opera was because he was forced to by her brother. She hoped Lord Rockhurst did not spoil it for her.

As if Rockhurst knew what she was thinking he replied, "Leicester has never been one to take orders well, my dear. If he was at the opera, it was because he chose to be not because he was coerced."

Catherine's face lit up at his words and Persephone silently mouthed the words, '*thank you*'. Rockhurst nodded in understanding. The three of them continued with their ride to Hawksford House.

Once they reached the duke's residence, Lord Rockhurst assisted both ladies from their mounts and escorted them up the steps and into the house.

Persephone paused in the grand foyer before she ascended the staircase to her bedchamber. "Thank you once again for your assistance today."

He nodded regally. "It is always a pleasure to be of assistance to such a lovely lady. Enjoy the rest of your day." He turned and walked away.

Persephone chuckled at his flirtations. As she turned toward the stairs, Billings came forward. "Lady Carlisle, a letter arrived for you this morning shortly after you left for your ride."

Persephone took the letter from the butler and started up the stairs. "I wonder who it could be from," she said to herself as she broke the seal.

Chapter Eight

Persephone knocked on Louisa's door holding the letter tightly in her hand. She opened the door slowly. "Aunt Louisa?"

"Persephone, come in child. Is something wrong?"

She bounced in excitedly. "No, not at all. I received a letter this morning. It was waiting for me when Catherine and I got back from our ride."

Louisa sat down on the settee and patted the cushion beside her for Persephone to join her. "A letter? Who from?"

"It's from Lady McDonough from Scotland. She claims to be a relative of mine. She says she is a distant cousin of my mother. Since you were my mother's dearest friend, I thought you might know if she is telling the truth. I have never heard her mentioned."

Aunt Louisa sighed heavily. "Lady McDonough is indeed a second or third cousin. Although she and your mother were never close. I'm not sure why she would be contacting you."

Persephone clutched the letter in her hand. "She wants me to come visit her family in Scotland. I never knew mother had Scottish relatives."

"Patricia McDonough is English. She married Laird McDonough, Duke of Sunbridge several years ago. What troubles me is how she found out about you and why after all these years she has reached out wanting you to come to Scotland." Louisa looked at her. "You aren't considering going, are you?"

Persephone looked down at the letter in her hand. "It would be nice to meet more of my family. It might be a fun adventure. Of course, I would wait until the close of the season. Perhaps you could travel with me."

Louisa shook her head. "Oh no, dear. Scotland is much too cold for my old bones." She then gave her a serious look. "Persephone dear, I am worried about you. You are so incredibly beautiful and I just knew you would find a husband your first season out. Has no one gained your attention?"

Persephone looked down. "You know that Catherine and I are not seriously seeking husbands this season."

The older woman scoffed. "Yes, yes, I know all about that silliness, and for Catherine I think that is an excellent idea. She is a year younger than you and not nearly as mature. But you are different. You will be twenty next season. I promised your mother I would see you settled well."

Persephone patted the older lady's hand. "I'm sorry for being so difficult. You know how much I care for you and I would not want you to worry over me. But I am not sure if I want to marry now or ever for that matter."

Louisa nodded knowing it was no use arguing further with her. "Promise me that you will take some time to think about it before you rush off to the wilds of Scotland."

Persephone gave her a hug. "Of course, I will write Lady McDonough but I will not promise to visit just yet."

Louisa smiled at her and patted her cheek. "You are a smart girl." But before Persephone could walk away, she said, "You know dear, your marriage does not have to be like your mother's."

Persephone paused considering the older lady's words then made her way out the door back to her own room. She didn't see the frown on the worried face of Louisa as she walked away.

Hawk was in his study with Lord Rockhurst when his aunt burst through the door. He quickly jumped to his feet. "Aunt Louisa, what's wrong?"

She began pacing in front of his desk. "I am worried about Persephone."

For his aunt to enter his study in such a state he knew it must be serious. "Stop pacing and tell me what you are talking about."

She stopped in front of him and put both hands on her hips. "Persephone received a letter today from a relative in Scotland."

"I didn't realize she had relatives in Scotland," he said crossing his arms over his chest.

"Persephone did not either. She has never met them before."

"So, what is the problem?"

Louisa frowned. "The problem is, by all reports, six feet six inches and handsome as sin."

Hawk closed his eyes and pinched the bridge of his nose trying to maintain his patience. "Please hurry and make your point, aunt."

She plopped down into the chair in front of him.

Lord Rockhurst raised an eyebrow. "You look like you could use a drink, my lady."

She waved him off. "No, no, perhaps later."

Hawk cleared his throat loudly. "Please continue, why is it such terrible news that Persephone has Scottish relatives?"

"Patricia Moorefield, who is Persephone's mother's second or third cousin, married the old Laird McDonough and Duke of Sunbridge several years ago. He was thirty plus years her senior and she was just barely seventeen. He was rich as Croesus and Patricia being greedy thought she could marry the older man, produce an heir quickly, and be a rich widow in no time. Unfortunately, she did not become with child right away, in fact it took nearly ten years for her to conceive. It is said that because the old

Laird was so intent on producing an heir, she was subject to his attentions nightly." She paused dramatically. "Serves her right for being so mercenary. Anyway, the old Laird died about three years ago and her son is now the new duke and Laird McDonough."

Hawk sighed heavily growing bored with the story. "What has all of this to do with Persephone?"

Louisa narrowed her eyes. "Pay attention, Ethan. Lady McDonough has always wanted her son to marry an English lady. Why else would she send for Persephone? She has made no effort to contact her through the years. Persephone is beautiful and being hailed as an incomparable, I'm sure word has reached Patricia and that is why she has asked Persephone to visit. And if my sources are correct, Laird McDonough is about your age, extremely handsome, and wealthy. I just know they have set their sights on our Persephone to marry him."

Hawk walked over and patted her arm. "There is nothing for you to worry about. Persephone will not be going to Scotland at least not without me."

Louisa rolled her eyes. "Don't be so arrogant, Ethan. Have you asked her to be your bride? And what makes you so sure she will accept. I'm sure Lady Sanderson rubbing up to you like a cat in heat last night at the opera didn't ease her mind any."

Rockhurst tried to cover up his laughter by clearing his throat. Hawk narrowed his eyes at him.

Louisa wasn't finished yet, "And don't think I didn't know about Lady Kingsley."

"I told you I will take care of it, aunt," he said growing irritated that his personal life seemed to be on display for all to see.

Louisa stood from her chair. "Well, I hope you do something soon before Persephone is on a stage to Edinburgh." With that she flounced out of the room.

"My how the plot continues to thicken," Rockhurst said drawing the ire of his friend. "You got rid of Barrington only to have the Comte Domingo step in and apparently there is some handsome Scottish duke to contend with now. I'm glad you feel confident that Persephone will accept your suit."

Hawk came around and sat at his desk. "I have work to do and I thought you had another meeting with your father this afternoon while he is still in town."

Rockhurst's face darkened. "Yes, the sooner I meet with him, the sooner he will leave for the country. I will see you later. If I find anything more of interest in the Comte, I will let you know."

Hawk sat at his desk for another hour before he decided it was time that he had a talk with Persephone. He was determined to seek her out and get their plans arranged. Once she agreed to be his wife, everything would settle down. His aunt would relax and the Comte would no longer be a threat if Persephone was his duchess. The thought made him smile. He had always known marriage was inevitable, but he never imagined that he would go into the institution willingly if not ecstatically.

After looking in the library and the downstairs drawing rooms, he decided to see if she was in her rooms. He hesitated only for a second. It wasn't proper to be in her rooms but since they would be married, he didn't see the harm. He knocked lightly on her door but there was no answer. He opened it just enough to see that she was lying on the chaise by the window and it appeared that she was sleeping. He quietly closed the door and made his way over to her. The sunlight coming through the window shone on her face. She was so lovely. Her hair was pinned up and his fingers itched to take out the pins to see exactly how long the golden tresses actually were. One hand was resting across her abdomen and the other was hanging down to the floor. He reached out and ran a finger along the side of her cheek causing her to turn into his touch. He bent down and took the hand that was hanging beside her and placed a kiss upon her open palm before placing it on her stomach. He saw her eyes begin to flutter.

"Darling," he whispered in her ear.

Persephone opened her eyes and sat up quickly. "My goodness, you scared me."

He chuckled as she tried to fix her skirts. "I'm sorry, my love. You looked so beautiful sleeping I almost didn't want to wake you."

Persephone sighed. "Since you did wake me, why are you here?" As if the reality of the situation just struck her, she surged to her feet. "You're in my rooms. Have you gone mad? Please tell me that you weren't seen."

He stood and put his hands on her shoulders. "No, I was not seen." He leaned down and kissed her forehead. "You know most young girls would be screaming the roof off hoping someone would catch me so they could become my duchess."

Persephone arched her eyebrows. "I'm not like other girls and I would make a terrible duchess."

He smiled. "You will make an excellent duchess."

Persephone narrowed her eyes a little. "You never told me the reason for being in my rooms."

He released her shoulders and took a step back. "I think it is time we made plans, my love."

"What sort of plans?" Persephone asked cautiously.

"I want you to be my wife, Persephone. I want you in my home and in my bed. I want you as my duchess." When she continued to stare at him, he continued. "We will be married by the end of the season. Then we will go to my estate in the country before taking a wedding trip."

Persephone held up her hand when he moved to take her in his arms once more. "I'm confused. Am I supposed to jump for joy or get on my knees and kiss your feet? I don't know the protocol for accepting such a lofty proposal."

"Damn it, Persephone!"

She closed her eyes and put her hand up to her forehead. "Forgive me. I don't mean to seem ungracious. But I told you that I didn't want you to feel as if you had to marry me because of what happened between us."

He ran his hand through his hair. "Bloody hell, is that why you think I want to marry you?"

"What other reason could there be? My dowry is pathetic, my father is an absent lord, I have no important familial connections, I come with nothing to offer."

He quickly wrapped his arms around her before she could move away. "I have more money than I could ever spend, I don't care about your father or your connections. I made up my mind to have you the moment you walked up to me with my aunt at Almacks."

She wanted to believe what he said, "You would grow tired of me."

He leaned down and kissed her then whispered above her lips. "I could never grow tired of you."

Persephone shook her head. He lifted her face to his. Persephone felt her resolve faltering. She didn't know what kind of power he possessed over her, but it made her lose all sense of reason. She searched his face and licked her lips before whispering, "I can't think when you kiss me like that."

"Do you want me to stop?" he asked in a husky voice.

She wrapped her arms around his neck and stood on her tiptoes. "No" She pulled his head down to her lips.

He returned her kiss until they were both panting for air. "We can't do this here," he said breathing heavily.

He grabbed her hand and went to the door. He opened it and looked down the hallway before pulling her from the room. Persephone struggled to keep up as they went down the hallway and up a third flight of stairs.

"Where are we going?"

He didn't say anything but continued to pull her along after him. Thankfully they didn't see anyone along the way. He stopped outside a door and turned back toward her. "Are you sure, Persephone?"

She nodded slowly and sucked in her breath as she was whisked up into his arms as he pushed open the door entering the room. He shut the door with his foot and gently set her back down on her feet.

She looked around the large masculine room and realized he had taken her to his bedchamber. Her boldness and bravado from earlier started to slip away. She turned around to see that he had removed his coat and was working on untying his cravat. Her breath started coming between her lips a little faster.

"Are you afraid, Persephone?"

She shook her head. "No,"

"Have you changed your mind? If so, tell me now."

She raised her head a notch higher. "I haven't changed my mind." And to prove herself she stepped toward him and placed both hands on his chest. She slowly moved her hands down marveling at how his muscles twitched beneath her touch. "But know that this does not mean I agree to marry you."

He wrapped his arms around her waist and pulled her into him as his mouth descended upon hers. Persephone felt the buttons on the back of her gown loosen before he slid the gown from her shoulders to pool at her feet. She wore only her chemise and stockings and instinctively crossed her arms over her chest.

"You certainly are proficient at removing a lady's gown. You would put many a lady's maid to shame," she said nervously as he stalked toward her.

He could see the uneasiness on her face. He put his hands on her shoulders and rubbed up and down her arms softly before lowering his head to her neck and nibbling behind her ear. When she started to relax, he picked her up in his arms and carried her to his bed. He laid her down never removing his lips from hers as he let his hands roam up her side to the strap of her chemise gently tugging it down until her breast was exposed.

Persephone arched her back as his mouth descended upon her breast and he began to suckle. His other hand moved slowly up her chemise to her thigh. "I want to touch you too," Persephone struggled to keep her breathing relaxed as her hands began to work the buttons of his shirt. He quickly sat up jerking the shirt over his head. Persephone let her hand slide through the dark hair on his chest down his stomach. She stopped when she reached the waist of his trousers.

"I want to see all of you, my love." And with that he whipped the chemise over her head leaving her in nothing but her stockings.

Persephone squeezed her knees together and wrapped her arms about herself. He leaned down and kissed her gently whispering in her ear. "You are the most beautiful creature I have ever seen. Don't hide yourself from me, Persephone."

She slowly lowered her arms as he kissed away her apprehension. He feathered kisses down her breasts to her stomach then back to her breasts again as his hands expertly pushed her thighs further apart. His fingers found her center and he rubbed slowly along her slit before slowly sliding one finger inside her. He swallowed her cry of pleasure as she lifted her hips and rolled her head backward. He raised his head.

"Do you like that, sweetheart?"

Persephone was beyond coherent speech. She could only nod as he continued his ministrations. He removed his hand from her long enough to unfasten the folds of his trousers so he could slip them down his legs to the floor.

He leaned over her. "Touch me."

He took her hand and placed it on his shaft. Persephone bit her lower lip as she allowed herself to close her hand around it, marveling at how hard it had become, but yet, it felt like silk. He placed his hand over hers and began to move it up and down the length of him.

Persephone watched his face as his eyes closed. He almost looked as if he was in pain. "Does it hurt?" she asked.

He lowered his forehead to hers. "God, no."

He covered her hand with his once more. "That's enough, love."

He saw the concern in her face so he explained his abruptness. "It feels too good, love. And I want you to feel pleasure."

He began pressing soft kisses from her breasts to her stomach. "Open your legs for me, darling."

When she hesitated, he gently nudged them further apart. He kissed lower until his lips lightly pressed against her mound.

Persephone nearly jumped out of her skin as his tongue flicked out over her most sensitive place. "Your grace," she moaned heavily as her fingers dug into the bedding beside her.

He moved over top of her. "Say my name."

"Hawk"

His tongue flicked over her earlobe. "Not my title, my name."

She arched her breasts up as his mouth descended upon her again. "Oh, Ethan!"

Suddenly there was pounding on the door. "Hawk!!"

They both stilled and Persephone covered her mouth with both of her hands. "It's Catherine!" she whispered.

"Hawk, are you in there? We can't find Persephone anywhere."

He closed his eyes and tried to gain a hold of his temper. "I'm going to kill her."

Persephone covered his mouth with her hand. "What are we going to do?!"

He jumped from the bed and quickly reached for his trousers. "Maybe she will go away."

But the pounding continued. "Hawk, I am afraid something has happened to her."

He blew out a heavy breath and let his head roll up to look at the ceiling. "I'll be down momentarily. I'm sure she is just out for a walk in the garden."

He glanced back over to the bed and frowned when he saw that Persephone had put her chemise back on. "Bloody hell!"

His sister called from the other side of the door. "I have all the servants looking for her. I'll go check again in the garden."

Hawk clinched his fists. "Remind me after we are married to send my sister to the continent. She can be Bonaparte's problem for a while."

Persephone had both of her hands covering her face. "My God, the entire household is searching for me. How are we going to get out of this situation?"

He put on his shirt and his boots. "Don't worry, darling. I have a plan."

He helped her dress quickly. She did the best she could do with her hair before slipping her shoes back on. When she turned around, she was surprised to see Hawk looked as if he had just walked out of a drawing room after having tea.

"How do you do that?" she asked.

"What?"

She held her hand out to him. "You look as if you could be taking tea with the queen and I look like I have been, . . ."

"Ravished," he finished for her with a wicked grin. "Lots of practice, my dear."

She put a hand to her forehead. "What do we do now?"

He held her hand then brought it to his lips and kissed her palm. "Follow me." He took her hand and led her to a panel beside the bed. He pushed and it opened. "It's a secret passageway, it leads out to the garden."

Persephone held onto his hand as he led her through the dark passage. "I told you I would make a terrible duchess. What sort of duchess slinks around through secret passageways to keep her amorous escapades a secret?"

His laughter was deep. "You would be surprised, darling."

"Of course, I forgot to whom I was speaking," she replied rolling her eyes heavenward.

When they came to the end of the passage, he pushed open another panel and sunlight flooded into the dark passage. She squinted until her eyes adjusted to the light.

"There is a bench to the right underneath the rose arbor. You can wait there until I come to find you, or one of the servants finds you."

Persephone nodded.

But before she walked away, he kissed her quickly. "Do we have an agreement?"

She looked back at him. "I will think about it." She then hurried through the door to find the bench where she would wait until she was discovered.

It didn't take long for her to hear Catherine's shrill voice crying out her name. "Persephone? Oh Persephone! Where have you been? We have been looking everywhere for you!"

Persephone got to her feet just as Catherine reached her. "I'm sorry. I have been outside enjoying the fresh air."

Catherine eyed her curiously. "Did you fall down?"

Persephone shook her head. "No, why would you say that?"

Catherine squinched up her face. "You look disheveled and your hair is all over the place."

Persephone blushed. "I took a nap on the bench."

"Well, we better go inside and let everyone know you are safe. Hawk will have everyone in London searching for you."

Persephone followed her inside but she couldn't hide her embarrassment as Catherine declared the search was over and she had been found safe and sound.

Hawk came toward her. "I'm glad you are safe, Persephone. Perhaps you should inform one of the staff the next you decide to disappear."

She narrowed her eyes at him in irritation. "Yes, I apologize. I most certainly should have let someone know."

He gave her a wink and a devilish grin. "We are all pleased that you were found unharmed."

Aunt Louisa came up and gave her a hug as Catherine and Hawk walked away. "Yes dear. I am so happy we found you. Catherine feared the dreadful Comte had come and taken you." She snickered. "Catherine has such an imagination."

Persephone smiled tentatively. "Yes, she does."

Louisa gave her a knowing grin before speaking softly in her ear. "But I would go have your lady's maid rebutton your dress before anyone else notices that the buttons aren't aligned."

Persephone blushed crimson.

Louisa patted her hand. "Men are always experts at getting a dress off but not nearly as proficient helping one put it back on." She chuckled once more before ascending the steps back to her rooms.

Chapter Nine

"**I** received word that you had information for me," Hawk said as he entered the Duke of Leicester's residence.

Leicester gave a nod to his secretary, Mr. Franklin, to leave them. "Yes, and Persephone was right to fear the Comte."

Hawk sat down in the chair opposite his friend. "Rockhurst has already discovered some disturbing things about the man. He is a degenerate."

"I found out a good deal more through my sources. He is here in England to find a bride and by all accounts he has set his sights on Persephone. He has even reached out to members of the ton to ask about her father. It seems he is ready to seek his permission to marry her."

Hawk shook his head in disgust. "He will never have her. Have you discovered anything else of importance?"

Leicester gave him a grave look. "Yes, and you aren't going to like it. Many of the women that Comte Domingo encounters somehow suffer mysterious disappearances or death."

Hawk's frowned deepened. "He is a murderer?"

Leicester leaned back further. "No evidence has ever linked him to the disappearances or the untimely deaths of the young ladies, but our friends in the foreign office are watching him closely. He has also been married before. His young wife is said to have killed herself."

Hawk stood from his seat and began pacing the room. "From what Rockhurst has told me, I imagine she thought it a better alternative than being married to the bastard." He stopped pacing and turned back to face his friend. "I will need to add extra security around the house. I will not take any chances with either Persephone or Catherine's safety."

Leicester nodded in agreement. "I think that is a wise decision."

Hawk resumed his pacing.

"Is there something else troubling you, Hawk?"

He shook his head. "I am thinking it might be time to move the family to the country. They would be safer at Hawk's Hill than here in London"

"Before the end of the season? I don't know about Persephone, but you will have to drag Catherine away. She will not want to leave all the enticements the season offers."

Hawk knew it would be difficult to convince Catherine to leave London but if Persephone's life was in danger, she wouldn't have much of a choice. "I know, but it is necessary. I will make the arrangements and hopefully be ready to go by the end of the week."

"I am here if you need any assistance."

Hawk nodded toward him. "Thank you, Michael, I will let you know. If you see Rockhurst, make him aware of my plans."

Bond Street

Catherine and Persephone were once again at the modiste with Aunt Louisa having their final fittings for their gowns for the Carrington's ball.

Persephone was a little worried that she was spending too much money on the season. She knew her father set aside some money for her every year and Aunt Louisa's solicitors handled it for her. But she knew it could not be much and she was worried that her expenses were becoming more than she could afford.

"Are you sure I need another gown, Aunt Louisa? I feel as if I am spending more money than is prudent."

Louisa waved off the comment. "My dear, you must stop worrying. Trust me, it would not do for you to only have one ballgown. Besides, it's the dressing that attracts the men like moths to a flame. A good modiste knows exactly how to fit you so that all of your best assets are on display."

Persephone blushed. Knowing full well the gown was displaying more of her *assets* than she thought was necessary.

Catherine laughed. "Oh Persephone, even if you didn't have a penny to your name Hawk can definitely afford a few dresses."

Persephone frowned at her friend. "It would not be right for your brother to buy my dresses." She looked quickly over at Louisa. "Please tell me that the duke is not financing my season."

"Of course not, dear."

Persephone was about to ask Louisa just how much money she had to spend when the front door to the shop opened and Lady Sanderson, the lady from the opera that apparently knew the duke quite well, came into the shop.

The lady glanced over at the three women and the jealousy became apparent on her face. "Good afternoon, Lady Gray and Countess Mulford," she said completely ignoring Persephone.

"Good afternoon, Lady Sanderson. Have you had the pleasure of meeting my dear friend Lady Persephone Carlisle?" Catherine said forcing the lady to acknowledge Persephone.

The lady took a quizzing glass from her reticule and put it to her eyes as she looked at Persephone from her feet back to her face as if she were inspecting her. "Yes, I believe she was with your group at the opera."

Catherine didn't like the way the lady looked at Persephone. "Yes, she is my guest in London."

"My apologies for not recognizing you sooner, Lady Carlisle."

Persephone nodded then looked down to avoid the woman's gaze.

Catherine took her hand. "Let's make our final purchases, Persephone. I'm sure we should hurry home soon. It does look like rain again."

Aunt Louisa walked away with Catherine as Persephone moved over to a table full of silks. Lady Sanderson moved behind her.

"Do you truly think you can hold his attention? A little young thing like yourself, he will grow tired of you soon and where will you be then? You had better stay away from Hawksford, my dear. He is too much man for you to handle. Leave him to his more experienced lovers," Lady Sanderson whispered in a spiteful voice behind her.

Persephone at first paled at her words then she grew angry. How dare this woman threaten her. "I can assure you Lady Sanderson that I am no threat to you and your kind. But I am certain that the duke has better taste than to associate with someone of your ilk."

Lady Sanderson sucked in her breath. "How dare you? You are nothing more than a little harlot."

Aunt Louisa came to her side. "That is enough! Come, Persephone, let's leave before the atmosphere becomes more disagreeable."

Once outside Louisa said, "My goodness, Persephone. Do not let a woman like Lady Sanderson get under your skin. When dealing with the ton it is important to have a backbone but you mustn't let anyone push you to the point where you behave as badly as they do."

"I'm not sure I can do that."

Louisa laughed. "Oh yes you can. You must if you want to survive in the ton. Aristocratic ladies of the beau monde can be vicious, but you must hold your head high and let them know that you are not afraid of their malicious tongues. You are the daughter of a viscount and the granddaughter of an earl. Your blood is just as blue as theirs. It is not that they think you aren't good enough for their company, they are jealous of you."

Persephone scoffed. "Jealous of me? There is nothing for them to be jealous of, Aunt Louisa."

"Don't be a fool, my dear. You have a mirror; you must know that you are exceptionally beautiful and you have captured the attention of a duke. The next time one of those vipers attacks you, you must be ready to defend yourself with more dignity."

Persephone smiled. "Maybe I should take lessons from Catherine."

Louisa chuckled. "Catherine definitely takes it too far, but perhaps somewhere in the middle."

They reached the carriage just as Catherine caught up to them. "I should have punched Lady Sanderson in the nose for how she treated you, Persephone."

Louisa gave Persephone a wink. "See, somewhere in the middle."

As the carriage came to a stop in front of Hawksford House, the ladies were assisted by a footman and Billings met them at the door.

"His grace has asked that all of you meet him in the library as soon as you have returned."

Aunt Louisa looked worried. "My goodness, Billings. Is everything alright?"

He stood very stoically at the front door. "I am not privy to his grace's reasons, my lady."

Catherine and Persephone exchanged worried glances and followed Aunt Louisa into the library. "He isn't here, Billings," Aunt Louisa said as she turned back toward the butler.

"I will inform his grace that you have arrived."

Catherine looked about the room nervously. "This doesn't bode well I'm afraid. Hawk has never summoned all of us like this before."

Persephone nervously clasped her hands in front of her hoping it was nothing serious. Aunt Louisa paced the room impatiently waiting for the duke's arrival.

When the doors of the library opened both Catherine and Louisa rushed forward toward the duke.

"What is wrong, Ethan?" Louisa asked anxiously.

"Please have a seat. There is something I want to discuss with all of you." He glanced at all three ladies but let his eyes linger as he stared at Persephone.

Persephone and Catherine both sat together on the settee while the countess sat in the chair by the windows.

Hawk came to stand before them. "I think it would be a wise decision for us to leave London as soon as possible for Hawk's Hill."

Catherine jumped up. "Before the season is over? Have you gone mad, Hawk? We can't leave London now. There are still several more weeks left."

Louisa studied her nephew's face. "Catherine do sit down. I would like to hear from your brother his reasoning behind such a hasty withdrawal to the country."

Hawk looked over at Persephone. "I think it would be better for Persephone's safety if we left London."

"My safety?" Persephone asked in confusion.

He moved closer to stand in front of her. "I have been looking into Comte Domingo and have discovered some unsavory details concerning him. I would feel better if the three of you were kept as far away from him as possible. So, I have made arrangements to have the household move to Hawk's Hill by the end of the week."

Catherine's face paled and her mouth fell open slightly. Persephone could see the panic on her friend's face. She had been looking forward to the season for several months and now her brother was threatening to take it all away from her. Persephone couldn't allow that to happen, especially because of her.

Persephone stood. "I can't ask all of you to disrupt your plans because of me. I think I might have a solution. Perhaps this would be a good time to visit Lady McDonough in Scotland."

Hawk came closer to her. "You are not going to Scotland. We are all going to Hawk's Hill."

Persephone looked over toward Aunt Louisa hoping to find an ally. "Louisa, you read Lady McDonough's letter, she asked me to come. It's a good solution to the problem. I will be safe away from London and Catherine can still enjoy the remainder of the season." She looked back toward Hawk. "And I'm sure you would much rather be in London than in the country. I could write Lady McDonogh now and accept her invitation."

Catherine took a deep breath and came to stand beside her. "As much as I hate to admit it, Hawk is right. I would worry terribly about you if you were in Scotland." She hugged her friend. "Besides there are lots of things we can do in the country. Since we are missing the remainder of the season perhaps, we can convince Hawk to host a house party."

Persephone shook her head. "Catherine, you have been looking forward to coming to London for months. It would not be fair to ask you to miss out because of me. I will leave for Scotland as soon as possible."

Hawk gave her a serious look and firmly said, "No! and I will not discuss that further."

Louisa stood from her seat. "When are we leaving?"

Hawk glanced at his aunt before turning back to Persephone. "I think the servants can have everything ready to go in two days' time. I have already sent word ahead to Hawk's Hill informing the staff there of our arrival."

"Two days! Can't we please stay one more day and attend the Carrington's ball? Please?" Catherine asked pleadingly.

"No, it's best for us to leave as soon as possible."

Persephone crossed her arms over her chest. "What can one more day hurt? We can stay ensconced safely here at Hawksford House until the ball. I feel dreadful being the cause of Catherine missing the rest of the season, can you please allow her to attend this one last ball before we leave?"

Hawk looked into her deep blue eyes and felt a moment of alarm as he realized that when she looked at him like that, he would find it hard to refuse her anything. "You will not leave this house and at the ball you will remain within my sight the entire time. That goes for both of you."

Persephone sank back down on the settee as Catherine wrapped her arms around her brother's neck. "Thank you, Hawk."

Louisa had already started for the door. "Come with me Catherine, if we are to leave in three days' time, I need some help getting ready." She gave Hawk and Persephone a knowing look as she took Catherine by the arm and led her from the library.

Persephone let out a sigh. "It would have been better if you had allowed me to leave."

"I will not discuss you leaving again. However, there are other ways in which to keep you safe from the Comte."

Persephone looked up at him as he stood before her. "What other ways do you suggest?"

"You could agree to marry me. As my wife and duchess, you would be protected. The Comte would not dare approach you once you were mine."

Persephone shook her head. "I have already said that you would soon grow tired of me." She bowed her head slightly before changing the subject. "Tell me, what do you know of the Comte? I was right to fear him."

He sat beside her but did not move to touch her. "Yes, you were. I along with Rockhurst and Leicester made some inquiries and he is indeed a dangerous man. I will spare you the details of what I know but he is a threat."

"I want to know everything. Why has he set his sights on me?"

Hawk hesitated contemplating exactly what he should share with her. "The Comte is known to be a cruel man. He was married once before and his wife died by her own hand." He saw her face pale. "Many of the women he has been associated with have disappeared or met unfortunate ends."

She looked over at him, her face pale. "Oh my, I would never have imagined anything so horrible, but I could feel that evil radiated from him. You should have just agreed to let me go to Scotland."

He narrowed his eyes. "Do you really think I would allow you to leave me?"

"I saw Lady Sanderson today at the modiste. She advised me to leave you to your more experienced lovers."

"Lady Sanderson means nothing to me nor does she know anything about me," he replied.

Persephone turned to look at him. "She called me a harlot." She saw his face darken with rage.

"I will deal with Lady Sanderson," he said in a tight voice trying to hold onto his temper.

"No need for that."

He stood from the settee and paced the floor in front of her. "There is every need. No one will disparage my duchess. Lady Sanderson will rue the day she spoke to you so scornfully."

"I meant that I do not need your help. If I am to deal with the ladies of the ton, I have to do so on my own, not with you hoovering behind me like an avenging angel, and I am not your duchess."

He sat beside her again and took her hand in his. "You know what I want, Persephone but I will not ask you again. The decision must be yours. But once you make that decision and decide to become my wife, there will be no going back. You will be mine and I will protect what is mine with a vengeance." With that being said, he stood from the settee and made his way to the door of the library. "The Carrington's ball is in three days and we will leave the following morning. I have much to do between now and then. I must have your word that you will remain inside the walls of this house until we attend the ball. Do I have your word?"

Persephone nodded and quietly said, "You have my word."

"If you decide that you would like to see me before then, Billings will know where I am." He bowed at the waist. "Good afternoon, Persephone."

Persephone watched as he walked out the door. He was leaving the decision up to her. A decision that would alter the course of her life. She put her head in her hands hoping she would make the right one.

Chapter Ten

It had indeed been a busy three days and the week passed by quickly. Persephone had not seen the duke since he left her in the library the day he had informed them of the move to Hawk's Hill. Catherine had been disappointed at missing the rest of the season, but the promise of a potential house party had lifted her spirits and she had been talking non-stop about it and the upcoming Carrington's ball. The arrangements had all been made and their belongings packed and ready to go. They were to leave the following morning after the ball. She had offered to not attend the ball, but Catherine would not hear of it. She insisted that Persephone attend with her or she would not go either. Persephone did not have the energy to argue with her friend so she had allowed Sarah to help her dress in her new turquoise evening gown. Aunt Louisa had brought in a black velvet box with a beautiful diamond necklace with matching earrings and a bracelet that Hawk had sent for her to wear. She couldn't help but marvel at how they sparkled in the candlelight and silently chastised herself for her vanity.

"My lady, everyone is waiting for you downstairs," Sarah said as she opened the door.

Persephone gave her a brief smile. "Thank you, Sarah."

Her maid returned her smile. "You look lovely, my lady. Are you happy to be leaving London?"

"I haven't been to Hawk's Hill since I was a young girl. It will be nice to see it again," Persephone said as she made her way to the door.

"I will get all of your things ready to travel, my lady."

"Thank you, but please don't wait up for me. I'm sure we will be late. Lady Catherine can help me with my dress if I need assistance."

The maid bobbed a curtsy. "Yes, my lady"

Persephone made her way down the stairs; she was surprised to see only the duke waiting for her. "Am I so late that Catherine and Louisa left without me?"

He grinned and moved toward her. "No, they are already in the carriage." He took her hand and raised it to his lips. "I love seeing you wear my family's jewels."

She returned his smile trying to ignore the way his touch made her warm inside. "They are very beautiful."

"I wanted to remind you that I will be keeping you in my sight tonight. Leicester and Rockhurst will also be there. You will be well protected."

She sobered at the reminder of the danger the Comte presented. "Thank you. I'm sorry to be so much trouble. Do we even know if the Comte will be in attendance tonight?"

Hawk's eyes darkened as his lips turned into a thin lined frown. "He will be there."

Persephone placed her hand on his sleeve. "We should join Catherine and Louisa."

He escorted her outside to the carriage and helped her inside. Catherine and Louisa were there waiting for them. "You look lovely, Catherine. I'm sorry to keep everyone waiting."

Catherine smiled at her before sending her brother a sly look. "We haven't been waiting long."

Louisa opened her fan. "I hope we take more than one carriage tomorrow, Ethan. It is much too cramped for a long journey."

"I have made arrangements that I am sure you will find suitable."

Louisa began fanning herself more vigorously. "I hope Carrington has some decent refreshment tonight."

Persephone leaned back against the cushions and tried to relax. She didn't look at Hawk but could feel his gaze upon her. She hoped this night would be over quickly. Catherine was so excited about the ball but honestly, Persephone had no real interest in attending especially knowing that the Comte was expected to be there. Hopefully once they arrived at Hawk's Hill things would get back to some sort of normalcy.

The ball was indeed the crush it had been expected to be and Persephone had danced almost every dance, all under the watchful eyes of Hawk and his friends. She had not seen the Comte and hoped that Hawk had been wrong about the Comte's expected attendance. Louisa had disappeared into the card room as was usual, and Catherine was busy talking to a young lord Persephone had yet to be introduced. It was quite warm inside the ballroom and she flipped open her fan hoping to cool off a bit.

"Are you alright?"

She had not heard Hawk come up behind her and she was startled for a moment. "Yes, I do think I would like some air."

"I will escort you."

Persephone shook her head. "No, I will be alright. Besides, you know very well that the two of us outside alone would cause gossip."

He smiled that cheeky grin she had come to find so appealing. "Perhaps I'm willing to take that chance. It would hasten the inevitable."

She couldn't help but laugh at his self-assured remark. "You are so sure of yourself. While the threat of having your name in the scandal sheets obviously doesn't bother you, I on the other hand, would prefer not to be mentioned in a disreputable way."

Hawk stared down at her laughing eyes and fought the urge to kiss the dimples that appeared when she smiled right there in front of the world. There was nothing he would rather do. He leaned down closer to whisper near her ear. "A little wickedness might be good for you, Persephone." He loved watching her cheeks blush and his fingers itched to pull her closer.

Persephone couldn't help but smile. "I'm not sure you are capable of just a little wickedness."

Hawk was surprised at her cheeky repartee. "Let's go somewhere a little more private."

Persephone shook her head and took a step back. "I am going to the lady's retiring room."

He took her arm. "I will escort you. Remember, I want you in my sight."

Persephone looked surprised. "To the lady's retiring room? I think it best that you wait for me here. I will not be long."

Hawk shook his head dismissing her request. "I will keep my distance."

Persephone rolled her eyes. "As you wish."

She started down the hallway hoping Hawk would realize how ridiculous he was being and she could have a minute or two alone to gather her wits. The banter between the two of them was dangerous. At one point she had thought he was going to kiss her right there in front of everyone and the scary thing was that she would have allowed it. The hallways were crowded with people. She was pushed and bustled around a little when suddenly someone shoved her a little harder and she stumbled into an open door to one of the sitting rooms.

She turned around expecting an apology from whoever had pushed her but was surprised when the doors to the room shut suddenly and she was face to face with Comte Domingo.

"It seems my luck has finally turned. I have been watching you from afar all evening. How would I guess that you would wander right to me?"

the Comte said as he stalked toward her and Persephone instinctively backed away.

"Comte Domingo, I had not realized you were in attendance tonight." She looked about the room surveying other ways of escape. "I should go back to the ball, but perhaps later I could save you a dance." She had no intention of dancing with the man but if a small lie would allow her to return to the ballroom, it was worth it.

"Not just yet, my dear. Were you aware that I have been denied access to you? Hawksford has made certain that I have not been admitted to his home." He stalked forward. "All of my gifts have been returned as well as the notes I sent for you. But what the duke does not realize is that his denying me access has only flared the flames of desire I have for you. You have consumed my thoughts from the first moment I set my eyes upon you."

Persephone kept moving, backing up hoping to circle the room and make it back to the door before he could reach her. "You flatter me with your compliments, but how can you feel so strongly about someone when we have only seen each other briefly."

His smile was evil. "I knew the first moment I saw you I had found what I was looking for and your hesitance only makes me want you more. I have been sent to England in search of a bride and you will do nicely."

Persephone kept her eyes on the Comte as she continued maneuvering herself back and around towards the door. "This is a highly inappropriate conversation, as you must know. I have no desire to marry you. While I wish you success in your search, I must insist that I return to the ballroom."

He moved a bit faster. "You will be pleased to know that I have already sent word to your father and requested that he give his permission for us to marry. Since I feel Hawksford will never give his approval. However, I don't need anyone's permission. There are circumstances where our marriage would be encouraged."

Persephone felt sick. How could this man ever think she would agree to marry him? She was almost to the door. She just needed to keep moving away from him. "I am sorry that I can't agree to your request for I am already engaged to be married. I accepted the Duke of Hawksford's proposal this afternoon."

She saw the Comte's face contort with anger and she truly felt a fear for this man that she never had before. "Engaged?" He lunged for her just as the door sprang open.

Hawk kept his distance as Persephone moved down the hallway. So far, the Comte had yet to make an appearance but he didn't want to take any chances.

"Hawksford!"

He turned to see Lord Netherfield coming toward him. "Netherfield, it is good to see you."

The older man pumped his outstretched hand. "It has indeed been a long time. How is your Aunt Louisa? I hear she is in town."

"She is quite well; in fact, she is probably in one of the card rooms." He craned his neck around to see Persephone still making her way through the crowd.

"You should come visit us at Netherfield this fall. We have excellent hunting and I would enjoy a bit of sport."

Hawk nodded but nervously turned around and this time he did not see Persephone. "I will do that. Excuse me, Netherfield."

"Certainly, your grace."

Hawk pushed his way through the crowd hoping to catch a glimpse of the top of her head. But she was nowhere to be found. He turned to his left and saw a closed door. He hesitated only a moment before pushing it open to have Persephone collide into his arms. He wrapped his arms about her to steady her.

"What the devil?" he said as he leveled the Comte with a murderous glare.

The Comte recovered himself quickly. "It seems that I must offer you my congratulations, Hawksford."

Hawk protectively pulled Persephone closer to his side. "Congratulations?"

Persephone swallowed a lump in her throat.

"Yes, Lady Carlisle was just telling me of your engagement."

Hawk looked from the Comte back to Persephone. "Our engagement?"

Persephone felt herself tremble and wished the floor would open up beneath her and swallow her. "Yes, I informed the Comte that unfortunately I could not accept his offer of marriage as I have already accepted an offer from you."

Hawk turned back toward the Comte raising one eyebrow. "Yes, I am a fortunate man."

The Comte glanced back over to Persephone. "Very fortunate." He bowed slightly then headed out the door.

Persephone breathed a sigh of relief as soon as they were alone. "I never saw him before he pushed me in here. Thank goodness you came when you did."

Hawk looked her over. "Did he hurt you?"

Persephone shook her head. "No, he didn't touch me. I kept moving out of his range."

He took both of her hands in his. "Smart girl. I feared the worst when I lost sight of you."

Persephone put a hand up to her chest trying to calm her rapidly beating heart. "He was so angry that he has been unable to see me and said he intended to marry me. He even alluded to the fact that there were circumstances where our marriage would be encouraged since he knew you would not grant permission."

Hawk wrapped his arms around her waist and pulled her into his chest. "Everything will be alright now. Come let's go back to the ballroom. We have an announcement to make."

Persephone pulled out of his grasp. "An announcement?"

"Yes, our betrothal announcement. Remember, I told you that I wouldn't ask again that it would be up to you. And with the Comte in attendance and after you told him we were engaged; this is the perfect time to let the ton know." He smiled knowing he had her.

Persephone's eyes widened. "You're serious?"

He leaned down closer to her face. "More serious than I have ever been. We wouldn't want the Comte to think you weren't truthful."

Persephone didn't know what to say. She should have known that Hawk would take her seriously and use this to his advantage. How would she ever get out of this mess?

She felt as if the next moments were all a dream and she was in a daze as he led her through the throng of people to the front of the ballroom. She heard the clinking of glasses and Hawk's strong firm voice as he announced that he had found his duchess. The next moments she was surrounded by well-wishers. She smiled faintly as people she had never met congratulated her. Catherine pushed her way to the front of the crowd and wrapped her in a tight hug.

"Oh, Persephone. I am so happy! We will truly be sisters now." Catherine leaned back and studied her friend's face. "Persephone?" She turned to her brother and then suddenly Lord Rockhurst was at their side. Catherine looked up at him. "I think she is going to faint."

Lord Rockhurst nodded then said in his booming deep commanding voice. "The future duchess is overjoyed, let's give her some air." He took

Persephone's arm and led her away leaving Hawk to accept the remainder of the ton's felicitations. Catherine followed right behind them.

Persephone felt as if she couldn't breathe. "I need to go outside. I have to get air," she said weakly.

Catherine came up beside her. "Of course, dear. My lord, will you escort us?"

Rockhurst nodded. "I'll have the carriage brought around if you would like."

Persephone looked up at him. "Yes, please. All of the excitement has me a little tired."

Catherine's smile grew wider. "Why didn't you tell me, Persephone? It is so exciting, but I knew Hawk was in love with you."

This pulled Persephone out of her fog. "He isn't in love with me, Catherine."

"Of course, he is."

Persephone knew there was no need in arguing with her so she waited patiently until Lord Rockhurst came to escort her to the carriage. "Thank you, my lord."

Lord Rockhurst nodded slightly. "My pleasure, my lady. May I also offer my congratulations and best wishes on your marriage. Hawk is a very lucky man."

Persephone managed to give him a weak smile before he closed the door of the carriage. She and Catherine had just gotten settled inside when Louisa and Hawk appeared. Louisa excitedly reached over to embrace her. "Persephone, I couldn't be happier. How did you ever keep it a secret from us?"

Hawk moved over to sit beside her. "That's enough questions for tonight. We have a long journey tomorrow. There will be plenty of time while on our way to Hawk's Hill for us to answer any questions." He reached over and placed his hand over hers.

Persephone gave Louisa and Catherine a small smile but did not try to answer their questions. Once they reached Hawksford House, she was assisted from the carriage by Hawk but Catherine was right at her elbow and wrapped her arm through hers. "We have so much to talk about, Persephone. I hope you have a huge affair at St. George's Cathedral. And we need to start planning for a wedding dress. There is so much to do."

Persephone glanced over her shoulder at Hawk as they made their way inside the house. He must have sensed her distress. "Catherine, go to bed. Like I said we will have plenty of time to discuss matters tomorrow."

Catherine gave her brother a frown and rolled her eyes at his command. "Men just don't understand how important a wedding is to a lady."

"I am tired after all of the excitement and we do need to get some rest. I promise we can talk more tomorrow." Persephone gave Catherine a quick hug then went quickly to her room. Once inside she leaned back against the wall and closed her eyes wondering what she was going to do now. She managed to remove her dress by herself and get into her night gown before going over to the chair by the fire. She sat there staring into the flames. The sound of the door opening caught her attention, but she didn't need to turn around to know who it was.

Hawk walked over towards her with a glass of brandy. "I thought you could use this."

Persephone shook her head. "I've never had brandy but thank you."

"It will steady your nerves."

She stood up from her chair to face him. "Why did you immediately make an announcement of our betrothal tonight? If you had given it time, we might have avoided this."

Hawk put both glasses down on the side table and walked over to stand against the wall across from her. He shrugged his shoulders arrogantly. "I made no secret of the fact that I wanted you, Persephone. At first it was just the desire to have you in my bed but eventually I decided that not only did I want you, but I didn't want anyone else to have you either." He crossed his arms over his chest and waited. When she made no reply he continued, "Since you were reluctant in accepting my proposal, I had to be patient. When you told the Comte that we were engaged, I pressed my advantage."

Persephone put her hands on her hips. "You did it on purpose so there would be no way to back out?"

He nodded once again. "I told you that you were mine, Persephone. I knew what I wanted and I planned a way to get it." He grinned roguishly and shrugged his shoulders. "It's a characteristic of being a duke, we tend to always get what we want."

Persephone clinched her fists. "And because you announced it to the entire ton, it would be impossible for me to deny it. Not without causing total ruin to my reputation and hurting your aunt and sister in the process."

Hawk moved away from the wall toward her. "Would you have rather accepted the Comte?" He saw her face pale slightly. "Now think rationally, Persephone. Did you really believe you could make such a statement to the Comte without anyone else ever finding out? Do you believe he would not have looked into the accusation to see if it were true?" He could see her mind working. "No, it would have been all over town by morning. My making the announcement saved us both embarrassment and added legitimacy to your lie."

Persephone sank back down knowing he spoke the truth. "I was not planning on getting married and if by chance I did I always said it would be for love."

"Love is overestimated. Most marriages do not take place for love. They take place for family allegiances, money, power, or even arranged for other purposes. If they are lucky there is a mutual respect between husband and wife." He moved to her and took her hand to help her stand before wrapping his arms around her waist. His lips lightly caressed her ear. "We are fortunate. Our marriage will be built on respect and a shared passion."

He let his lips trail further down her neck as his hands caressed her sides through the sheer fabric of her night gown.

Persephone couldn't stop her eyes from drifting closed as Hawk's teeth nipped at her collarbone. She wanted to be angry. She wanted to rage at him for the egotistical manner in which he tried to manage everyone around him. She wanted to push him away and declare that she would make her own decisions and that desire was not enough for her, she wanted love. But when his lips moved over her skin and his hands softly slid over her body, she found that she could not resist him. Surrender was inevitable. Her head fell backwards allowing him unobstructed access to her throat.

Hawk let his hands drift over her back to caress her perfectively rounded backside. He pulled her closer and felt himself growing harder with every second. When a soft moan escaped her lips, he knew he had won. He reached down and scooped her into his arms as his lips captured hers. He deepened the kiss as her arms came around his neck.

He pulled away slightly. "Are we in agreement, Persephone? Will you be my duchess?"

Persephone opened her eyes hating that he was no longer kissing her. She nodded in agreement.

He kissed her gently. "Say it"

Persephone looked into his eyes and replied softly, "I will be your duchess."

He smiled and kissed her again before setting her back on her feet. She held onto his arms to steady herself. "You must get some rest. We will be leaving early in the morning."

Persephone watched him as he made his way to the door. "If we are engaged, why is it still necessary for us to leave London. Catherine could still enjoy the season."

He paused at the door. "You will still be safer in the country than in London and until you are my wife, I will not take any chances. Besides I would prefer we were married at Hawk's Hill." He gave her a wink. "The sooner I have you in my bed the better, my love."

Persephone let out the breath she had been holding and sank down on her bed. When she had agreed to come to London with Catherine for the season, she had never planned on looking for a husband. She had only wanted to enjoy the parties and all the other attractions London had to offer, now she was about to marry one of the wealthiest and most powerful men in England. She was to become a duchess, the Duchess of Hawksford. Married to a man who desired her but did not love her, a man with a wicked reputation, a man that made her insides quiver whenever he looked in her direction. She pulled the covers over her and lay back against her pillows. But the thought that soon she would be sharing a bed with Hawk kept any chance of sleep away.

Chapter Eleven

Persephone was so tired of being in a carriage. It was now day two of their travels and by all accounts they had several more hours to go. They had left the following morning after the ball with Persephone riding alone with Catherine and her Aunt Louisa. The entourage traveling with them was impressive to say the least. There were three traveling coaches one for the ladies, one for their lady's maids and the duke's valet as well as the duke's private carriage which he travelled in alone. There was a separate carriage for their luggage and belongings and at least eight out-riders for their protection. When they neared a village, they drew quite a crowd of onlookers trying to get a glimpse of nobility.

The duke had made previous arrangements for their stay at a posting inn last night. The inn keeper and his wife were thrilled to have such an elite guest and practically fell over themselves trying make them comfortable and meet all their needs to the duke's satisfaction. Since they were all so exhausted from a hard day of traveling, they had eaten their supper quickly and went to their assigned rooms. She and Catherine had shared a room and thankfully Catherine had been too exhausted to continue talking about the upcoming wedding.

Persephone had only seen Hawk for a moment while at the posting inn and they had not been alone then. Aunt Louisa said they would stop to change out horses one more time before they reached Hawk's Hill.

Catherine was reading a book and Aunt Louisa was working on her embroidery. Persephone leaned against the side of the carriage faking sleep. It was the only way to get any peace from Catherine's constant talk of the wedding and romance. She hoped they would stop soon; she was getting a bit hungry and needed to stretch her legs.

"Persephone, wake up," Catherine said shaking her none to gently. "We are almost at the inn where we can change horses."

Persephone stifled a pretend yawn and stretched her arms out above her. "Thank goodness, I need to get out and walk a bit."

Aunt Louisa put her embroidery back into her basket. "I could use a drink and something to eat as well. I hope Ethan allows us enough time at this stop to do so."

"I'm sure we will have time. Hawk is not immortal. He must be getting hungry too," Catherine said causing Persephone to crack a smile.

"He may not be immortal but he certainly acts as if he has divine power," Persephone said jokingly.

"They all act that way," Catherine said as she adjusted her skirts. "Leicester and Rockhurst are no better. I think they are all pulled aside at school and given lessons on how to be arrogant and superior." She leaned over toward Persephone and whispered. "Although I must admit, I find Leicester's proud manner very tempting."

"Catherine, ladies do not speak of such things. My goodness, girl," Aunt Louisa said shaking her head disapprovingly.

Catherine laughed. "Aunt Louisa you have said worse yourself."

"Yes, but I am not a young lady in search of a husband. When you are my age, you may say and do as you like but until then try to act more circumspect."

Catherine and Persephone both giggled but made no further comment as the carriage came to a stop.

"Finally! This is our last stop before we reach Hawk's Hill. I can't wait to be back home. I hope Mrs. Potter will make us some of her famous lemon cakes." Catherine turned to Persephone. "They were your favorites when we were girls."

Persephone smiled as the memory came back to her. "I remember but it has been at least eight years since I have been to Hawk's Hill. Is Mrs. Potter still there?"

Catherine shrugged her shoulders. "It's been two years since I have been home and she was still there then. I am sure Hawk would have mentioned it if she had left. He loves her cooking. He always says there is no French chef alive that can match Mrs. Potter's sweet cakes." She grabbed Persephone's hand. "Now that you will be duchess, we can have sweet cakes as much as you want."

Persephone didn't have time to respond before the door of the carriage was opened and a footman assisted them down. The sun was bright and Persephone shielded her eyes from it as she looked around. It was another posting inn, one in which they could eat a bite and change horses before traveling the rest of the way to Hawksford's ancestral seat.

Catherine linked her arm through hers and began walking toward the inn. "I am famished. Hopefully we can find some fresh bread and butter or some cheese."

They followed Aunt Louisa as she led the way inside the inn while the horses were being changed out and preparations were made for the remainder of the journey. The innkeeper was a very polite older man and he promptly brought them out some cider to drink as well as some fresh bread and cheese. Persephone took some bread and put some fresh butter on it. It was warm from the oven and it seemed to melt in her mouth. She wondered if Hawk would come inside and eat or if he would continue supervising everything outside while the servants and outriders ate. She was just about to ask Louisa if she should take him something when the door opened and he came inside. He didn't look like he had been in a carriage for two days. He looked just as elegant as he would have in any ballroom. She tentatively put a hand to her hair hoping she looked better than she felt.

Hawk glanced over at her and grinned. "Ladies as soon as you have finished your meal and have seen to your needs, we can be on our way again. It looks like we will see some rain before we reach Hawk's Hill and I don't wish to be caught in a storm after dark. We are only about four more hours away."

"Aren't you going to eat anything?" Persephone asked as she gestured toward the loaf of warm bread.

He shook his head slightly. "I have already eaten but thank you for thinking of me." He gave her a wink which she hoped no one else saw. "I will be outside with the carriages. As soon as you are ready, we may proceed." He bowed to them slightly then left to go wait with the others.

"Well, we must hurry, girls. No one wants to traverse muddy roads and I am anxious to finish our journey," Louisa said as she began to gather her things.

Persephone took one more bite of bread and followed Catherine and Louisa outside to the carriages. She was about to get in the carriage behind Catherine when Hawk stepped in front of her.

"You will ride with me for the remainder of our journey."

"I'm not sure that would be proper for us to be alone in a carriage. Your aunt will not allow it," Persephone said as he turned toward the carriage containing his aunt and sister.

"Ethan, you know I can't allow Persephone to be alone with you for that amount of time with no chaperone. Have Sarah, her lady's maid ride with the two of you," Louisa said from inside the carriage.

"No," he said firmly causing all three ladies to stop and stare at him. "Persephone and I will continue in my carriage. There is no need for a chaperone as we will be married, . . . soon."

Persephone heard Catherine mumble. "I hope he is this lenient when I find a gentleman to pay his addresses to me."

Aunt Louisa frowned at him. "Behave yourself, Ethan."

He nodded in agreement as he closed the door before leading Persephone to his carriage. "I hope you don't mind riding with me. I was getting lonely and I selfishly decided that there was no reason the two of us couldn't enjoy each other's company for the remainder of the trip."

He assisted her as she got in and then followed behind to take the seat across from her. "I must confess that I don't mind taking a break from Catherine and all of her wedding planning."

"She is tenacious," he replied, causing Persephone to laugh.

The carriage started moving forward and suddenly she found herself pulled across the conveyance into his arms. "Now that I have you all to myself." He bent his head down and lightly feathered kisses down her neck.

Persephone let her eyes flutter closed and leaned her head over to the side. "Didn't you promise your aunt that you would behave?"

He sucked her earlobe in between his teeth before replying, "My aunt knows fully well that it is not in my ability to do so. She therefore has thrown you to the wolves or one wolf so to speak." He took her chin in his hand and turned her face to him. "Of course, I am certain that if we were not to be married, she would have put up much more resistance." He kissed her and if Persephone had any objections, they would have all melted away with that kiss. She leaned into him and wrapped her arms around his neck.

He pulled back just enough to shift her position on his lap. "I have been thinking of nothing else but having you for the past two days and now we are alone and unless we are set upon by highway men, we should not be disturbed for the next several hours."

Persephone couldn't help but laugh. "Highway men would be more my luck."

"If they disturbed us now, I would be forced to shoot each and every one of them." He reached around and deftly began releasing the buttons on the back of her bodice as he leaned forward and pressed kisses to her collarbone and the area just above her breasts.

Persephone felt his fingers at her back working the buttons letting the tips of his fingers slide along her skin as he popped each one free. She felt her skin prickle with each touch. When the last button was freed, he pushed her bodice down to her waist leaving her chemise exposed. He stopped kissing her long enough to watch as he placed his fingers under each of her chemise straps and slowly slid them down her arms until her breasts were free. She felt her blush rising as his eyes feasted upon her. She started to cover herself but he shook his head.

"Don't move, you are perfect." He bent his head and took one of her breasts in his mouth.

Persephone arched her back as he tugged her nipple between his teeth. His hands were busy making their way slowly up her skirt past her knees until they reached her garters. She felt her garter give way as he slowly rolled down her stocking before repeating the action with her other leg.

Hawk had never wanted a woman so badly in his life. He wanted to see her naked and feel himself inside of her. But he would be damned if he took his future duchess's virtue in a carriage. Restraint would be difficult but he would wait until he could take her properly in his bed. But he knew of other ways to bring her pleasure. He let his fingers slide up her leg slowly tracing circles on her silky-smooth skin while his lips feasted upon her breasts. She was an innocent and had no idea how erotic she sounded when she moaned as he touched her. He let his fingers travel up her leg until he reached the apex at the top of her thighs. Finding her slit, he let his fingers slide along it, causing her to buck upward.

Persephone bit her lip as his fingers moved up her thigh closer to her center but when he touched her there, she couldn't help but jump. His other hand pressed against her hip holding her steady.

"Do you want me to stop, Persephone?"

"No" It was the only word she could manage to get out of her mouth. Then she sucked in her breath sharply as he let one of his fingers press slowly inside her. Her senses heightened and she felt herself open further.

He continued to slide his fingers in and out of her as she grew wetter. Then suddenly he lifted her and shifted so that she was lying flat along the carriage seat. He lifted her skirts and put her knees over his shoulders.

Persephone scrambled to sit up. "What are you doing?"

"Be still, love. Trust me."

Persephone sat up on her elbows when she felt his lips press against the inside of her knee. His fingers once again moved inside her as his mouth slowly moved from her knees to the sensitive skin on the inside of her thighs. She felt a loss when his fingers left her but nearly jumped out of her skin as his mouth replaced them.

"You can't do that," she breathed heavily and tried to press her legs together. "This can't be proper."

He stopped and lifted his head. "Nothing I want to do to you is proper, but I promise it will give you pleasure. Lie back and let me pleasure you."

Persephone was not sure but everything he had done so far had been more than satisfying. Although she wasn't sure about this, she did trust him. She closed her eyes and felt her whole body tense as his tongue flicked over her. She arched her back and her fists clinched as he continued licking and sucking her most secret place. She felt a pressure building inside her, something she couldn't explain until finally it felt as if a million stars had burst within her. She cried out and her breathing grew heavier as her body convulsed.

Hawk continued to hold her as her body trembled. His cock grew harder within his trousers pressing uncomfortably against the fabric. He closed his eyes and willed himself to stay still. It took more will power than he had ever had to possess not to loosen the flap on his pants and thrust into her. She was panting and shivering so he lifted her up and placed her back in his lap so he could hold her close. He replaced the straps on her chemise and moved it and her bodice back into place. He looked at her face and kissed her pink cheeks as she rested her head against his chest.

Persephone wasn't sure what to say or even if she could form words. Hawk held her close and let his fingers rub up and down her back. After several minutes she managed to hold her head up and study his face. "I know I am naive and I don't know what I am supposed to do but shouldn't you find some kind of pleasure also."

Hawk kissed the tip of her nose. "I enjoyed giving you pleasure."

"That's not what I meant. What can I do for you?" She looked down embarrassed. "I'm sorry but I really have no idea what to do and your Aunt Louisa hasn't talked to me about what a wife and husband do together. Catherine and I have sneaked a peek at a few books but nothing was very helpful."

Hawk couldn't believe they were having this conversation. "I love your innocence and yes there are things I will teach you but not now. When you are my wife and we are in my bed there are many things we will do together. But I will not take you in a carriage." He gave her that wicked grin again. "At least not for your first time." He shifted her so he could button her dress and then sat her on the seat opposite him.

Persephone was surprised at the sudden distance he put between them. She hastily pulled her stockings back into place and fastened her garters. "Did I say something wrong?"

Hawk reached over and took her hand and placed a kiss on the inside of her wrist. "No, my love. It is just extremely difficult for me to be so close to you and not make you mine. You make me want to abandon my ideals and make love to you here and now."

Persephone couldn't hide a small smile. It thrilled her to know that he wanted her so badly. "Perhaps you could tell me about Hawk's Hill, it has been several years since I have been there and I'm sure there have been some changes made in the past eight years."

Hawk didn't want to talk about Hawks' Hill or anything else for that matter, but he supposed since his restraint was only holding by a thread it would be best if he could try to get his mind off of how good it would be to have Persephone naked beneath him.

"There haven't been as many changes as you might think. I haven't spent as much time in the country since I came into my title. Most of my time has been spent in London." He grinned. "But I'm sure that since you have read of my many exploits you already knew that."

She shifted a little closer to the window and moved the curtain back so she could see outside. "Weren't you the one that told me that most of what was written wasn't true?"

He shrugged his shoulders. "Unfortunately, some of it is." He saw her grin even if she was no longer facing him. "My steward handles most of the matters of my estates. He is very efficient."

"How many estates do you own besides Hawk's Hill?"

"Hawks' Hill is my family seat but I also own estates and properties in Yorkshire, Bath, Kent and Cornwall. Although I don't visit those properties very often."

Persephone turned to look at him. "You should visit them at least once a year. I'm sure the farmers and villagers would be happy to know that you were taking more of an interest."

He raised an eyebrow. "Are you going to be the type of duchess that tells me how to manage my affairs?" He was only teasing her, of course.

She lowered her eyes before turning back toward the window. "Certainly not, I merely meant it as a suggestion."

He watched her as she looked out the window. "You are right. We will make a point of spending more time at our estates, if that is what you prefer."

"I don't know what I prefer," she turned to look back at him. "I am not sure I will be a very good duchess."

"You will be a fabulous duchess and the staff will adore you. They will be very excited to finally have a duchess once again. Conway is the butler at Hawk's Hill, he has been there for ages and of course Mrs. Gregory is the head housekeeper and she will be instrumental in helping you adjust to your duties."

"How many servants are employed at Hawk's Hill?"

He thought for a moment. "At least fifty."

Persephone felt her stomach turning. She took a deep breath and steadied her nerves.

He reached across the carriage and took her hand in his. "Everything will be alright, Persephone."

She pulled her hand away. "How soon are we to be married?"

"If you are not opposed to a quiet ceremony with close family and friends, I would like to be married before the month's end."

Persephone's eyes widened. "That's only two weeks away!"

"Yes, I am aware."

"Catherine and Aunt Louisa have been making all sorts of plans in the carriage on the way here. They will not be able to do half of what they have planned in so short a time."

He saw the panic on her face and needed to ease her mind, so he pulled her back onto his lap and turned her face to his. "Did you have a hand in this planning, Persephone?"

She looked confused. "No, not really. Catherine was so excited. She talked about nothing else all the way here. I had not given a lot of thought to getting married. And yes, I already know that is the entire purpose of the season for young ladies."

He chuckled causing her to frown. "It is hard for me to believe that a lady as beautiful as you has given little thought to getting married. How did you ever think you would manage to maneuver through the season without a hundred marriage proposals?"

"Well as it happens, I only had two, yours and the Comte's."

He leaned forward and pressed a sweet kiss to her lips. "There were several others."

She pushed away. "What?"

"There were others. If I remember correctly about a dozen."

She was stunned. "Why did I never know?"

He tightened his hold. "They were not acceptable. Two were old enough to be your father and one had been married three times before. The others I sent away because I simply wanted you for myself."

She tried to pull away again but he kissed her quickly. "I don't know if I should be angry with you or not."

He nipped at her earlobe again. "Can I convince you to forgive me?"

She leaned up to kiss him when the carriage came to a stop.

He sat her on the seat opposite him and opened the door to see what had happened. "I'll be right back. Stay inside."

Persephone looked out the window at the darkening skies. It was not looking like they would make it to Hawk's Hill before the rain. As soon as the thought crossed her mind heavy raindrops started pounding the roof of the carriage. Suddenly the door flung open and Catherine jumped inside followed by her Aunt Louisa.

"The wheel on our carriage hit something in the road and broke. We will have to leave it behind to be repaired. Hawk said we could ride with the two of you," Catherine said as she gave Persephone a knowing look.

Aunt Louisa took off her hat and tried to wipe it dry but from the look of the sagging feathers, it was a lost cause. "Thank heavens we are only about an hour away from Hawk's Hill."

"Where is Hawk?" Persephone asked as she searched the window to see if she could find him.

Catherine shook out her damp skirts. "He is helping the footmen unhitch the horses and making arrangements to have the carriage repaired. He should be along shortly."

No sooner had the words left her mouth than the door opened and Hawk stuck his head inside. "I am soaking wet so I will ride atop to keep you ladies from getting soaked."

Persephone moved quickly from her seat. "You most certainly will not. There must be a blanket in here somewhere." She lifted the seat and indeed there was a blanket inside. She pulled his hand. "Come inside before you become sick."

Catherine scooted closer to her aunt. "Persephone can sit by me so you will have the whole bench to yourself, Hawk."

He moved inside the carriage as Persephone wrapped the blanket about his shoulders. He glanced up at her and his heart warmed at the sight of her pretty little worried face. "Thank you." He then looked over at his aunt. "She is behaving like an authoritative duchess already."

She took a seat beside Catherine. "I am behaving as I would to anyone in danger of catching their death of cold."

He pulled the blanket closer around him grateful for its warmth. Persephone sat very still and avoided eye contact with him but every once in a while, he would catch her glancing in his direction making sure he was alright.

They traveled mostly in silence for the remainder of the journey. The rain had slowed down quite a bit, and the sun was beginning to set leaving the sky painted in hues of orange and reds. They had been on his land for about an hour but they would be reaching the manor house in a few minutes.

"We are almost here, Persephone," Catherine announced excitedly. "Look there is the lake we used to swim in when we were girls."

Persephone laughed. "The very same one where you fell in and Leicester had to jump in and rescue you. He was so angry."

Catherine shrugged her shoulders. "It was very romantic."

"You were ten years old, Catherine," Persephone said amused at her friend's infatuation with his grace the Duke of Leicester. Of course, then he was simply Michael to them.

"He wasn't as mad at me as he was when you put that frog in his boot."

Persephone let out another laugh. "So many fun memories." She looked over at Hawk. "You were not around very much, your grace."

Hawk looked out the window. "I was the heir. There was always something I needed to learn. My father felt that as the future Duke of Hawksford, I should be concerned more with learning how to run an estate and manage servants and business matters than swimming and catching frogs." His look was somber then he turned and a smile replaced the frown. "I was learning to be a duke."

"Is that why once you went to Eton you went wild?" Catherine asked causing her aunt to gasp and nearly swallow her tongue.

"Catherine! A lady does not mention such things. My goodness I have been lax in your education."

Catherine rolled her eyes but didn't continue that same line of conversation. The house loomed in the distance now like a medieval fortress. Persephone had always loved the house thinking it looked like something from a story book. It was massive with probably fifty or more windows and two huge turrets. The gray stone walls were ornamented with carvings and the gardens were still as lovely as she remembered. She would soon be mistress of all of this and she felt the flutters in her belly once again.

"We are home, Persephone," Hawk said as he studied her profile as she looked out the carriage's windows.

'*Home*', it seemed like a lifetime since Persephone had called anywhere home. She had spent most of her life bouncing between her paternal aunt Grace and her mother's best friend, Aunt Louisa. But neither place had ever been her home. She swallowed a lump in her throat and felt her eyes mist with tears.

Catherine must have noticed and she silently reached over and squeezed her hand. Persephone sniffed and wiped at her eyes before giving her friend a sweet smile.

The carriage came to a stop and all of the servants lined up to greet the duke and his future duchess. Catherine and Louisa stepped out of the way to allow Hawk a chance to lead her inside. Persephone smiled and nodded to each of the servants as they curtsied to her. She hoped they couldn't tell just how nervous she really felt. Hawk introduced her to Conway the butler and to the head housekeeper Mrs. Gregory.

"We are so excited to have a new duchess, my lady," Mrs. Gregory said all smiles as she curtsied deeply.

Persephone reached over and gave the older lady a quick hug. "Thank you, Mrs. Gregory. I hope that I can live up to your expectations. I will need your help as well."

With those words Persephone had just won the heart of the older servant and Hawk knew the others would come to adore her as well.

"Why don't you show the ladies to their chambers. I'm sure they would like to freshen up before supper tonight," Hawk said as he stood aside to allow Mrs. Gregory to take over.

"Of course, your grace." She looked over at Persephone. "Forgive me for not mentioning it sooner. There is a warm tub waiting for each of you in your chambers."

Catherine moved forward. "Thank goodness. I can't wait to get out of these traveling clothes."

Aunt Louisa let out a frustrated breath. "Really Catherine."

Persephone followed them up the stairs to their rooms. A long hot bath sounded like heaven right now. She looked back over her shoulder to see Hawk watching her. She gave him a quick smile then hurried to catch up with Catherine.

Chapter Twelve

Persephone closed her eyes and leaned her head back against the rim of the tub. The water was steamy and it felt so good to just relax. She heard the door open behind her but didn't bother opening her eyes.

"Sarah, would you mind getting the bottle of lavender oil from the table. I would love a few more drops in my bath water." She heard footsteps across the floor and the sounds of the drops of oil as they plopped into the water. "Thank you, Sarah. I am just going to soak for a while so please see to whatever you need to do. I will call you when it's time to dress for dinner."

"Take as long as you need, sweetheart. I am enjoying the view."

Persephone's eyes flew open as she crossed her arms over her chest quickly sloshing water onto the floor. "What are you doing in here?!"

He began rolling up his shirt sleeves. "I came to see if you were settling in. It is just my good fortune that you were still in the bath."

Persephone pointed to the door. "You had better leave before Sarah returns. She will be scandalized."

"I have no intention of leaving and your maid will not return for some time." He moved over closer to the tub. "Lean forward and I will wash your back."

Persephone cautiously leaned forward resting her chin on her knees as Hawk reached into the water letting his hands move slowly over her wet skin and began soaping her back. "Even though this feels delicious, you know you shouldn't be here."

His hand dipped lower. "I have spent most of my adult life doing things I shouldn't have done. Why stop now? Besides, everyone is preoccupied with other things. I will not seduce you tonight. I just had the urge to see you. If I had known I would be seeing so much of you, I would have hastened up here sooner."

Persephone turned her head to the side but kept her eyes closed as his hands moved over her skin.

"Your skin is so soft. I will have a larger tub commissioned tomorrow. One big enough for both of us."

Persephone blushed. "You are a rake."

He leaned over and pressed a kiss to her wet shoulder. "I have never tried to deny that fact. But I should leave you for now. I believe a warm bath waits me in my chambers as well. I will see you at supper."

Persephone wrapped her arms around her knees when she heard him leave and the door close behind him. He may not love her but could desire be enough for a happy marriage?

Supper was not nearly as peaceful as her warm bath had been. When Hawk announced his plan to have the wedding take place in two weeks, both Catherine and Louisa did not hesitate to voice their objections.

"Two weeks is ridiculous, Hawk. How are we to get everything ready by then and the guests will have to travel from London?" Catherine said raising her voice.

"Not to mention Persephone's wedding gown and trousseau. How are we to get everything made she will need in so short a time span?" Aunt Louisa added.

"We have a perfectly excellent seamstress in the village who would be more than pleased, if not flattered, to make Persephone's gown and trousseau. It will be a very small ceremony and the guests will be very close family and friends. I do not want an entourage showing up at the estate to entertain. We will marry in the chapel here in a small intimate ceremony," Hawk said patiently as he sipped his wine.

"This just will not do. Getting married by special license without the banns being read will certainly have people gossiping about the hastiness of the marriage," Louisa said as she glanced over at Persephone.

Hawk put down his glass. "I don't care about the gossip and once we are married there isn't anyone in the ton that would dare to speak ill about my duchess."

Aunt Louisa snorted unladylike. "So you think, Ethan."

He stood from his chair. "This is really a matter between Persephone and me." He turned to her. "Persephone, what are your feelings and please do not feel bullied by either myself or my family?"

Persephone glanced at Catherine who was urging her to agree to more time. She then glanced at Hawk. There was no pressure in his eyes, he was simply waiting to hear what she had to add to the conversation. "I think I would prefer a small intimate ceremony. I don't have any family to attend and I already have more than enough clothes, I see no reason to commission more to be made." She picked up her wine glass hoping no one noticed the slight tremble in her fingers. "Two weeks is fine with me."

"Then it is settled. Two weeks ladies." He nodded to each of them. "My finances of course are at your disposal and my secretary will make any arrangements." He paused behind Persephone's chair putting his hand briefly on her shoulder. "Enjoy the rest of your evening ladies, I have some business to attend to."

Catherine waited until he had left the dining room before saying, "He would have agreed to more time, Persephone if you had asked."

"I don't need any more time. I really do not want a large ceremony with half the ton staring as I walk down the aisle. If I am to be married, I would like to just get it over with."

"My goodness, Persephone, it's a wedding not an execution. If Leicester would propose to me, I would be beyond excited," Catherine said as she motioned for a footman to refill her glass.

"Well, we have a lot to do, ladies. Two weeks will fly by before we know it. Tomorrow we will visit the seamstress in the village. I dare say Ethan is correct and she will be overjoyed at having been chosen to outfit the new duchess," Louisa said as she stood from her seat.

"I truly do not see a reason to buy more dresses, Aunt Louisa. I have enough," Persephone insisted.

"Nonsense, you are about to become a duchess, the Duchess of Hawksford no less. You must be dressed as is fitting for your station. Not to mention a few intimate pieces for your husband to appreciate." The older lady blushed scarlet. "Your life is about to change my dear."

Persephone sat there for a moment pondering that statement. Her life was about to change, she hoped it would be for the better.

Two weeks did go by quicker than Persephone imagined. She had seen very little of Hawk as the wedding preparations had consumed most of her time. Aunt Louisa had kept her at the dressmakers and commissioned several new day gowns as well as two more ballgowns along with several other items for her trousseau. Persephone had been surprised to learn that Hawk had already commissioned several gowns and instructed his secretary to see to all of their needs and handle any arrangements that they required. The special license had not been difficult for him to acquire and when he returned from getting it, he had Leicester and Rockhurst with him. Catherine had been overjoyed to have the Duke of Leicester under roof but Aunt Louisa had once again cautioned her about appearing too eager.

Persephone's wedding dress was made of sky-blue silk with a white lace overlay on the skirt. The tiny puff sleeves had pearls sewn around them and the bodice had a darker royal blue ribbon that tied just underneath her breasts. Aunt Louisa had brought her a diamond tiara from the Hawksford collection as well as a delicate lace veil worn by all of the former Duchess's of Hawksford on their wedding day.

The guests had been arriving for the past hour and her nerves were starting to fray. They had invited only close family and friends so it would be a simple ceremony. The only family Persephone had was her aunt Grace who had declined to attend due to an illness so really there was no one attending for her.

Aunt Louisa had been kind enough to step in the role for her mother and explain what would happen between a husband and wife on their wedding night. Persephone had tried to follow the awkward conversation that drifted back and forth between flower petals and bees. She had tried to control her amusement at the older lady's discomfiture until finally Louisa took a deep breath and blurted out, "It will hurt the first time but after that it will be more enjoyable."

Catherine had helped her get dressed but had left to go to the chapel and now she was all alone waiting for Lord Rockhurst to come fetch her when it was time for the ceremony to begin. He had agreed to escort her down the aisle since she had no one else.

As she looked upon herself in the mirror, she couldn't believe it was her. She looked like a princess. The diamond tiara sparkled and felt heavy on her head. The lace framing her face made her appear almost angelic and she wondered if her mother would be happy for her. She jumped as a heavy knock sounded on the door.

Persephone stood and crossed her hands in front of her. "Come in."

The door opened and Lord Rockhurst appeared. She smiled as he stood there a bit stunned for a moment. "Do I look alright?" she asked questioningly.

He blinked his eyes and smiled. "You look magnificent, as if a goddess has descended from Mount Olympus to grace us mortals with your presence."

She laughed and the sound was very melodious. "You are very skilled at flattery, my lord."

He walked toward her taking her hand and raising it to his lips. "It's not flattery if it's true, my dear."

She felt her cheeks blush. "Is it time for the ceremony?"

He offered her his arm. "Indeed, I am here to collect you. Unless you would like to reconsider and run away with me instead."

Persephone laughed again. She knew he wasn't serious, but she appreciated his attempt at humor to lessen her nerves. "Don't tempt me, I am already so nervous."

"We would never make it out the front door I'm afraid. Hawk is anxiously waiting your arrival." He put her hand on his sleeve and began leading her out the door and down the stairs toward the chapel.

Persephone felt her breathing grow heavier with every step and stopped the moment they stood in the chapel doorway. It was full of those family and friends that had warranted an invitation as well as several of the long-time servants who anxiously waited to see the duke marry his duchess. She felt herself growing weak and blew a slow steady breath through her lips. She was frozen. Hawk was waiting for her at the end of the aisle. Catherine was her only attendant and Aunt Louisa was seated up front smiling at her encouragingly, but she couldn't move.

She felt Lord Rockhurst cover her hand with his and whisper to her. "Everything will be alright, Persephone. You will be a wonderful duchess and Hawk cares for you very much."

At his words she turned her face to look at him. He gave her a soft reassuring smile. His words pulled her free of her petrified state and when he moved forward, she moved with him. As they reached the end, Hawk took her hand and held it as they faced the clergyman.

Hawk felt her hand quiver as he held it in his and he could see the look of panic on her face. He leaned closer and whispered. "I was afraid you had changed your mind when you hesitated."

She looked up at him and his assuring smile instantly made her feel more at ease. "Lord Rockhurst said we would never make it past the front door if we tried to escape so I figured I might as well continue."

He looked startled for a moment until he realized she was teasing him. He pulled her a little closer as the ceremony began. Persephone repeated the words of the marriage ceremony and moved forward to sign her name in the registry when it was time to do so. The clergyman announced that they were man and wife and Hawk turned her to face him. He placed a soft chaste kiss to her lips before those in attendance cheered for them.

The wedding breakfast seemed to last forever. She and Hawk received so many congratulations and gifts it was exhausting to keep up with everything. After several hours everyone began to disburse.

Aunt Louisa came up and kissed her cheek. "Catherine and I are moving to the Dower House but will come to visit in a few days."

Persephone was taken off guard. "You are leaving?"

Louisa gave her a quick hug. "Of course, my dear. You and Ethan need time to be alone and you can't have the privacy a young married couple needs with Catherine and I underfoot."

Catherine was all smiles. "Leicester and Rockhurst are escorting us to the dower house before they leave for Lord Rockhurst's estate. Maybe I will find some time to be alone with Michael."

Louisa rolled her eyes. "My goodness, child. He is 'your grace' now. It isn't proper to call him by his given name and you will in no way be alone with him."

Catherine gave Persephone a wink. "We shall see," then she leaned forward and whispered in her ear. "You will have to tell me all about the marriage night."

Aunt Louisa grabbed her arm. "Come along, Catherine. On the eve of your wedding, I will give you the same speech I gave Persephone."

"The one about flowers and pollination? I would prefer more details," Catherine said as her aunt nearly dragged her from the room.

"You will be the death of me, Catherine," Persephone heard Aunt Louisa say as they walked out the front door.

Persephone looked around. Almost everyone had gone. Only Lord Rockhurst and Leicester were left. They each came up to offer their congratulations one more time before following Louisa and Catherine out to the carriages.

The butler closed the front door and the servants all went about their work. Persephone stood there looking at the closed door for a minute or two before Hawk took her hand and led her to the sitting room where a bottle of champagne and something to eat was waiting for them.

"You should eat something."

Persephone took a seat but didn't reach for any of the food Mrs. Cooper had been good enough to set aside for them. "I'm not very hungry."

He took the seat opposite her. "Yes, it has been an exhausting day. You looked very beautiful by the way and I feel very fortunate."

Persephone smiled weakly. "I was very nervous."

"Are you still nervous?" he asked watching her intensely.

"A little. I would be a fool to lie and say I wasn't. But if I am correct most brides are nervous on their wedding night."

He grinned. "I wouldn't know, as this is the first time I have ever been with a bride on her wedding night." He saw her lips slowly turn up into a smile. "I don't want you to be nervous, Persephone."

"I think I will go to my room for a bit and perhaps I'll eat something later," she said as she stood from her seat.

He stood as well. "Your things have all been moved to the duchess' chambers. I hope the rooms meet your satisfaction, but if there is anything you would like to change you have my permission to do so. Afterall they are your rooms now."

Persephone nodded. "Thank you."

"However, you will sleep in the duke's chambers with me."

Persephone curtsied. "As you wish." She then turned and left to make her way up to the duchess' suites. She needed a few minutes to herself before Hawk joined her.

Hawk watched her go. He didn't know why he had said that she would sleep in his chambers. In most society marriages it was common for the husband and wife to sleep in their own separate rooms. The man would visit his wife's bedchamber and then return to his own once his needs had been fulfilled. His own father and mother had that arrangement. And while he had not given much thought to doing anything different, when he saw Persephone today, he knew that he did not want to sleep apart from her. He wanted her in his bed, and he wanted to wake up to her in his arms. He didn't care what other ton marriages did, he wanted his wife with him.

He smiled to himself thinking how his feelings had changed on that matter. A year ago, if he had thought of finding a bride, he would have wanted a wife that would make few demands on him. One he could wed, bed, and produce an heir. A duchess that would not disrupt his life overly much. Now, it was different, Persephone was different. He poured himself a glass of brandy and willed himself not to go upstairs too quickly.

The duchess's chambers were much larger than she had expected. In addition to the bedroom there was the duchess' private sitting room as well as an extremely large dressing room. The bed was intricately carved with a delicate yellow coverlet. It was lovely and she couldn't believe it was hers. She had dismissed her maid and dressed in her nightgown herself. It was sheer white gauze with delicate lace around the bodice. The gown was embarrassingly sheer, but Aunt Louisa insisted that Hawk would like it. She blew out a breath wondering what she should do now. While she was naturally nervous about the bedding, she couldn't help but be a little excited as well. She paced her bedchamber for a few minutes then decided to be bold. Crossing the room to the connecting door that led to the duke's bedchamber, her hand trembled a little as she turned the doorknob. The door didn't make a sound as she slowly opened it and walked inside. The chambers were empty so she took a few minutes to look around.

The duke's rooms were even larger than her own. The rooms had a definitive masculine feel. There was a private study as well as the duke's own dressing room. The bed was enormous with a dark blue coverlet over crisp white sheets. She forced herself to move closer to the bed letting her hand glide over the pillows. She was startled when she heard a door close behind her.

Hawk had not been expecting to find Persephone in his rooms. As a nervous bride he imagined her waiting for him in her chambers. But there she stood wearing a sheer white confection, her long blonde curls hanging loose down her back nearly reaching her waist. She was letting her fingers slide over his pillow and he imagined those same fingers touching him. He swallowed and took a step further into the room.

"I wasn't expecting to find you here waiting for me." He threw his jacket over a chair. His valet would not be happy about it, but right now he didn't give a damn about anything but getting his wife into his bed.

Persephone took a step toward him. "I didn't know what else to do. It was driving me mad waiting for you and since you had already said I was to sleep in your chambers I decided to see if you were here."

Hawk smiled at her comment. "I'm glad you came to me." He began loosening the buttons on his shirt. He saw Persephone's eyes watch his movements.

She tore her eyes away and moved back toward the bed. She pulled the covers back. "Should I get into bed and wait for you? I must confess it is giving me a bit of anxiety not knowing what I should do."

He chuckled as he whipped the shirt over his head tossing it in the same direction as the jacket. "Come here and let me see if I can ease your anxiety."

Persephone slowly moved toward him. "I'm not sure seeing you like this is going to ease my anxiety. My goodness you must be very athletic." When she reached him, she couldn't help but let her hands roam over his chest and down the muscles of his abdomen.

Hawk let her explore willing himself not to touch her yet. He was relieved that Persephone was not one of those weeping frightened brides he had heard others speak about. He liked that she was bold and even if her touch was tentative, he admired her for her courage. He cupped her face in both his hands and turned it up to his. His lips drifted down until they lightly touched hers.

"You look very beautiful, Persephone," he said as he continued to press soft kisses down her cheek to her neckline. "That nightgown is very lovely but I would prefer to see it pooling on the floor at your feet."

He let his hands slowly slide down her shoulders to her wrists. Then he took her arms and held them over her head as he gathered the hem of the nightgown in his hands and swiftly whipped it over her head and tossed it to the floor.

Persephone did not cover herself but she did feel herself blush. "That nightgown was very expensive you know. We really shouldn't leave it on the floor."

He wrapped his arms around her. "I can afford to buy you a hundred nightgowns, but I prefer you not wear them at all." He kissed her again this time with more possession than before. "You have no idea how perfect you are." He bent down and swept her into his arms. "And you are mine!" He carried her over to the bed and gently laid her back against the pillows. He stood back and let his gaze move over her. "I have been longing to see you just like this, naked in my bed with your hair spread out about my pillows."

He moved onto the bed to lie beside her letting his fingers slowly move over her chest causing her nipples to pucker. He bent his head closer to suck a nipple in between his teeth causing her to arch her back upwards.

Persephone closed her eyes as his hands moved over her skin and when he began to nibble on her breast, she felt herself growing warm inside and moisture pooling between her thighs. But he had given her pleasure this way before, she wanted to touch him. She reached up and ran her hands down his spine marveling at how his muscles twitched under her touch. He was still wearing his trousers and the thought irritated her.

"Shouldn't you be naked as well?"

Hawk stared down at her. "Since you have only seen me once before I thought I would give you more time to make sure you were ready."

Persephone returned his stare. "I'm ready."

He swiftly moved to undo the flap on his pants before sliding them down his legs. His shaft sprang free and he saw her eyes widen. "Are you alright?"

Persephone bit her bottom lip. Perhaps she was being too bold. She had seen pictures and had an idea of what happened in the marriage bed, she had no idea how this was going to work. He was very large and for this first time she did feel a little bit frightened.

Being daring was working for her so far so she decided it would be best to continue. "Do you mind if I touch you?"

She surprised him at every turn. Hawk turned to lay on his back. "I am all yours, my love."

Persephone pulled the sheet up covering herself and sat up to stare down at Hawk. She reached out and let her fingers slide over his hips. She hesitated briefly then reached with her fingers to touch his cock. She quickly removed her hand when it jumped at her touch. When he didn't say anything, she moved her fingers once again marveling at hard he was underneath the smooth skin.

He took her hand and wrapped it around his member and showed her how to move her hand up and down his cock. He closed his eyes and his breathing grew heavier as her tempo increased and she became more sure of her movements.

Persephone marveled at how he felt in her grip and watched his face as she continued to stroke her hand over him. Her voice squeaked when he suddenly flipped her over onto her back and moved on top of her.

"Enough," he said in a rough voice.

"Did I do something wrong?"

He leaned over and kissed her. "No, darling. You were doing everything right, but now it's your turn." He let his fingers drift lower to find the center at the apex of her thighs. "Open your legs for me," he whispered against her lips.

Persephone did as he asked and gasp as he slipped a finger inside of her. She arched her neck over to the side as he pressed kisses behind her ear as he let his finger move inside her.

"You are ready now, Persephone. I will go slow and try to make it hurt as little as possible," he whispered near her ear as he positioned himself at her entrance.

Persephone tensed as he pushed a little further. She began to feel a sense of panic and tried to push herself away.

Hawk caught her hips and held her steady. He stopped moving and kissed her, taking advantage of her parted lips, he let his tongue slip inside to mingle with hers. He felt her relax and pushed forward more. She sucked in her breath and he held still letting her body adjust to his intrusion before pushing into her fully. When he felt her relax further, he thrust forward more forcibly and felt her maidenhead give way.

Persephone stiffened at the sharp pain that shot through her. She would have cried out but Hawks' mouth had descended on hers and swallowed any cries she might have made. He held still and the sting gradually faded away.

"That's it, sweetheart. There will not be any more pain only pleasure." To reassure her he pulled back slowly and then pressed back into her. "Does it feel better?"

She nodded. "Yes, but is that it?"

Laughter rumbled in his chest, "No, darling." He then pulled out and pressed back in again, this time a little faster.

Persephone tried to match his rhythm as he moved inside her, his thrusts becoming harder and faster. She felt something building inside her until finally it burst forth. Her body convulsed underneath him as he reached his climax soon after collapsing on top of her.

Persephone was breathing heavily and didn't know if her legs would hold her if she stood. Hawk rolled to his side and pulled her into him. He pressed kisses to her shoulder and the back of her neck as he let his hands caress her. "I'm sorry, darling. I tried to make it as good as I could but you were driving me mad and I couldn't wait any longer."

Persephone turned in his arms to face him. "Can we only do that once a night?"

Hawk grinned and kissed her. "No, my sweet we can do that as many times as you like. But tonight, I think it would be best to give your body some time to heal."

She reached up and wrapped her arms about his neck. "I would rather try that again."

He turned her to her back and began kissing her again. "You are going to be the best duchess ever."

Chapter Thirteen

The next morning Persephone had a little regret. Her body ached and she did have a good deal of soreness. Sarah had seen that a tub of hot water was prepared for her to soak in before going down to breakfast. She and Hawk had made love at least three more times. Now she knew why the mommas and dowagers kept the secrets of the marriage bed secret until young ladies were about to marry. If young girls knew how delightful the marriage bed could be she imagined there would be a lot more elopements to Gretna Green and a good many more scandals.

Hawk said if she felt like it, they could take a ride in his phaeton around the estate today. Persephone was excited about that. She was anxious to see how much Hawk's Hill had changed and excited about spending more time with him. Since they had stayed in bed much longer than usual this morning, she supposed it was time to drag herself out of the soothing water before it got cold and dress to go downstairs.

After drying off, she pulled the bellpull for Sarah to assist her. She had already laid out one of her new day dresses with a lovely matching bonnet.

Sarah came in quickly. "His grace is waiting for you downstairs."

"We must hurry then. I don't want him to grow tired of waiting for me. I'm ashamed to admit that I could have stayed in the tub for hours longer."

Her maid blushed. "Yes, your grace."

Persephone stood still. This was the first time she had been referred to as 'your grace', it seemed odd to her. It was like the title didn't really fit someone of her manner. She gave the maid a sweet smile and continued getting ready. It took longer than she had hoped and when she hurried down the stairs, she didn't see Hawk waiting for her.

Conway came forward bowing deeply. "May I be of assistance, your grace?"

"I was looking for the duke."

"I believe his grace is still in the dining room reading his paper."

Persephone smiled, "Thank you, Conway."

She made her way to the dining room where she did indeed find Hawk reading *The Times* and drinking tea. When he heard her enter, he looked up from his paper and set it aside. "Good morning, duchess."

Persephone smile brightly. "Good morning, I'm sorry I have kept you waiting so long."

He stood and walked around to pull the chair out for her. "You are certainly worth the wait. Did you enjoy your bath this morning?"

She blushed. "I did, thank you. Please don't let me keep you from your paper. Did you still want to take a ride today in your phaeton?"

He sat back down and took the paper in hand. "It is being made ready now. We can leave as soon as you have eaten something." He gave her a wicked look. "I know you are exhausted from last night's activities and we need you to keep your strength up."

She laughed as she reached for one of Mrs. Cooper's sweet cakes.

He folded the paper and held it out to her. "I thought you might want to read this."

She took the paper from him. "What is it?"

"Our marriage announcement. I had my solicitor make certain it would be in the paper today. So, by now most of London knows that you are my bride."

Her eyes scanned the announcement. "Including Comte Domingo."

"There is no need for you to fear him now. He will know there is no longer a reason to pursue you." He took the paper from her. "When we return to London, the Prince Regent will have a dinner for us at Carlton House. He is anxious to congratulate you. I had informed him before we wed so it would not come as a shock."

She looked surprised. "I'm not certain I will fit in at Carlton House."

"My darling, you're a duchess, you will be welcomed everywhere. Doors will open for you that you previously had thought closed. You will be a leader of the ton."

Persephone's smile faded. She had never wanted to be a leader of the ton. This was exactly what she had feared when Hawk had first mentioned marriage to her. She took one more bite of her cake and pushed it aside. "I'm ready to go whenever you are."

He stood from his seat and pulled her chair out for her. "It looks to be a lovely day but you should grab your cloak in case the weather changes."

He escorted her out into the hallway where Sarah was waiting with her cloak. She placed her hand on his arm as they walked outside where his phaeton was waiting for them hooked up to two beautiful grays. "I thought we might take a ride to the old ruins, if you would like."

Persephone took his hand as he helped her up to her seat. "The old ruins? Catherine and I were never allowed to go there when we were girls. The duchess always said it was much too dangerous and young ladies had no business climbing about ancient stones all day."

"But you and Catherine went to the ruins anyway, didn't you?" he asked as he took his seat and picked up the reins.

Persephone laughed as the memoires began to come back to her. "Of course, we did. Telling Catherine not to do something made her want to do it even more. We almost got caught a time or two. One time Catherine fell and skinned her knee. It was very bad and she limped the entire way home. When her nurse saw it, she told Catherine she was going to tell the duchess.

Catherine told her that if the duchess sent her away to a convent, she would lose her employment. The nurse kept her mouth shut but made Catherine promise to be more careful in the future."

"As it so happens, I am on very intimate terms with the new duchess and I believe she is a bit more adventurous than the former." He leaned over and kissed her lips causing her pulse to quicken.

"Your mother was so regal. I always thought she looked more like a queen than a duchess. I don't think I will ever be able to fill her shoes."

Hawk reached over and took one of her hands and brought it to his lips. "My mother was not born a duchess. I'm sure she had her struggles as well. I have no doubt that you will be a great duchess, one that both I and the staff admire greatly."

"I appreciate your confidence. I will endeavor to do my best." She did however notice that he used the word 'admire' rather than 'love'.

As they continued their drive she listened as he talked about Hawks' Hill. Occasionally they would pass a farm and he would stop to introduce her to the tenants. The estate was just as lovely as it had been when she was a girl. It was nearly noon by the time they reached the ruins. Hawk secured the horses and came to assist her as she climbed down from the phaeton.

The ruins were little more than fallen stones and pillars covered in grass and debris from the centuries. "Catherine said it used to be an old abbey, is that true?"

Hawk came to stand behind her. "It is a rumor. Some say it was an old castle but I'm not sure if we will ever know exactly what it was. When we were children, Leicester and I would meet here. The villagers believed it was haunted and of course we were determined to discover if it was true."

She turned her head to look back at him. "And? Did you discover anything?"

He wrapped his arms about her waist. "No, only that it is freezing out here at night." He kissed the top of her head. "It is said that William the Conqueror passed through here on his conquest of England and perhaps he sought refuge here, but I have never found any record to support that rumor."

"There is a small pond beyond those trees that is fed by a natural underground spring. Catherine and I would walk down to it and dangle our feet in the water while waiting for our knight in shining armor to come find us and rescue us from the dragon that lived in the cave beyond the hill." She pointed to the location of the cave.

"I never knew there was a cave there."

She nodded. "It is covered with foliage and if you don't know where the entrance is, it would be easy to pass it up."

He turned her to face him. "Why did you or Catherine never mention it?"

Her lips twitched in amusement. "And have you or Leicester ruin all of our fun? No, we kept it our secret. Besides if your mother had ever found out Catherine was climbing about in dark caves fighting dragons, she would never let her leave the house and quite possibly would have sent her to the convent. Your Aunt Louisa would have been very disappointed in me as well, and I did not want to do anything that might cause her to send me away."

He saw sadness cross her features briefly before she smiled up at him again. "I suppose it is safe to show you where it is now. If you feel like a bit of adventure today."

"I'm always ready for adventure. Let's go back to the phaeton and drive over closer to the cave." He took her arm and helped her maneuver across the fallen stones back toward the phaeton. When they reached it, he swiftly lifted her in his arms and sat her on the seat before jumping up beside her.

They rode the short distance to the hill where Persephone had pointed out the location of the cave. Hawk once again secured the horses and helped her down from the carriage. Persephone led the way pushing through the overgrowth until she came to the hill. She moved the foliage out of the way searching for the opening. It took her several minutes but eventually she cried out, "I found it."

Hawk watched her and loved the way her eyes sparkled with joy. There were so many estate matters and business dealings he could be working on, but right now seeing her face light up with delight at being able to share a memory with him, he knew there was no place he would rather be.

"Be careful, Persephone. It doesn't look very safe." He moved to stand in front of her and looked inside the dark hole.

Persephone came to stand beside him. "It seemed much larger when we were younger."

He frowned down at her. "Yes, I'm sure it does. I'm not certain it is safe enough to explore."

But Persephone wasn't listening. She bent down and squeezed herself through the hole inside the cave. "It is really dark and it goes back pretty far."

She felt Hawk behind her. "Let me go ahead of you."

Hawk took the lead as they moved slowly through the dark. Suddenly Persephone bumped into him and squealed. "Hawk something just ran over my foot!"

"It was probably just a mouse."

She tightened her hold on his jacket as they continued further. "At least it wasn't the dragon."

She heard Hawk chuckle. They moved further inside until they both heard a rumble ahead. Hawk turned and quickly wrapped his arms around Persephone as some dirt and debris rained down on them. "That's enough of an adventure for today." He pushed her back toward the entrance.

Once they were outside the cave, he turned Persephone towards him. "Are you hurt? Some of those rocks were big enough to injure you."

Persephone was busy brushing dirt and dust from her hair and dress. "I'm fine just filthy." She glanced up and gasp when she saw the tear in his jacket. "Oh no, your jacket is torn."

He was dusting off his clothes. "Yes, it will need to be repaired."

Persephone reached up and brushed some debris from his hair. "I'm sorry. I didn't remember it being so dangerous."

"I can definitely see why you and Catherine kept it a secret because if I had known about it neither of you would have been allowed to play here." He took her arm and began leading her back to the carriage.

"See, that is why we didn't tell you. You would have ruined all of our fun," she said as they reached the phaeton.

He didn't say anything but lifted her back into her seat and then took the seat beside her. "We should start back for the house now. It appears we are both in need of a bath before we dine tonight." He gave her a wicked wink and Persephone thrilled knowing exactly what he had in mind.

For the next two weeks they seldom left the house and spent most of their time in bed. Persephone loved spending time with Hawk, but it was time she started attending to her duties as duchess. So, when Mrs. Cooper told her about one of the farmers on the estate and how his wife had been told by the physician to stay in bed until the birth of their baby, she decided that she would go visit her and take some food to help the family out. Hawk had agreed that it was a good idea, as long as she took her maid and a footman with her for protection. He had some estate matters to attend to and was expecting Leicester to arrive sometime today to discuss some horses at Tattersalls that they were contemplating purchasing.

She had Conway have the grooms hitch up the barouche for her and Sarah to ride in and the footman would follow on horseback. Mrs. Cooper had prepared a picnic basket full of food and sent several other food items as well for the family.

Hawk escorted her to the waiting carriage and kissed her cheek before handing her up. He then went over to the footmen and gave him instructions to keep her in his sight and to watch for any dangers on the way.

"We will be fine. Do not worry so much, Hawk," Persephone said as she clicked to the horses and they took off down the drive.

Hawk watched her go and debated on whether or not he should saddle a horse and go with her. He shook his head and dismissed the thought. She would not be leaving his lands and she was doing exactly as his own mother used to do when one of the tenants became sick. Besides, it was time for him to get back to the business of running his estates.

He walked back into the house and told Conway to have his steward meet him in his study as soon as possible.

Persephone loved being out in the sunshine. She had lived in the country most of her life and enjoyed being outdoors. When she arrived at the farmers cottage, she was met by three smaller children who rushed out to the carriage to greet her. The farmer followed behind them urging them to not bother her. When Persephone informed him of the reason for her visit he was overcome. With hat in hand, he led her into the cottage to where his wife was resting. Upon seeing her, the woman tried to get out of the bed embarrassed to be seen in such disarray. Persephone put the woman's fears to ease and sat with her to visit while Sarah put away the food they had brought into the kitchen. She stayed and visited with her for about two hours.

When she left, Persephone assured her that after the baby was born, she would be back to visit again. The farmer was so appreciative of the food she had brought them she could have sworn there was a tear in his eye.

When she got back into the barouche she looked over at Sarah, "I think we should bring toys for the children the next time we come."

Sarah smiled, "I'm sure they would love that, your grace."

Persephone's smile grew wider. She couldn't wait to get home so she could share her day with Hawk and clicked to the horses to increase their speed. Her heart seemed to flutter when she thought of him and she realized that she was so happy, happier than anyone had a right to be.

Hawk was still ensconced in his study with his steward when Conway came to the door. "Your grace, you have a visitor."

Hawk narrowed his eyes. "I wasn't expecting anyone other than Leicester. Who is it, Conway?"

"It is Lady Farthington, your grace."

Hawk glanced at his steward. "We will continue our business tomorrow." His steward stood and bowed deeply before retreating the room.

"Please show Lady Farthington in, Conway."

Lady Eloise Farthington was an old friend. Years ago, he had courted her briefly before her marriage to Viscount Farthington and after her marriage they had remained friends. When her husband died over a year ago, he had written to her and offered his condolences but she had been to overcome with grief to respond. Why she would appear at Hawks' Hill today was a mystery to him. He moved to stand in front of his desk as Conway escorted her through the door.

"Lady Farthington, your grace," Conway announced before backing out of the room closing the door behind him.

Hawk moved forward taking her hand and raising it to his lips. "Eloise, it is good to see you again. What brings you to Hawk's Hill?"

The lady smiled. "It is good to see you as well, Hawk. I thought you would be in London. It is the height of the season," she moved gracefully over to the settee and took a seat. "I have heard a rumor that you have married. I came to find out if it is true."

Hawk stayed where he was standing. "You came all the way to Hawk's Hill to discover if a rumor was true?"

She raised one of her eyebrows. "You should know me better than that. I was on my way to London. My mourning period is over and I thought I might join the festivities for the remainder of the season." He saw a look of sadness cross her face. "I can't stay in this state of depression forever. Clayton would not have wanted that. Besides since I was never able to produce an heir, the estate now goes to his brother Marcus."

Hawk nodded knowing full well how the succession worked. "I am sorry, Eloise."

"You didn't answer my question, are you married? Does Hawk's Hill have a new duchess?"

Hawk walked over to a decanter of brandy on the edge of his desk. He poured himself a glass the held it up to her. She shook her head and declined. "It is true. I married just over two weeks ago to Lady Persephone Carlisle."

Eloise studied his face. "Was it a forced marriage?"

"No," he stated simply as he took a drink of his brandy.

She nodded her head and smiled. "I'm happy to hear that you were not trapped by an ambitious female. I must confess that was what I feared."

Hawk chuckled. "I'm too smart for that, Eloise."

"So, tell me about your wife."

Hawk paused as he started to lift his glass back to his lips and smiled as his thoughts drifted to Persephone. "She is out visiting tenants this morning. Perhaps she will return before you leave."

Eloise got up from her seat and moved to stand before him. "How ever did she manage to get one of London's most elusive bachelors to the altar willingly?" She studied his face as he smiled once again with a faraway look. "You are in love with her, aren't you?" she said rather stunned.

Persephone climbed down from the carriage with the help of a footman. "Sarah, I'm going to go find, 'his grace' so please go ahead and take some time for yourself."

Sarah followed her up the steps to the house. "Thank you, your grace. I do have some letters to write."

Conway opened the door for them. Persephone removed her cloak and handed it to Sarah as the maid went up the stairs. She turned to the butler. "Where is the duke?"

"His grace in in his study with a guest. Shall I inform him that you have returned?"

Persephone shook her head and removed her gloves. "No, don't disturb him. I can speak with him later." She walked toward the library but paused as she neared the study and heard a definite female voice. A part of her knew it was unladylike to listen at doorways, but she couldn't help herself. With her back to the wall, she stood beside the door listening.

Hawk was stunned at Eloise's words. "In love? Don't be ridiculous, Eloise. People of our station do not marry for love. I have a great deal of respect for my wife and I care for her but love, no I don't believe so." He shook his head and took a drink of his brandy.

Eloise turned her head to the side and didn't look convinced. "I can't agree with you on that, Hawk. Clayton and I found love."

"With all due respect, Eloise, Clayton was a viscount. I am a duke with many more responsibilities. Persephone and I suit each other and that is all we need for a happy marriage."

Eloise shook her head sadly. "We have been friends for a long time, Hawk and I hope we can continue to be even after I say what I feel I must. Just because you suit each other in bed doesn't make a marriage. You will grow tired of her if that is all you have."

Hawk frowned and replied a bit sharper than he intended. "My marriage is none of your concern, Eloise."

She held up her hands in surrender. "I didn't come here to make you an enemy, I apologize. I was hoping to find you deliriously happy and in love. It is what I wished for you when I heard of your marriage. I do hope you will forgive my impertinence and know that I wish you my best." She picked up her gloves from where she had sat them on the settee. "I hope to see you and your wife in London. I also heard Catherine is out this season. Perhaps I will see her as well."

Hawk followed as she made her way to the door. "I will be happy to introduce you to Persephone once we return to London. I am glad to see you joining the living again, Eloise. Allow me to escort you to your carriage and if there is anything you need to finish your journey to London, I will have Conway make arrangements to help." Hawk opened the door and led her down the hallway.

When Persephone heard them moving toward the door, she quickly walked down the hallway and darted into the library. She quietly shut the door and leaned back against it. Her hands were shaking and she wasn't sure how much longer her legs would hold her. She shouldn't be surprised; Hawk had never professed love to her and had even stated that ton marriages were not based on love. As she looked around the library at the portraits of all the former duchesses of years passed, she wondered if at one time they all felt the way she did or if she was truly naïve. She closed her eyes as the reality started to set in, she had made a monumental mistake. She had fallen in love with her husband.

Chapter Fourteen

ersephone didn't know exactly how long she waited in the library. She had heard Hawk reenter his study after informing Conway to send Leicester directly in once he arrived. Thankfully, Conway didn't mention that she had returned from her visit and Hawk had not asked either. Once she was sure he was back in his study, she quietly left the library and headed for the front door. Only a footman was waiting there and he didn't ask any questions as she went outside.

Persephone headed straight for the stables. Upon entering, the grooms in attendance jumped to their feet.

"Saddle me a horse, please and I will ride astride, no sidesaddle. I have decided to go to the dower house."

One of the grooms came forward while another one jumped to do as she had asked. "Would you like for one of us to ride with you, your grace?"

She smiled at the older man. "Oh no, that will not be necessary. I am just going to visit Lady Catherine."

The older man looked around nervously. "If you don't mind me saying, his grace will sack all of us if we allow you to go unescorted."

Persephone had wanted to be alone, but she didn't want anyone to get into trouble over her. "Of course, you are right, please have someone join me." She saw obvious relief flash across his face as he gave orders for one of the grooms to saddle another horse.

Once the horses were brought around, the older groom helped her into the saddle and she urged the mare into a canter toward the road to the dower house with the groom close behind her. It was an hour ride to the dower house and it would be pushing it to get back before dark, but she needed to get away and a talk with Catherine might make her feel better.

They arrived at the dower house and rode straight to the stables. She left the groom with the horses and she ran up the stairs to knock on the door. The door was opened by their butler who was startled to see her.

"Is Lady Catherine at home?"

He bowed deeply, "Yes, your grace. Shall I show you to the drawing room?"

"Yes please," but before she could follow the butler, she heard Catherine's voice as she hurried down the stairs to greet her.

"Persephone?! I wasn't expecting to see you today or for the next few weeks for that matter." Then she saw the look on her friend's face. "Please excuse us, Jefferies."

"Yes, my lady," as he hurried away.

Once they were alone Catherine reached out and took both of her hands in hers. "What has happened?"

Persephone felt her bottom lip quiver and tears gathering in her eyes. Catherine grabbed her hand and together they went upstairs to the privacy of Catherine's bedroom. Once they were alone behind closed doors, Catherine wrapped her friend in a big hug as Persephone finally let her tears fall.

Her shoulders shuttered as she tried to get control of herself. When she finally felt that she had cried all there was for her to cry she wiped her eyes and took the handkerchief Catherine offered her.

Catherine urged her to take a seat on the bed. "Now, suppose you tell me what this is all about?"

Persephone hiccupped a few times. "I'm such a fool, Catherine."

"A fool? Why would you say that?"

"I knew I shouldn't but I couldn't help it," Persephone said wiping her red rimmed eyes again.

"Persephone, what are you talking about?"

Persephone took a deep breath. "I love him."

"Who?!"

"Hawk"

Catherine gave her a strange look. "Persephone, he is your husband. I don't understand. Perhaps you should start from the beginning."

Persephone told her about her day and how she had arrived home to overhear Hawk speaking to a lady in his study and how he said he did not love her. When she finished retelling the events, she sighed heavily and fell backwards on the bed throwing her arm over her eyes. "And now I have done exactly what I said I couldn't allow myself to do, I have fallen in love with a man who does not love me. How long before he decides that he would prefer his amusements in London to being with me?"

Catherine stood and walked over to the table to pour her a glass of water. "Here drink this." She handed the glass to Persephone. "Do you know who the lady was in the study with him?"

Persephone shook her head. "No, I hid in the library. I never even saw her."

Catherine came to sit back down on the bed with her. "Persephone, I know you don't believe me but I do think Hawk loves you. He just may not realize it yet. Men are rather slow when it comes to the intricacies of love."

"I don't believe he will ever love me and how am I to comport myself now? Do I pretend I do not know, live a lie? Should I try to make myself not love him so it doesn't trouble me so much? I don't think I can face him right now."

Catherine sighed. "Everything will be fine but it will be dark soon. You should head back now so you can make it home before it gets too late."

Persephone gave her a pleading look. "Can I stay here tonight? We can come up with some sort of excuse. I can send the groom back with a note saying that time had slipped away from us and since it was so late, I was just going to stay at the dower house. Leicester was supposed to arrive today so Hawk will have him to keep him occupied. He probably will be happy to have some time without me."

Catherine didn't look too convinced. "The dower house is technically yours, Persephone. You are the duchess. You don't have to ask my permission to stay here."

Persephone went to the desk and found some writing paper. "I will say you aren't feeling well and that I am going to stay to keep you company. Surely, he will not object to that. It will give me some time to compose myself."

"I still don't think this is a good idea, Persephone. Hawk does love you; I just know it. And I don't think he will be happy about you staying here rather than at Hawk's Hill."

Persephone ignored her friend and finished composing the note. She then went downstairs and had one of the footmen take the note to her groom in the stables. When finished she went back upstairs to Catherine's room and sat in the chair by the fire. "I feel so tired, Catherine."

"Are you going to talk with Hawk about this?" Catherine asked as she took the seat opposite her.

"And tell him I was eavesdropping on him while he was in his study? That makes me look crazy and I'm certain he would not be happy about that either. I just wish I had not overheard it, then I would never have known."

Catherine patted her hand. "I think everything will be alright in time, dear. Why don't you lie down and get some sleep? I will have something brought up for you to eat later if you do not wish to come down. I will come up with something to say to Aunt Louisa to let her know you are here. She has been under the weather and I'm not sure will come down for supper."

Persephone took a deep breath. "Thank you, Catherine. I am exhausted but I'm not sure I can sleep."

"Try, if nothing else, it will help clear your mind so you can think," Catherine said as she quietly closed the door behind her.

"I think we will have a winner on our hands if we can purchase the horse for a fair price. Both the sire and dam are of running blood. If we could get a win at Newmarket next year, it would boost our breeding program," Leicester said as he looked over the horse's paperwork.

Hawk smiled as he leaned back in his chair. "Yes, it certainly would. By the way, have you any news on Comte Domingo?"

Leicester took a note from his pocket. "I received this from Rockhurst yesterday before I left to come here. He says that the Comte has left London supposedly headed back to Spain. I think the announcement of your marriage to Persephone in *The Times* must have convinced him that he was too late."

Hawk read the note. "Probably but I will be happier once he is out of England."

"Yes, he is a rotten sort. It would be justice for all those women he has made to suffer over the years if his ship sank on the way back to Spain."

Hawk nodded in agreement. "Yes, well we can hope. Anyway, I do think the horse is a good investment and I trust your judgement. Let me know once you have made the purchase from Tattersalls. Persephone will enjoy Newmarket. I think I will take her with me."

Leicester sighed heavily. "And so it begins."

Hawk studied his friend's facial expression. "Whatever do you mean by that?"

"You my friend are now domesticated."

Hawk laughed. "Hardly, what a ridiculous thing to say just because I want to take my wife to see the horse races."

"That's exactly the reason. You want to take your wife. Only a man that has decided to give up on his wicked ways would take their wife with them to the races."

Hawk shook his head. "I enjoy spending time with Persephone. I look forward to sharing my life with her."

Leicester smiled. "You love her."

"You are the second person to accuse me of that emotion today. Why should everything I say make people think I have fallen in love?"

"It's not just the things you say, it's the way you look at her, the way your eyes instantly find her in a room of a hundred people. Can you imagine being without her?"

Hawk listened intently to his friend and gave his words considerable thought. He pulled out his pocket watch. "It has gotten very late. Cook will be more than a little angry if her food gets cold before we can eat it. Besides, Persephone will be waiting on us as well."

Leicester followed him as they left the study. They had just reached the dining room doors when Conway came forward carrying a note. "Excuse me, your grace but a note just arrived from the duchess."

Hawk took the note from the butler's hand. "Is she not home yet, Conway?"

"She did return from her visit to the tenants but upon arriving she had a horse saddled and went to the dower house. I was unaware until this note arrived."

Leicester watched as his friend's frown darkened. "What does it say?"

He crumbled the note up in his hand. "Have the carriage brought around for me."

The butler nodded. "As you wish, your grace."

He turned back toward Leicester. "Please go ahead and enjoy supper without me."

"Has something happened, Hawk?"

He walked over to get his greatcoat. "My wife has apparently just sent me word that she will be staying over at the dower house with my sister and aunt tonight."

Leicester shrugged his shoulders. "What the hell is wrong with that?"

Hawk stared at him. "I want her here with me, that's what is wrong with it. I am going to collect her."

"I would offer to go with you but I am not in the mood to fend off your sister tonight and to be honest, I am too hungry to disappoint your cook."

Hawk nodded and made his way to the front door while Leicester turned toward the dining room mumbling to himself. "And he thinks he isn't in love."

By the time Hawk reached the dower house he had worked himself into a foul mood. Instead of enjoying a superb supper with his wife and best friend, he was out on a cold night to retrieve Persephone. He didn't bother knocking as he barged into the front entranceway. Servants jumped to their feet, some to scurry away from him.

"Where is the duchess?" he stated louder than he intended.

Catherine came out of the dining room. "My goodness, Hawk. There is no need to shout."

He moved toward his sister. "You don't look as if you are feeling unwell, Catherine. So, tell me, why has my wife decided to spend the evening here instead of with me?"

"Perhaps you should ask her," Catherine said crossing her arms over her chest.

"I plan on doing just that as soon as you tell me where she is." He looked to the stairway and saw his Aunt Louisa coming down to join them.

"Ethan, what on earth are you doing here this time of night?" Her hand quickly went to her throat and her face paled. "Oh my, is something wrong with Persephone?"

He closed his eyes briefly and blew out a steading breath. "I'm trying to find that out right now." He turned back toward his sister. "Tell me where she is, Catherine."

Aunt Louisa rushed forward. "Has Persephone gone missing?"

Catherine took her aunt's hand. "No, she is upstairs resting."

Her aunt looked confused. "Persephone is here?"

"You didn't know?" Hawk asked spearing his sister with an intense frown.

Louisa shook her head. "No, I had no idea. I've been upstairs resting today. I have been ill." She looked at Catherine. "What is going on?"

"I'll tell you later, Aunt Louisa. After Hawk has left." She met her brother's frown with one of her own.

"I'm not leaving without her."

"I didn't think you would. She is in my room. It's the second door on the right after you reach the top of the stairs. But I would not go in there like a raging bull if I were you."

"I do not need advice from you, Catherine." He took the stairs two at a time and didn't bother knocking when he reached his sister's room. He opened the door expecting to demand an explanation from Persephone about what was going on but she was asleep. He closed the door and walked over to the bed where she was laying. Her hands were resting under her head. Her eyes were swollen and red rimmed, she had been crying. His anger swiftly faded replaced with concern. He moved her hair away from her face and quietly whispered her name. She stirred slightly and her eyes fluttered open. At first, he saw surprise in them but that changed quickly to resignation. She sat up slowly.

"I sent you a note."

He sat beside her on the bed. "I know, I got the note."

"Then why are you here?" she asked curiously.

He took her hand in his and moved closer to her. "Because you are my wife, Persephone and I want you home with me. I came in the carriage."

"I'm sorry, I didn't mean for you to come all the way here." She stood from the bed and started to walk to the door but he grabbed her hand to stop her.

"Persephone, what has happened? You have been crying," he said causing her to turn back toward him.

She gave him a weak smile. "I have had an exhausting day and I don't want to disturb Aunt Louisa; she has been under the weather. So can we just go home. I really didn't think you would come out tonight after I sent a note. Leicester is still there, isn't he?"

He stood from the bed and walked closer to her still looking at her curiously. "Yes, he is still there. I left him and told him to go ahead and eat without us. He is staying a few days before heading to London."

Sadness crossed her face again. "Oh dear, I made another lapse in judgement. I am sorry, I should have returned home."

"Why did you not tell me you were coming to the dower house, you could have taken the carriage," he said as he placed his hands on her shoulders.

"It was a spontaneous decision. I am sorry to have caused so much trouble." She turned back toward the door. There was little to no emotion in her voice. "We should go. If my guess is right, you haven't had any supper and I'm sure you are hungry."

Hawk wanted to rage and tell her he didn't give a damn about supper or anything else for that matter, he was only concerned with what had happened to make her behave in such a way. But there would be time for that later. He certainly didn't want to have this conversation here. He would wait till they got in the carriage or were home first. He took her arm and escorted her down the stairs.

Aunt Louisa came forward to give her a hug. "Persephone, why did you not tell me you were here?"

She smiled. "You were asleep and I didn't want to disturb you. I'm sorry." She then turned to Catherine. "Catherine, thank you."

Catherine returned her hug. "Anytime, my dear. I will come over day after tomorrow and we can take a nice long ride. It will do you good."

Persephone nodded. "I would like that very much."

Hawk gave his sister one last look of disapproval before saying, "Ladies, enjoy the rest of your evening." He wrapped Persephone's cloak around her shoulders and escorted her out to the waiting carriage.

Once inside the carriage he could hold his tongue no longer. It was killing him, not knowing what had happened. "Now that we are alone, tell me. When last I saw you this morning you were happy and excited about visiting the farmer and his wife. Did something happen on your visit to upset you. Is it something I need to deal with?"

Persephone pulled the cloak tighter around her to avoid the chill. "Oh no, the visit to the farmer was wonderful. They were so appreciative of the food we brought them. I visited for over an hour with his wife and promised to come back once the baby is born. I also would like to bring the children some toys, if you have no objection to that."

"Of course not. Take them whatever you like. So, if it wasn't the visit, what was it to make you so melancholy."

He sat across from her and stared into her eyes willing her to tell him. Persephone knew she would have to eventually and she might as well get it over with. "When I came home this afternoon, I overheard your conversation with the lady visiting you."

Now things were starting to make sense. She had overheard Eloise and must be jealous. "Persephone, Lady Farthington is an old friend. She stopped by to offer her congratulations on our marriage before continuing on to London. There is nothing for you to be worried about, darling."

Persephone squinted her eyes in confusion. "I wasn't worried about that, Hawk. It was the part of the conversation I overheard that upset me."

Hawk still didn't understand. "Enlighten me. What was said that has you so upset?"

Persephone took a deep steady breath and faced him. "I heard you tell her that you didn't love me." She saw understanding dawn on his face and held up her hand to silence him. "I know that when you first mentioned marriage that you told me love was a ridiculous emotion. That ton marriages were based on respect and very few were based on love. So please do not think I am angry with you. I knew exactly how you felt about it when I agreed to become your wife."

Hawk didn't exactly know what to say. "Persephone, I, . . ."

She held up her hand again. "No, please you do not have to explain anything. As I said I am not upset with you. I am angry with myself."

"Why are you angry with yourself?"

Persephone knew she must be completely empty of tears because she was able to answer in a clear strong voice that barely shook and no tears gathered in her eyes. "Because I foolishly allowed myself to fall in love with you."

Hawk was stunned into silence. He didn't know what to say. The silence stretched between them. Every creak of the carriage, every bump in the road, or noises made by the horses seemed to be magnified in the silence. He sat across from her watching her. She did not cry or offer any further explanation for her words. They continued the journey in silence.

When they got back to Hawk's Hill a footman rushed to open the carriage door. Hawk stepped down and then offered her his hand to assist her.

"Thank you," she said simply as they walked up the stone steps together.

Leicester was standing in the entryway. "Ah, we have recovered our missing duchess."

Persephone gave him a timid smile and went over to him. "My apologies, your grace for not being here to greet you. You must think me lacking in hospitality."

He raised her hand to his lips. "Nonsense, but I must confess supper would have been more delightful if I had someone as lovely as you to dine with."

"Tomorrow night you shall have my undivided attention." She turned back to Hawk. "I hope cook saved something for you. I believe I will skip eating tonight and go to bed early."

Both Hawk and Leicester bowed deeply as she turned to head up the stairs to her rooms.

"You want to tell me what the hell is going on?" Leicester asked once she was out of hearing.

"Let's go into my study. I don't want anyone to hear," Hawk said as he led the way to his study closing the door behind them.

"I had a visitor today, Eloise Farthington."

Leicester took a seat. "Is she out of mourning, then?"

"Yes, and she stopped by here on her way to London. She wanted to congratulate me on my marriage. Well, that isn't entirely true, she wanted to see if it was true. She thought it might be a rumor and was also afraid I had been trapped by an ambitious young lady."

"And Persephone was angry about that or was there something more between you and Eloise?" he asked narrowing his eyes at his friend.

Hawk gave his friend a fierce look. "Nothing happened between Eloise and myself. I would not be unfaithful to my vows regardless of my past deeds and reputation. No, Persephone unfortunately heard a part of a conversation."

"What did you say?" Leicester asked cautiously.

"Eloise stated that I was in love and I denied it, emphatically I might add," he said raking a hand through his thick black hair. "Persephone heard it and it upset her."

"You are a fool," Leicester said simply.

"You know men have been called out and shot for saying less," Hawk stated as he slumped down into his chair.

"She is angry, perhaps some new jewelry will make her forgive you." Leicester offered helpfully.

"That's the problem, she isn't mad at me. If jewelry would fix it, I would buy her the most expensive necklace on Bond Street. She is mad at herself."

Leicester snorted. "Mad at herself, why on earth is she mad at herself?"

Hawk closed his eyes before lowering his head to his hands. "Because she allowed herself to fall in love with me."

Leicester sat still for a moment. "She is mad because she loves you, women make no sense at all."

"She is angry at herself for loving me when she knows I don't love her. It stems from her damned father and his treatment of her mother. This was the reason she was reluctant to marry me because I told her love was ridiculous."

"It seems to me that the solution is rather simple, just go tell her you love her."

Hawk shook his head. "She will know it for a lie, I can't do that."

"But is it a lie? Rockhurst and I have been saying you love her from the moment you laid eyes on her. Don't be a fool, Hawk. You have a chance to have what most people long for, an extremely beautiful wife who loves you and is devoted to you."

"You know I never heard my father tell my mother he loved her. He respected her and cared for her I am sure of that, but love was never mentioned."

"Hawk your parents were happy," Leicester said hoping to ease his friend's mind.

"They were content and that is what I always saw my marriage as being a state of contentment. Love complicates matters."

"Well, I suggest you figure it out soon. Persephone may love you now but love can die just as quickly as it blooms." Leicester stood from his chair. "I will leave you with that and head off to bed. I will see you and Persephone at breakfast. If you are in a mood to, we could sharpen our pugilist skills tomorrow. It has been some time since either of us have been to Jackson's and I could use some exercise."

Hawk nodded but didn't respond. All he could think about was Persephone. He couldn't stand seeing her unhappy. He sat in his study alone thinking for another two hours before heading up to his room. He was surprised to see Persephone asleep in his bed. He had half expected her to try and sleep away from him in the duchess' chambers. Of course, after retrieving her from the dower house in the middle of the night, she probably saw the futility of trying to sleep away from him. He removed his clothes and slid under the covers. She didn't move as he wrapped his arm around her pulling her into his side. He just wanted to hold her tonight. Tomorrow he would know what to do, but tonight he needed sleep. He pressed his nose into her hair loving the way she smelled of lavender and how her warm body molded perfectly to his. He lay awake for a while but eventually sleep did come.

Chapter Fifteen

Hawk stretched his arms out only to find the opposite side of the bed cold and empty. He opened his eyes adjusting to the light coming through the draperies.

He sat up in the bed and looked around at the empty room. "Persephone?" When he got no answer, he jumped out of bed and hastily dressed.

He hurriedly went down the stairs and heard laughter coming from the dining room. He entered the room to find Leicester and Persephone having breakfast together. She was smiling brightly at something he was telling her and he felt an instant stab of jealousy that he had caused her such sadness yesterday while Leicester had been the one to put a bright smile on her face.

When she turned and saw him standing in the doorway, her smile faded a bit. "Good morning, Hawk. Michael was just telling me stories from when the two of you were at Eton."

Leicester stared at him in astonishment. "Did you sack your valet?"

Hawk turned his gaze from Persephone to his friend. "No."

Leicester smirked and sipped his tea. "Your appearance suggests otherwise."

Hawk looked down to see his clothes in disarray. "I woke up alone."

Persephone looked down at her plate avoiding his eyes. "Breakfast is very good this morning."

Hawk nodded, "If you will both excuse me, I will go make myself more presentable and join you momentarily." He went back upstairs to properly dress. He wanted to talk to Persephone. After breakfast he would find some time to spend with her. Things needed to be settled. There seemed to be a distance growing between them and he didn't like it. When he came back downstairs, he found that they had another uninvited guest this morning. His sister was sitting at the table beside Persephone.

"Catherine, we were not expecting you this morning," he said as he moved to the head of the table.

She gave her brother an innocent smile before turning back toward Michael batting her eyelashes flirtatiously. "Last night when you said Leicester was visiting, I thought I might ride over to be polite and of course to check on Persephone. I was hoping he would like to join me for a ride around the estate. It has been a long time since I beat him in a horse race."

Leicester rolled his eyes. "You were twelve and I was much older. How ungentlemanly it would have been if I had trounced you?"

Catherine smiled and lowered her lashes demurely. "So, you let me win. That is so gallant."

Hawk cleared his throat loudly and gave his sister a disapproving look. "That's enough, Catherine."

Catherine shrugged her shoulders defiantly. "It is just as well; Persephone is going to ride with me to the village and help me pick out some material for a new dress. Aunt Louisa wants to go to Bath when all the ton leaves London at the end of the season and I just have to have something new."

"Will you be needing the carriage?" he asked looking at Persephone.

"No, that will not be necessary. I enjoy riding and it looks like it will be a nice day. We shouldn't be gone long," Persephone said as she took her napkin and delicately wiped the corners of her lips. "I'll go change into my riding habit. I will be right back, Catherine."

"No need to hurry. Michael will keep me company till you get back." Catherine said dreamily looking across the table at Leicester.

Hawk stood from his seat and followed Persephone from the room. Once they were out of hearing he caught up with her. "I would like to speak with you before you leave with Catherine."

Persephone allowed him to take her arm and lead her into his study. Once inside he turned her to face him. "I wanted to talk about last night, Persephone."

She shook her head. "There really is no need, I am fine. I know that just because there will not be love between us doesn't necessarily mean we will be unhappy. Respect can be enough. We do get along rather well together."

Hawk leaned down and pressed his lips against hers. She returned his kiss but it was not as warm as it had once been. He raised his lips and studied her face. "We will take a wedding trip. Where would you like to go? We can go wherever you like."

She gave him a small smile. "That would be nice. I'll give it some thought." She moved out of his grasp and walked out the room leaving him still feeling like everything was wrong. He had never felt this way over a woman before. But this one was driving him mad.

Persephone hurriedly changed into her riding habit to join Catherine. She needed this ride to get out of the house that seemed to be closing in around her. The fact was she didn't know if respect would be enough and that she was in love with a man who would never love her made her ache deep inside. So, an afternoon with Catherine, even if it meant listening to her constant chatter of her feelings for Leicester, would be a most needed distraction.

Catherine was waiting for her by the front door when she came downstairs causing Persephone to ask, "Did Leicester manage to escape your clutches?"

Catherine laughed softly. "Hawk rescued him. He said if they were going to get practice in for Jackson's they needed to get it in early."

"Jackson's? The boxing club in London?" Persephone asked as they made their way outside to their waiting horses.

"Yes, they are members and used to go quite frequently for the exercise. Leicester is quite the pugilist I hear although of the three they say Lord Rockhurst has never been beaten."

They were assisted onto their horses with the groom Catherine had brought with her from the dower house following close behind them for protection. They rode for about twenty minutes in silence before Catherine could hold it in no longer.

"I was worried about you last night. Was Hawk very angry?"

Persephone sighed heavily knowing she could not avoid Catherine's questions. "He was very worried but not angry."

"Did you tell him what happened?"

"Yes, I told him."

Catherine maneuvered her horse closer. "What did he say?"

Persephone didn't look over at her but stared straight ahead. "I told him that I was not angry at him or upset that he was with the lady in question. I was angry at myself for falling in love with him."

"Oh my goodness, and how did he take that?"

"I think he was rather shocked. He didn't say much and I was so exhausted I went to bed early. It seems as if he doesn't know what to say. He did suggest we would take a wedding trip soon."

Catherine shook her head. "He is an idiot. I am beginning to think all men are foolish. He loves you Persephone, and he will come to realize it soon."

"Even if he doesn't, I will be alright. Truly, I will." She gave her friend a smile. "So, you are going to Bath?"

"Yes, but it will be different without you there. Aunt Louisa isn't as lenient with me when you aren't around. I think she knew you kept me in line."

Persephone smiled. "Please take care, Catherine."

"Don't I always. Now let's have some fun. I'll race you to the tree line." Catherine took off and Persephone laughed as she kicked her horse into a gallop to chase after her friend.

Catherine easily beat her but Persephone knew she never had a chance. Catherine had always been an expert rider. "You win again. Now we have to wait for your poor groom to catch up."

Catherine laughed. "Yes, we had better walk the rest of the way. Sam doesn't like it when I race the horses. When I was a little girl, he would threaten to tell my father."

The groom finally caught up to them. "I would ask you to please not do that again, my lady."

"I promise, Sam no more racing today. We will canter or walk the rest of the way to the village," Catherine said turning her horse back toward Persephone.

Suddenly there was a loud report that startled the horses. Persephone struggled to keep her horse under control as it spun around nearly unseating her.

Catherine screamed and jumped down from her horse when she saw her groom lying face first on the ground. His horse running down the hill.

"Sam!" Catherine knelt beside him and turned him over. Blood oozed from his left shoulder. "Persephone, he has been shot!"

Persephone jumped down from her horse and went over. "Is he dead?!"

Catherine leaned over and listened for a heartbeat. "No, he still has a heartbeat. But he is bleeding badly. You have to go back to the house for help."

Persephone nodded her head and went to climb back on her horse when a voice stopped her. "I don't think you will be going anywhere, duchess."

Both Persephone and Catherine jerked their heads around to see Comte Domingo and another man they didn't know on horseback emerging from the tree line.

Catherine got to her feet quickly and went to stand beside Persephone. "Did you do this?"

The Comte jumped down from his horse and moved to stand before them. "Ah, Lady Gray. I see you haven't lost that sharp tongue of yours. My associate is quite a good shot is he not?"

Persephone watched him warily as he moved closer to them taking a step backwards. "Why are you here?"

He narrowed his eyes. "I came for you, my dear."

Catherine moved to stand in front of Persephone. "This is my brother's land. You have no right to be here."

She was not prepared for the hard slap across her face and stumbled backwards. Persephone shrieked and moved to catch her but the Comte grabbed her by her hair and yanked her to him.

"Not so fast, duchess." He leaned closer to her face and Persephone closed her eyes as his lips pressed against her cheek. "I have been waiting for a moment to catch you away from your husband. He took what should have been mine and now I'm going to reclaim it."

He grabbed her arm and pulled her to her horse. "Get on your horse. You are going with me, duchess."

Catherine jumped to her feet wiping blood from her lip. "She isn't going anywhere with you." She launched herself into the Comte. He threw Persephone to the ground and hit Catherine again hard enough to leave her stunned. Persephone screamed as he pulled a pistol from his jacket and pointed it at Catherine.

"You either go with me, duchess or Lady Gray takes a bullet right now."

"No! Please! I'll go with you. Just please don't hurt her," Persephone cried.

He lowered his pistol and turned back toward her. "That's more like it. I'm glad you are being reasonable." He looked at the other man and pointed at Catherine as she lay on the ground. "Make yourself useful and tie her up. I don't want her found anytime soon."

The man got down from his horse and roughly grabbed Catherine by the arm. She fought him as he dragged her into the trees. Persephone heard her scream again and then silence. She looked at the Comte. "I thought you wouldn't hurt her."

He gripped her arms tightly and roughly gripped her chin in his hands. "She will live." He kissed her roughly squeezing her check to force her mouth open as he shoved his tongue inside.

Persephone felt nausea rising as he plundered her mouth. She pushed against him and he released her laughing cruelly. "We are going to have so much fun, duchess. Now get on your horse."

"What about the groom? He needs a surgeon," Persephone asked as she mounted her horse.

The Comte's man came out of the tree line and she feared for Catherine. "I tied her up so she can't get free and gaged her so she can't cry out for help. It will take them a long time to find her by then we will be long gone from here."

"Excellent. Drag the groom into the trees and hide his body. He still lives but he is in no condition to cry out," the Comte said as he mounted his horse taking Persephone's reins from her.

They waited as the man dragged Sam into the trees and covered the blood on the ground with sand and dirt. Once that was done, they started off heading north away from Hawk's Hill and the village. Persephone's mind started reeling wondering where they could be heading then she thought they were only a day and a half ride from the coast. Surely, he wasn't planning on taking her away from England. Tears rolled down her cheeks as she contemplated her fate and that of Catherine. She didn't know what the man had done to her when he dragged her into the woods but she was afraid for her.

"We will keep to the trails through the woods away from main roads as much as we can. We don't want anyone to see us with her. If we are caught, we will hang," the man said a little nervously to the Comte.

"No one will ever find us to hang us. Stick to the plan and you will be paid handsomely," the Comte replied glancing over at Persephone as he reached over placing a hand on her knee. "Soon, my love you will know the full extent of my desire for you."

Persephone closed her eyes and tried to stop her body from trembling. "My husband will find me and he will kill you for this." He reached across and slapped her. Persephone's head jerked back and she tasted the coppery taste of blood on her lips. But she would not give him the satisfaction of crying and pleading with him. She faced straight ahead taking in her surroundings in case she was able to make an escape, but as they continued riding farther and farther away from Hawk's Hill her hope started to fade.

"Have you had enough, Leicester?" Hawk asked as he landed another punch to his friend's abdomen.

Leicester grimaced but managed to land a hard left to Hawk's cheek. "No, have you?"

They had taken care of some estate business after breakfast and it was almost noon before they had found time for some boxing. "The ladies should be back soon and we both need to freshen up," Hawk said grabbing a towel and tossing it to his friend.

They both turned suddenly when Conway burst into the room. "My apologies, your grace, but I think something might have happened to Lady Catherine and the duchess."

Hawk rushed forward. "What is it, Conway?"

"A horse rode in without a rider just now. It was the one the groom was riding. He went with her grace and Lady Catherine," Conway said nervously.

Leicester came to stand beside him. "He was probably unseated, Conway. Lady Catherine is reckless on a horse and he probably couldn't keep up with them."

Conway twisted his hands in front of him. "Yes, your grace, but there was quite a lot of blood on the saddle."

Hawk felt his heart drop into his stomach. "Have two horses saddled for me and Leicester as well as four guards to ride along with us."

Conway nodded. "I will see to it right away, your grace."

Leicester followed Hawk as he threw his shirt over his head and walked quickly to his study. He took two pistols out of a case handing one to Leicester. "Here we might need these."

Leicester took the pistol from him as they both put on their coats and went outside to the stables. "We will find them, Hawk. Hopefully it is nothing serious."

Hawk didn't feel as if it was nothing. Something wasn't right.

Catherine's eyes fluttered open. Her head throbbed where the man had struck her. She must have lost consciousness. It would be dark soon, and she had to get loose so she could find Persephone and get help for Sam. She worked the bindings on her hands rubbing them against the tree hoping to cut the rope. She cringed as the splinters of the wood dug deep into her wrists. She continued until she felt blood running down her hands. It was no use. She couldn't free herself that way. She decided to try to loosen the gag over her mouth. She worked it to where it became loose enough for her to let out a muffled scream.

"There is no sign of them, Hawk. We should split up to cover more ground," Leicester said as he scanned the horizon.

"I'm not going back till I find them." He looked at the four men that rode with them. "Two of you head east and two of you head west toward the dower house. Leicester and I will continue on this track." He turned his horse toward Leicester. They had already ridden into the village and their concern grew when they discovered that the ladies had never made it to the dressmakers. "I know we checked the village, but I feel like we must find some clues along the road. I want us to check again."

Leicester nodded and they headed down the road looking for any signs that they might have headed in that direction.

Suddenly Hawk pulled his horse to a stop. "Did you hear something?"

"No," he looked toward the tree line. "Wait, I do hear something." Leicester pointed to the trees along the side of the road ahead. "It's coming from the trees."

Hawk urged his horse in that direction and stopped again to listen when they got closer. "I don't hear anything. Maybe my mind is playing tricks on me." Then they heard it again.

"No, that's no trick." Leicester said rushing forward then jumping to the ground. He moved forward then yelled, "Hawk!"

Hawk had already gotten down from his horse and was rushing toward him when Leicester called his name. They both rushed through the trees nearly tripping on the body of the groom. "Bloody hell, he's been shot."

Leicester was leaning over the body of the groom. "He still lives but his pulse is weak and his breathing is shallow." He stood up as he heard the muffled sound again. "Over there behind those trees." They both hurried over and stopped suddenly at the sight of Catherine tied to a tree. Her face was bruised and her lips bloodied.

Hawk raced forward removing the gag from her mouth. "My God, Catherine. Who did this to you and where is Persephone?"

Leicester went behind her and began loosening the bindings around her wrists cringing as he noticed the blood and raw flesh where she had tried to free herself.

Once her hands were free, she threw her arms around her brother and sobbed. "It was Comte Domingo. He and another man ambushed us on the way to the village. They shot Sam and took Persephone!"

Hawk took her by the shoulders and held her away from him. "Where did they take her? How long have they been gone? Which direction did they go?"

Catherine shook her head and cried harder. "I don't know! When he said he was going to take her, I tried to fight him but he pulled a pistol and threatened to shoot me. Persephone said she would go with him if he would not hurt me. His hired man dragged me here and clobbered me over the head. When I woke up, I was tied to the tree and they were gone." Hot tears ran down her cheeks stinging her busted lips.

Hawk stood up. "You need to get Catherine back to Hawk's Hill. Send for a physician and get help for the groom. His injury is grave and his recovery will be in the hands of God. I'm going after that bastard and getting my wife back."

Catherine had gotten to her feet by that time. "Hawk you have to hurry. He is going to hurt her. I'm afraid he means to. . ." She couldn't finish the statement but from the look in her brother's eyes he knew what she was trying to say.

Leicester grabbed his arm. "I will take Catherine home and then come back to help you search. Be careful, Hawk. They have already nearly killed one man. They will not hesitate to put a bullet through you."

Hawk's eyes burned with fury. "He will not get a chance. I'm going to kill him."

Leicester put an arm around Catherine and helped her walk to the horse as Hawk rode away. Before helping her mount, he took her face in his hands and turned it to examine the bruises on her face then took each of her hands and looked over the bloody scratches from the rope and the tree. There was dried blood in her hair from where she had been struck.

"Domingo did this to you?" he asked as he gently rubbed his thumb over her bleeding lip.

Catherine nodded. "He and the man that was with him."

"I may have to kill him myself," he said as he lightly touched her cheek.

"Oh Michael, I am so afraid for Persephone."

He wrapped his arms around her. "It will be alright. Hawk will find her and when he does no one will have to worry about the Comte again." He lifted her into the saddle then mounted behind her. She leaned back and rested against his chest as he turned his horse back in the direction of Hawk's Hill.

"I hope he finds them quickly. I don't know how much of the Comte's abuse Persephone can withstand," Catherine said wiping more tears from her face.

Leicester wrapped an arm around her waist to hold her steady and give her comfort. He wanted to tell her not to worry but the truth was, he was afraid for Persephone as well. He hoped Hawk found her quickly.

Chapter Sixteen

Persephone shivered but she didn't know if it was from fear or from the cold. She was beginning to lose hope that Hawk would find her as she looked around at her surroundings wondering if there was any way she could get away. She glanced over at the other man riding beside her. The Comte had never called him by name, but he kept staring at her. They would be getting closer to the coast but she didn't know how long it would take to get there. A gust of wind picked up and she felt the chill to her bones.

"Getting cold, duchess?" the Comte asked as he reached over and gripped her arm cruelly. "I will warm you up soon enough."

Persephone jerked her arm out of his grasp. "Why are you doing this?"

"Why? Because when I first saw you, I knew I had to have you. I tried to be a gentleman but my dances were refused. I sent gifts and letters only to have them returned unopened. Every time I tried to see you, Hawksford prevented it, all because he wanted you for himself. He took what should have been mine!" He became angrier by the second and Persephone saw him flex his hands into fists. "I will make you pay for his disrespect."

Persephone looked away from the evil she saw in his eyes.

"I need to go into the next village and get more provisions. We can find a place to hide her and you stay and keep an eye on her. But don't touch her! She is mine! I will come back for you under the cover of darkness," the Comte said to his companion.

"Why should I take the risk of being caught with her? If we are discovered, I will hang for this. You aren't paying me enough money to risk my neck," the man said as he dismounted his horse.

The Comte narrowed his eyes. "You will do as I tell you or I will kill you now." He pulled a pistol out of his jacket and pointed it at the man.

His companion held up his hands and relented. "I'll stay with her. You can put that away."

The Comte smiled and moved back to where Persephone sat on her horse. "I will help make it easier for you. When I am done with her, she will not be able to give you any problems."

They maneuvered the horses into a deeply forested area away from the roads. When they reached a clearing. The Comte moved over and roughly pulled Persephone from her horse. The other man dismounted and came around to take the reins of both her horse and the Comte's. He tossed some rope on the ground at her feet. "Just tie her up and get going. The sooner I get my money and I am rid of the two of you the better."

The Comte grabbed her hair and pulled her further into the woods. He pushed her against a tree and kissed her letting his hands roughly squeeze her breast through the fabric of her riding habit.

Persephone pushed against him but he wouldn't budge. She felt his hand ripping at her bodice so she kicked him as hard as she could in his shin. Then pushed hard again catching him off guard, he stumbled backwards and fell to the ground. Persephone took advantage of the moment and ran as fast as she could. But she didn't get far before he caught her from behind knocking her to the ground.

"You will pay for that, duchess." He stood up and kicked her hard in the side twice before dragging her by her hair over to a tree. He wrapped his hands around her throat and squeezed. Persephone clawed at his hands as she gasped for air. When he finally released her, she collapsed on the ground at his feet. He kicked her again causing her to cough and sputter as she wrapped an arm around her waist.

He knelt beside her. "That will teach you a lesson, duchess. Fight me again and you will receive the same."

Persephone curled into a ball to protectively shield herself and mumbled. "I will never submit to you even if you kill me."

He laughed cruelly as he moved a hand up her skirts, "You will submit or that is exactly what I will do."

Persephone kicked at him again and tried to crawl away as his hands passed her knees and moved up her thighs. He grabbed her ankles and pulled her back to him. He pulled her arms behind her and bound them tightly before binding her feet. Once he had her bound, he back handed her across the face. "Perhaps when I return you will have decided that it would be in your best interest to be more receptive to my advances."

Persephone turned her face away from him but she heard his deep sadistic laughter as he moved away to join his companion. "She won't give you any trouble now. Keep your eyes open and remember what I said. If you touch her, I will kill you. She will be mine and mine only."

She heard his horse ride away and felt rain start to fall. Her body hurt everywhere and she was having trouble breathing. Her ribs had to be broken.

The man that had been told to guard her came closer. She flinched as he pulled her hair to make her look at him. "I haven't ever had a woman like you before, but even your sweet cuny isn't worth dying for. The Comte is crazed and I have a feeling he has no intention of letting me see any of the coin I have been promised." He let go of her hair roughly letting her head hit the ground. "I'm not staying here and waiting for the duke to find us. He has probably sent for Bow Street Runners by now. Good luck to you, duchess. I'm leaving."

She tried to roll onto her side but every movement was excruciatingly painful. "Please untie me," she managed to get out in a whisper.

He walked back to her and took out a knife. "I'll cut you free, but you won't get far. I'm taking your horse. I have to get something for my trouble." He cut her feet and hands free then mounted his horse and grabbed the reins of her mount leaving her alone.

Persephone tried to stand but fell to her knees as a wave of pain shot through her chest. She began to shiver uncontrollably as the rain seeped through her clothing. Hopefully the rain and cold as well as her injuries she had sustained would take her life before the Comte returned. She closed her eyes and thought of Hawk and how she would never see him again. The thought hurt her worse than any injury the Comte could subject her to. She loved him so and even if he never loved her, it would have been enough just to be with him for the rest of her life. Now she would never get that chance. Fresh tears ran down her face mingling with the rain drops as they continued to fall. She forced herself to stand and took a few more steps before collapsing again. She felt her head growing fuzzy and everything was getting dark. Her fingers dug into the cold damp ground and she tried to drag herself. But it was no use. She closed her eyes as the darkness overcame her.

With every minute that passed, Hawk's anger and fear grew. He knew what the Comte was capable of, Rockhurst had shared with him the sordid details of his investigations. The thought of his Persephone being used in such a perverse way made him sick. It was beginning to get dark and the temperature was dropping fast. Panic was starting to set in. He couldn't stand the thought of Persephone spending the night in the clutches of that degenerate. He would not stop looking for her and when he found him, he would take pleasure in killing him.

He turned when he heard horses riding up behind him. He pulled his horse to a stop seeing it was Leicester and Rockhurst had joined him. When they reached him, he asked, "How is Catherine?"

Leicester shifted in his saddle. "She is resting at Hawk's Hill. I sent for a physician and had someone go to the dower house to collect your aunt. She is so worried over Persephone that I'm sure the doctor will give her some laudanum to relax her. I sent some men to get the groom. I am not sure of his health as I left to join you before they returned."

Hawk looked at Rockhurst. "I don't know how you came to be here but I am grateful. Let's not waste any time talking. I think we should ride into the village again."

Rockhurst nodded as he fell in beside him. "I had no idea anything had happened. I decided to come up from London for a few days. I was waiting for the two of you at Hawk's Hill when Leicester came back with Catherine. He filled me in. I'm sorry, Hawk."

Hawk nodded trying not to focus on what could be happening to his wife. "I want to go back to the village and start questioning people. There has to be someone who has seen something."

Leicester and Rockhurst shared concerned looks as they followed their friend back toward the village. They both knew that the longer it took to find her and the longer she was in the mad man's clutches the outcome was bleaker by the minute. But they knew Hawk would not give up until they found her and when they did, they would send the Comte to hell where he belonged.

Persephone slowly opened her eyes when she felt a sharp pain in her back. She blinked rapidly trying to get her eyes to focus. When her vision finally cleared, she saw a young boy of about twelve maybe thirteen years of age standing over her poking her with a stick.

"I thought you were dead, miss." He bent down. "You need help."

Persephone tried to stand but couldn't. The boy took her arm and helped her to her feet. Persephone winced with the pain in her ribs. Her body ached all over and she was so cold.

She sucked breath in when she took a step. "I need to get away from here but I don't think I can travel very far. A very bad man did this to me and I have to get away before he comes back.

"I can take you back to my farm. My mother and father will know how to help you," the boy said as he helped her take a few more steps.

Persephone almost collapsed again. "No, he is a very bad man. If he found me, he would hurt your family. Is there somewhere close where you can hide me and then perhaps go to my husband. He will be looking for me." She closed her eyes. Every step she took hurt and she was so cold her teeth were chattering.

The boy looked over his shoulder. "There is an old, abandoned hunting lodge not far from here. I can take you there and then go get some help. But you need a doctor, miss."

Persephone didn't argue with him. "The lodge will be fine. I don't know how much time I have before he returns so we must hurry."

The boy continued to support her as she struggled to drag herself through the forest. She wasn't sure she had the strength to make it all the way to the lodge but she had to try.

They had to stop a few times to let her catch her breath but eventually they made it to the lodge. It was dark and dusty. There was no furniture or anything for her to lay on but at least she was out of the rain. The boy led her further in the room and helped her lay on the floor.

"I can't lite a fire, it might draw the attention of the man looking for you," he said as he looked around the room for something that might be used to keep her warm, unfortunately there wasn't anything.

"It's alright. What's your name?"

"It's Thomas."

Persephone tried to give him a smile. "Thank you, Thomas. My name is Lady Persephone Gray, my husband is the Duke of Hawksford. Please try to get word to him. I know he is looking for me."

Thomas immediately ripped his hat off his head. "A duchess?" He looked panicked. "I will, your grace. I will go get help."

Persephone closed her eyes; her breath came out as a vapor in the cold air and darkness overcame her again.

Hawk felt a renewed sense of hope. When they returned to the village, they did find a farmer that had seen two men traveling with a woman heading toward the coast. They were not traveling the main roads and the farmer just happened to see them by chance. At least Hawk knew what direction they were traveling in. The weather had taken a turn for the worse not only had it gotten colder but rain had set in. They had changed horses in the village and headed out in the direction pointed out by the farmer. Leicester had directed the footmen and grooms at Hawks Hill to spread out and search the surrounding areas as well. The more people they had searching the better the odds of finding her.

With each passing minute his worry grew. He had hoped to find Persephone before the night was over. They had ridden through the night and dawn was beginning to break when he saw a horse tied to some trees off the road.

He pointed towards it. "Look over there. I don't see anyone but it might be worth investigating."

Leicester nodded and turned his horse toward the tree line with Rockhurst right behind him.

When they got closer, Rockhurst pulled his pistol. "Something doesn't feel right, Hawk. Keep your eyes open."

Hawk pulled his pistol as he dismounted his horse. "Leicester be careful."

Leicester had moved around so he could come up behind whoever was in the trees. He disappeared into the trees and undergrowth as Rockhurst moved to the other side. Hawk remained in the front. They walked carefully and slowly staying alert to any danger that might be present.

Suddenly there was a shot and Leicester yelled, "It's him, Hawk!"

Leicester marched through the trees dragging the Comte by the collar. Hawk launched himself into the Comte taking him down with one swift punch to the face.

"Where is she?!" he yelled as he hit him again.

Leicester placed a hand on his shoulder. "He can't tell us where she is if he is dead, Hawk."

Hawk pulled the bloodied Comte up by his cravat. "Where is my wife?"

The Comte wiped the blood from his mouth. "What makes you think I have your wife. Perhaps she wasn't happy being your duchess and left you. Maybe you weren't satisfying her needs."

Hawk hit him again. "I found my sister; I know you have Persephone."

The Comte narrowed his eyes. "I knew I should have killed that bitch."

This time Leicester moved forward and punched the Comte hard breaking his nose. "Bastard. You aren't worthy to be in the same room as her. Now tell us where the duchess is or we will take you apart piece by piece."

Rockhurst moved closer taking his pistol out from underneath his coat. "There are places on the human body where a man can be shot and not die right away. He just suffers in horrible pain begging for death as his life blood slowly seeps away."

The Comte laughed. "Trying to frighten me, my lord? It isn't going to work."

Hawk had never wanted to kill a man so bad in his life but he couldn't give in to the urge until Persephone was found. "Where is she?!" He grabbed his coat and shook him roughly.

The Comte's maniacal laughter grew louder. "You will never find her, Hawksford. You will never know what happened to her. I want you to suffer with that for the rest of your days always wondering, always searching," the Comte said before he broke down in a fit of crazed laughter.

Hawk went over and picked the man up by the lapels of his jacket. "Son of a bitch! Tell me or I will beat it out of you." He began shaking the Comte which only caused the man to laugh louder.

Rockhurst came forward. "Hawk you have to stop. I don't think he is going to tell us anything."

Suddenly the Comte reached for the pistol Rockhurst was holding in his hand. The two struggled until a loud report caused everyone to stand still. The Comte dropped to his knees, a gaping hole in his chest near his heart.

Hawk dropped to his knees beside the dying man. "For God's sake, ease your conscious before you stand before God and tell me where my wife is."

The Comte smiled, blood oozing past his lips. He coughed a few times. "The devil will welcome me to hell." He spit blood from his mouth as he gasped his last breath.

Hawk stood with his head in his hands. "My God, how will we find her now."

Hawk walked away to have a moment to himself. He was still no closer to finding Persephone. He wanted to have her back in his arms. He wanted to tell her how much she meant to him, that he loved her. Now he may never get the chance and the thought that she might never know how he truly felt and that he loved her was more than he could stand. He lowered his head feeling defeated.

Leicester walked up behind him placing a hand on his shoulder. "We will find her, Hawk."

He took a deep breath and nodded. "We need to get started looking again." He looked back toward the Comte's body. "Leave him for the buzzards."

They went back to their horses and turned back toward the village when Rockhurst caught sight of some movement out of the corner of his eye.

He turned, dismounted, and moved over closer to an area covered in large bushes and vines. "You there! Come out, we won't hurt you."

A boy slowly came out through the bushes. "'Ow do I know you won't hurt her?"

At his words, Hawk flung himself down from his horse and moved quickly to stand before the boy. "Do you know something, boy."

The lad defiantly stood taller. "Who might you be?"

Hawk was not in the mood. "I am the Duke of Hawksford and if you know something I demand that you tell me now."

Leicester put a steady hand on his shoulder. "Let him speak, Hawk."

The boy looked over at Leicester. "Is he really the duke?"

Leicester nodded. "Yes, and he is looking for his duchess. Two bad men took her and he is trying to find her."

The boy seemed to accept that as the truth. "I can take you to her. I helped her escape from that man when they left her last night. She is hurt bad and will not be able to travel on horseback."

Hawk looked at Rockhurst. "Go make arrangements for a carriage from the village." He then turned back to the boy. "Is she close by?"

"Aye, I couldn't get her far away so I hid her in an abandoned hunting lodge hidden back in the woods. I'll take ye to her." He didn't wait for an answer but headed off through the woods knowing they would follow.

Hawk looked over at Leicester who shrugged his shoulders as they followed the boy through the thick underbrush. "How did you find her?" he asked the boy as they followed him.

"I thought she was dead."

Hawk felt his heart sink at his words.

The boy continued. "I poked her with a stick and she opened her eyes and told me what those men had done to her. So, I helped her walk to the lodge. It isn't much, but I couldn't carry her any farther by myself. I was going to go get help when those two showed up looking for her. I stayed hidden until you found me."

"How bad is she hurt?"

The boy stopped and turned to look at him. "She is hurt really bad, your grace."

Hawk hoped he was not too late. They continued to follow the boy until they came to an old, dilapidated building. It looked as if a good stiff wind could blow it down any minute.

The boy opened the door then stood out of the way as both Hawk and Leicester rushed in to find Persephone lying on the floor.

Hawk knelt beside her. "Persephone? Darling, I'm here and you're safe." He took her hand in his. "She is so cold." He took his coat off and wrapped it around her.

Leicester also knelt down to feel for a pulse. He feared the worst upon seeing her. She had lost all color in her face and with the coldness of her body he feared they had been too late but there was a pulse, it was faint but there was a pulse. "She lives, Hawk but she needs a doctor immediately."

Hawk put an arm under her to lift her into his arms. With the movement she cried out in pain and slowly opened her eyes. "Hawk?" she whispered faintly.

Hawk leaned over and pressed a kiss to her cheek. "Yes, my love. I'm here. Everything is going to be alright."

"Catherine?" she asked weakly.

"Catherine is safe at Hawk's Hill. She is worried about you and I'm sure once I get you home, she will talk incessantly about this whole ordeal."

She managed a small smile before closing her eyes again and going limp. "Persephone!"

"She has fainted, Hawk. We need to examine her and make some way to get her out of here. I don't think she can take the pain of you carrying her."

Leicester took off his coat and laid it on the floor so Hawk could carefully lay her body back down. He then took the boy outside so Hawk could remove her riding habit and search for injuries.

Her riding habit was damp and had a few rips in the material. He carefully rolled her to her side to unbutton it so he could remove it. Once he had her in her shift, he carefully lowered the straps so he could see the extent of her injuries. Her wrists were rubbed raw from the ropes and her legs had some bruises but the extent of her injuries was in her chest and midsection. She was bruised badly and from the way the bruises darkened along her ribs he knew she must either have cracked or broken ribs. There was no wonder she had passed out from the pain. Her body was too cold to stay uncovered for long so he wrapped his coat back around her and went outside to get Leicester.

"The bastard tried to kick her ribs in. She is badly bruised from her hips to her collarbone. But her ribs I am certain are either broken or cracked. We need to get a fire built if we can and warm her up." He looked at the boy. "What's your name?"

"Thomas, your grace."

"Thomas, I owe you a debt of gratitude for helping my wife and you will be rewarded handsomely. But we need your help. Go gather some sticks and anything that will make a good fire. I want to warm her up.

Leicester, you need to go find Rockhurst and if he doesn't have a doctor with him, go get one."

Both Leicester and Thomas nodded and did as they were instructed.

Hawk went back inside and knelt beside his wife. He pushed her hair away from her face. "Persephone, we are going to get you a doctor and take you back home." She stirred slightly as he ran a finger slowly down her face to her bruised cheek. He took his handkerchief from his vest and wiped at the dried blood on her cheek and lips. He thought of the Comte and wished he was still alive so he could make him suffer the way his Persephone had suffered at his hands.

"You will get better, Persephone. I won't allow anything else to ever happen to you, darling. I love you, Persephone. Can you hear me? I love you and when you are better, I will tell you every day how much you mean to me." She didn't stir and he wasn't sure she had heard his words. He squeezed her hand softly and pressed a kiss to her forehead.

Chapter Seventeen

Persephone felt as if she were trying to pull herself out of a fog. She could hear voices around her, but her eyes were too heavy to open. She could see light through her eyelids. Her head hurt terribly, but she felt as if she needed to try to open her eyes. She forced them open blinking rapidly to adjust to the light in the room. She tried to sit up further but it was much too painful. She turned her head slowly to see Catherine asleep in a chair beside her bed. She pushed aside her disappointment that Hawk was not there with her. At times when she was in and out of consciousness, she thought she had heard his voice calling to her but she supposed it was just her imagination. She opened her mouth noting how dry her throat was.

"Catherine?" she said weakly then again a little stronger, "Catherine."

Her friend opened her eyes and looked shocked to see her awake. "Persephone, your awake!" She rushed over to the bed taking her hand then touched her forehead. "And your fever is gone! Oh Persephone, I have been so afraid."

"Can I have some water?" Persephone asked as she struggled once again to sit up.

Her friend helped her into a sitting position and propped some pillows behind her back. "Yes, of course." She went over to the table and poured her a glass of water then brought it back and held it up to her lips. "I have to go get Hawk; he will be furious if I wait any longer."

Persephone grabbed her hand. "No, don't disturb him. Tell me what happened. I must confess that my memory is fuzzy."

Catherine smiled. "I'll tell you all about it later, right now I'm going to get Hawk. He has hardly left your bedside the entire time you have been recovering."

Persephone closed her eyes and laid her head back against the pillows. She knew it was no use in arguing with Catherine, but she didn't know if she was prepared to see Hawk now.

Hawk had scarcely left Persephone's side once he had gotten her home. It had taken much longer than expected. When Rockhurst arrived with a carriage, the doctor had insisted on examining Persephone in the village before transporting her back to Hawk's Hill. Hawk had been relieved to hear that she had not been raped as he had feared, but she did have numerous bruises and a broken rib possibly two. It had been slow going not wanting to jostle her overly much. Then the fever had set in. The doctor had given her laudanum for the pain and with the fever she had not been fully conscious in over two weeks. He had feared the fever would take her life and he had spent many nights by her side bathing her body with cool water to cool her down. His aunt and sister had offered to relieve him, but he couldn't leave her. He never wanted to leave her again. His nights had been tormented with thoughts of losing her forever.

Occasionally, she would cry out in terror and it was a suffering he hoped neither of them would ever go through again. He had not wanted any scandal connected with Persephone, so the entire incident would remain secret to avoid any disgrace. The Comte's death had been widely accepted as a robbery by highwaymen and as far as he was concerned no one would ever know what had happened to either Persephone or his sister. But Persephone was his number one priority right now and he needed to return to her side as soon as possible. He had only left her room this morning when Catherine had convinced him that he needed a bath badly.

So, he reluctantly left the duchess's chambers to bathe and dress in some clean clothes and grab a bite to eat before going back to her bedside.

He walked into the dining room to see both Leicester and Rockhurst already there. They had arrived from London two nights ago and were staying for a week or so before returning to their own estates.

"Any change?" Rockhurst asked as Hawk entered the room.

"No, she still sleeps," he said as a footmen set a plate of food before him.

"Perhaps you should get outside and get some exercise today, Hawk. It has been two weeks and you haven't left her side except to eat and bathe," Leicester said as he took a sip of tea.

"I will not leave her. I want to be the first face she sees when she wakes up. I owe her that."

All three men jumped to their feet when Catherine came running down the stairs. "Hawk!"

Hawk knocked his chair over as he rushed around the table to meet his sister fearing the worst. "What is it, Catherine? Persephone?"

Catherine smiled brightly, tears misting her eyes. "She is awake and wanted something to drink. And the fever is gone."

She didn't get a chance to tell him anymore. He was already running up the stairs to her room.

Rockhurst laughed in relief. "Thank god! She will recover now and Hawk can stop being a recluse."

Catherine moved over to stand by Leicester. "Yes, she will be fine now and Hawk can finally tell her how much he loves her." She looked up at Leicester fluttering her lashes at him causing Rockhurst to laugh again and Leicester to move away from her.

Persephone's eyes flew open as Hawk burst through the doors of her room. He stood there for a moment just staring at her before moving to her side falling on his knees beside her bed. He took her hand and raised it to his lips.

"You scared the hell out of me, Persephone."

She removed her hand from his and moved some hair from her face. "I am sorry, it has been hell for me as well."

He sat beside her on the bed and wrapped his arms around her gently trying not to hurt her bruised ribs. The wounds on her face had healed and her bruises were fading but the doctor had told him it would take weeks for her ribs to heal completely. "I know sweetheart. But you are going to be alright now."

"What happened to the Comte?" she asked.

"You have no reason to fear him ever again. He is dead and the world is better for it. He will never hurt anyone again," he could not disguise the anger in his voice.

A concerned look crossed her face. "Sam? The groom. He was shot."

Hawk reached out and took her hand. "It was a grave injury, but you will be happy to know that even though it was close, the bullet missed any internal organs and he is recovering although very slowly. He is at the dower house, and I hear he is making a fine recovery. Catherine has been riding over to visit him once or twice a week. You will also be happy to know that the young boy Thomas who thankfully led me to you has been compensated for his help. I have made arrangements for him to attend school as he now wants to be a doctor. His family was very proud of him." He kissed the top of her head. "But enough of that, are you hungry, love?"

"I actually am, but I would love a bath first. If you will send Sarah in to assist me, I would be grateful."

He went to the bellpull and rang for a maid. "Have a warm bath brought up for the duchess in her changing room." He then went back to join Persephone in her bed. "There will be no need for Sarah, I will assist you."

"You don't have to do that, Hawk. I know there must be more important things for you to do."

His face became serious. "Persephone, look at me. There is nothing more important than you. I have been a fool and I have been in my own personal hell these past few days afraid that I would not be able to tell you."

Persephone looked at him curiously. "Tell me what?"

He took her face in his hands and gently kissed her lips before saying, "When that bastard took you from me, I felt a fear I had never known before. I was afraid I would never see you again. I would never be able to hold you again or kiss you again." He let his lips lightly kiss hers again. "I worried for your safety at the hands of that mad man, but I was tormented by something else as well. I was terrified that I would not be able to tell you that I love you. I love you, Persephone with all my heart and I do not want to be parted from you ever." He wiped away the tears as they rolled down her cheeks. "Don't cry, my love."

Persephone couldn't help it. "I thought I had imagined it."

He pulled her closer to his side. "Imagined what, darling?"

"I heard you telling me you loved me while I was sleeping and I thought it was a dream. I was so afraid I would never hear you say those words to me."

"It was not a dream, I told you countless times while you were sleeping that I loved you and there will never be a day that you will not hear it from me, Persephone. I don't give a damn about other society marriages or what anyone in the ton thinks, I am in love with my wife and I want everyone, especially her to know it always."

Persephone squeezed his hands. "I love you too, Hawk. I think I always have."

They lay together for several minutes then he kissed her again and got up from the bed carefully lifting her into his arms. "Now, let's go see if your bath is ready. My duchess will be moving back into the duke's bedchamber tonight. I know it will be some time before I can make love to you again, but I want you by my side. I want to hold you in my arms every night from here on out." She laughed and he continued. "I will be such an attentive husband that you will grow tired of me."

"You don't think you will grow tired of me?" she asked as he carried her into the other room.

He smiled down at her, "Never, my love." Now let me be your lady's maid and after your bath we will get some food in you. You have lost quite a bit of weight over the past few days. Aunt Louisa and Catherine will be dying to see you as will Leicester and Rockhurst but I want you all to myself for a bit. I find I am reluctant to share you with others even if it is family and close friends.

"That's alright with me. I am just happy to be back home."

He kissed her once again. "You are home. I love you, my duchess."

Epilogue

It had been almost two months since Persephone's kidnapping. Her ribs were a little sore but for the first few weeks since she woke up from her unconscious state, Hawk had insisted on carrying her almost everywhere she went in the house. She finally had to tell him, that while she loved being in his arms, it was getting a bit embarrassing to be carried about like an infant from room to room. He of course protested not wanting her to overdo it but had eventually given in with some coaxing from Aunt Louisa and Catherine.

He had some business in London to attend to and she had convinced him that she was well enough to travel with him and they were making preparations to return to Hawksford House in Mayfair. Aunt Louisa would be leaving for Bath in the next day or so then on to Brighton and Catherine was trying to determine if she would like to go with her aunt or return to London with Persephone.

If Catherine chose to go to Bath, she knew she would miss her, but it would be nice to have some alone time with Hawk. They had been invited to a dinner at Carlton House given by the Prince Regent before he joined the rest of the beau monde in Brighton. She was anxiously looking forward to attending and seeing Carlton House. Hawk had told her about the prince's extensive art collection and she was looking forward to seeing it.

Hawk had promised her a wedding trip as soon as she was fully recovered, but with things heating up on the continent with Bonaparte, they might have to wait it out. Persephone hated the thought of war and prayed that the conflict would soon be ended. Perhaps they would go to Brighton and visit the Royal Pavilion before returning to Hawk's Hill.

She was putting the finishing touches to her hair when a strong pair of arms gently encircled her waist. She sighed as Hawk pressed slow kisses behind her ear. "Good afternoon, Hawk."

He turned her around to face him. "Hello my beautiful duchess." He said before kissing her possessively. "Luncheon will be served soon. I came to see if you will be joining me. Leicester and Rockhurst are both already downstairs and I'm sure once Catherine has discovered that Michael is here she will descend upon him."

Persephone giggled. "She is persistent, I'll give her that." She wrapped her arms around his neck and pulled his head down for another kiss."

Hawk kissed her passionately. "Forget luncheon. Let's go back to bed. I'm finding myself hungry for something else."

Persephone playfully slapped at his arm. "We can't leave our guests downstairs alone. What kind of hostess will they think me?"

He whisked her up into his arms. "Darling, right now I don't care what they think. I want my wife in my bed."

Persephone giggled and kissed him quickly. "Later, my love."

He put her back on her feet and reluctantly stepped away. "I will hold you to that promise, duchess." He walked back toward the door. "I will see you downstairs."

Persephone smiled and went back to finishing her hair.

Catherine's lady's maid had just informed her that the Duke of Leicester had arrived and would be having luncheon with the duke and duchess before continuing to his estate. Catherine had been hoping to see him again before she left Hawk's Hill. She had decided that in order to see him more often she should probably return to London with Persephone. Aunt Louisa would be disappointed but if she was going to convince Michael that he loved her, she couldn't be away in Bath.

She had changed into her prettiest day dress and had her maid redress her hair. She moved gracefully down the stairs toward the dining room. She paused at the door when she heard Michael's voice.

"I'm glad Persephone is feeling better Hawk and I am even more glad that the two of you have decided to return to London. I just wished your sister was not coming with you," Leicester said as he and Hawk waited for Persephone to join them.

"She is young, Leicester. Eventually she will discover you for the arse you truly are and seek love elsewhere," Rockhurst contributed to the conversation.

Catherine jumped when she heard Persephone come up behind her. "What are you doing, Catherine?"

Catherine put her finger up to her lips to signal for her friend to remain quiet as she continued listening at the door.

Leicester snorted. "I know she is your sister and please do not take offense, but there is no way I could ever love Catherine. She drives me crazy. I'm almost afraid to come to Hawk's Hill if I know she is going to be here. I feel like a fox being chased by the hounds whenever she is around."

Hawk smiled. "She is here at present so you may have to get ready to run."

Leicester sighed heavily. "Perhaps she will find a suitor next season. I may have to start recruiting gentlemen myself in order to find any peace at all."

The three of them laughed.

Catherine turned to face Persephone her eyes filled with unshed tears. Persephone wrapped her arms around her. "Oh Catherine, I'm so sorry you heard that. I'm sure he didn't mean any of it."

Catherine sniffed and wiped a stray tear from her cheek before taking a deep breath and raising her chin up a notch. "We really should stop listening at doors shouldn't we, Persephone." She took a step away. "I believe I will pass on luncheon today. Please give my regards to your guests and I have decided to go with Aunt Louisa to Bath and then on to Brighton. The ton will be there soon and it will be a nice distraction."

Persephone gave her friend a worried look. "Catherine, please don't do anything you will regret."

Catherine gave her a sad smile. "Don't worry. The only thing I regret is all the time I wasted on his grace the Duke of Leicester. Now I am free of him and can concentrate on myself. And I plan on having fun Persephone and when I return to London for my second season, I will be the woman everyone is talking about."

"Oh, Catherine. Now I am really worried."

Catherine gave her a quick hug. "I will be fine, Persephone." She then hurried back up the stairs to her room.

Persephone hesitated, watching her friend until she was out of sight before heading in to join the gentlemen in the dining room. All three rose to their feet immediately upon seeing her. Hawk moved forward to hold a chair out for her to sit beside him.

"I'm sorry to keep you waiting. I was talking with Catherine." She looked over at Leicester with a frown.

"What is keeping her?" Hawk asked as he retook his seat.

"She will not be joining us for luncheon. She is preparing to leave for Bath and then travel on to Brighton. She has decided to join your aunt there instead of going to London with us."

Rockhurst raised his glass toward Leicester. "Looks like your problem has been solved."

Leicester rolled his eyes. "We shall see."

The footmen served the food cook had prepared and they ate talking mostly about the plans they had for horses and the races next year. Persephone listened but she was worried about Catherine. Hopefully she could convince her to be careful and not do anything that could cause a scandal and get her into trouble.

When lunch was over, she excused herself to go upstairs to speak with Catherine. She found her busily packing her trunks with her lady's maid.

"Don't try to stop me, Persephone. I have made up my mind and what's better I feel relieved not to have to worry over Leicester any longer."

Persephone sat on the bed and watched her friend throw her belongings into her trunks. "I wasn't going to try and change your mind, Catherine. I just want to caution you about being careful. Please don't let some fortune hunter or reprobate get you into a bad situation. I would be broken hearted if something like that happened to you."

Catherine paused. "I will be careful, dear. Please don't worry and when it is time to return to London for the season, we can enjoy it together. This time you can be my chaperone since you are now married." She went back to gathering her things.

Persephone knew there was no need in trying to reason with her. She would just have to hope Aunt Louisa kept a watchful eye on her and maybe she could talk Hawk into going to Brighton or Bath for a few weeks to check on Catherine. "When will you leave?"

"Tomorrow I will return to the dower house. I'm not certain when Aunt Louisa will want to travel to Bath but hopefully soon. I don't want to miss any of the festivities."

Persephone nodded then headed back to her chambers. She was surprised to see Hawk waiting for her. "What are you doing here?" she asked with a smile.

"I'm here to seduce my wife."

"What about your guests?"

He moved forward taking her hand and leading her through the connecting door to his bedchamber. "I told them they would have to entertain themselves for the rest of the day and evening. It has been too long since I have made love to you, Persephone and I wouldn't care if the King himself came to visit, there is nothing that will keep me away from you tonight."

After he closed and locked the door, he turned her around and started loosening the buttons of her day dress. Persephone sighed as his hands slid slowly down her skin as her dress fell to the floor. She turned around in his arms and pressed a kiss to his lips. "Hmm, I am more important than the King?"

Hawk lifted her into his arms and carried her to the bed. "My darling, you are more important than anyone. I love you, Persephone. You might get tired of hearing it, but I will never get tired of saying it."

Persephone kissed him again as his body covered hers. "I will never get tired of hearing it."

The next morning Persephone and Hawk were joined by Rockhurst and Leicester in the grand entryway to say their goodbyes to Catherine. Hawk had the carriage prepared to take her to the dower house but as usual Catherine was late. He looked up at the clock in the hallway before glancing at Persephone.

"Here she is," Persephone said brightly as Catherine made her way down the stairs. She noted that Catherine looked very lovely this morning and did not have a hint on her face that she had been upset by Leicester's words the day before. She descended the steps very gracefully looking regal in her manner.

Catherine went first to her brother. "Thank you for use of your carriage, Hawk."

He bent down and kissed her cheek. "Be safe, Catherine and we will see you soon."

Persephone reached over and gave her a tight hug. "Please take care of yourself and write to me often."

Catherine smiled and gave her a wink. "I will keep you updated on all my adventures."

She then moved to Lord Rockhurst. He raised her hand to his lips. "Safe travels, Catherine."

"Thank you, my lord. I hope to see you again in London during the season."

"You might see me sooner. I have a feeling that Brighton might be more interesting with you there, my lady."

Catherine laughed then sailed right past Leicester out the door to the carriage. The four of them followed her out and Hawk helped her climb inside the conveyance. She waved at them out the window as the carriage started down the drive.

"What the hell was that all about?" Leicester asked crossly. "She didn't even look at me."

Rockhurst patted him on the back. "Perhaps you are getting what you wished for. You did want her to leave you alone." He grinned over at Persephone before turning back to Michael. "She looked lovely did she not."

Leicester frowned. "I hope your Aunt Louisa is up to properly chaperoning her."

Hawk wrapped his arm around Persephone's waist as they began walking back toward the house. "She will be fine."

Leicester followed the three of them back toward the front door but before walking inside he turned back once again to see the carriage moving farther away. Something didn't feel right and he didn't know exactly what it was, but he was determined to find out.

Later that evening Hawk held Persephone in his arms after making love to her for the second time. Rockhurst and Leicester had left earlier to return to Leicester's estate to check on some new horses they had purchased. Hawk declined the invitation to go with them. He had no desire to be anywhere away from Persephone. He leaned over and kissed the top of her head. She snuggled closer and pressed a kiss to his chest.

"Hawk?" she said sleepily.

He rubbed a hand over her bare arms. "Yes, my love."

"Do you think we should start to think about filling the nursery?"

He stilled. "I would love nothing more than to see you carrying my child, but it frightens me."

Persephone sat up to look at him. "Frightens you?"

He reached up and brushed a stray lock of hair behind her ear. "Childbirth is dangerous, Persephone. And the thought that I might lose you terrifies me. When you were taken from me it was the worst fear I could imagine and I never want to feel that way again. I love you with my whole heart, and I do not want to live without you."

Persephone brushed her lips over his and tried to ease the frown on his face. "I love you with my whole heart too. But as your duchess, it is my duty to produce an heir."

"I don't give a damn about the duchy and continuing my lineage. I just want to love you all the days of my life."

Persephone smiled. "But I want to give you a child. I want to give you a son that looks just like you. He will be part of us and every time I look at him, I will see our love."

"Or perhaps a daughter that is just as beautiful as her mother. Of course, I will have to lock her away because there will not be a man worthy of her."

Persephone laughed and snuggled back against him. "So will you give me a child, one day?"

He rolled her to her back and moved over top of her. "I would give you the moon and stars if I could, my love. If you want children, we shall have them but I warn you, I will be an overprotective husband and father."

"I love your protectiveness. I love everything about you."

He kissed her again. "As I love everything about you, my duchess.

Thank you for reading Hawk and Persephone's story in the book, *A Duke Always Gets What He Wants*. I hope you enjoyed the first installment in the, *A Duke Always* series. Be sure check out Leicester's story in the next book in the series, *A Duke Always Has A Secret,* coming soon.

Rebecca Leigh